THE TRADE

Thomas Kirkwood

The Trade

Before moving to Amazon, Thomas Kirkwood was published by Macmillan, Collier Macmillan (Europe), Donald I. Fine (an imprint of Penguin), Signet (an imprint of NAL), Brilliance (audio), and Stjerne-Spenning (Europe). No part of this book may be reproduced or transmitted in any form or by any means, graphic, electronic, or mechanical, including photocopying, recording, taping, or by any information storage or retrieval system, without the permission in writing from the publisher.

***

This novel is a work of fiction. Names, characters, places, and incidents either are the product of the author's imagination or are used fictitiously; any resemblance to actual persons, living or dead, events or locales is entirely coincidental.

ISBN-13: 978-1461141471
ISBN-10: 1461141478

.

Copyright 2012 Thomas Kirkwood

For Natasha

♦ **Books by Thomas Kirkwood** ♦

The Quiet Assassin

Lacking Virtues

SAVE ITALY Forget the Rest
(Writing as Tommy Vilar)

The Svalbard Passage

The Thirteenth Disciple: A Requiem for America

The Poppy Broker

FAITH A Secret Life
(Writing as Chub Yublinsky)

PROLOGUE

Slovenia
November, 2002

When the vehicle in which Stepan Mikhailovich Obruchev was traveling crested the hill, he saw the silhouette of the abandoned factory. Orange light from the coal fires inside leaked through broken windows and projected a faint glow onto the sagging night sky. He doubted the residents of Žiri would notice. And if they did, so what? An explanation was already on record with the authorities.

His first cousin, Bogdan, maneuvered the truck over pockmarked asphalt and muddy stretches of washed-out road. Obruchev lowered the passenger window and breathed deeply of the cool night air. A refreshing mist blew across his face. When he returned there would be snow instead of mud. No problem. These eight-wheel-drive Czech military transporters could go anywhere in any weather.

Žiri was an impoverished Slovenian town west of the capital, Ljubljana. The Austrian Alps with their exclusive ski resorts were less than 100 kilometers away. Hard to be poor in a place like this, Obruchev thought. Hard for the townspeople but good for business.

Bogdan shifted down to cross a stream where a bridge had caved in. "Care for a smoke?"

"Black Russians?"

"What else? I read you can order these things in the States now. Did you know?"

"Yes."

Obruchev raised his window, lit up and took a long drag – but he said no more. He never shared the details of his private life with his cousin, no matter how small. He and Bogdan had spent their childhoods together. They were associates in Obruchev's most profitable business. But their lives had taken off in different directions. What Obruchev did in East

Europe was one thing; what he did in the West, another. From the start, he had been careful to build no bridges between the two.

Why, he thought, should he tell Bogdan about his American socialite wife, about the symphonies, ballets and charity dinners he attended several times a week, about his respectable vodka import business? Why tell him what he did or where he lived in the US? Why bother trying to explain that smoking Black Russians in America, where he was admired his for old-world sophistication, would give off the odor of his modest Ukrainian origins? Nothing worth the effort could come of it. Nothing at all.

They passed through a series of checkpoints manned by Slovenian policemen or soldiers, all on the corporate payroll. At the factory entrance they parked in a dark lot amid a convoy of trucks belonging to the business, the only vehicles allowed on the heavily guarded road. The merchandise, once bought and prepared for travel, would be delivered to the buyers in equally secure but more accessible holding areas.

In normal circumstances, the lot would have been empty. Bogdan always arrived at 9:00 p.m., well before the other employees. He was running late tonight because he had insisted on picking up Obruchev at the airport.

"We need to talk," Obruchev said before they got out. "Isn't there a dome light? I can't see a goddamn thing."

Bogdan fumbled overhead for the switch. "Better?"

"Better." Outside, the mist had turned to rain. It hammered the roof and hood of the truck, driven by an angry wind. Obruchev studied the dark shadows on Bogdan's face.

"I'm going to ask a favor of you. Tell me now if you're not up to it."

"Not up to it? What are you talking about, Stepan? We're in this together. That means we help each other. You need it done, I'll do it." Bogdan stared out the windshield, mesmerized by the crazy patterns into which the gale whipped the rain. "Cough it up," he finally said. "We should be inside by now."

"A package is coming. I'll be gone when it arrives. I want you to dispose of it."

"You could tell me what's in it."

"A kid."

"No problem. I'll pitch the thing into the incinerator."

"The kid is still alive."

"Alive? In a package?"

"She is the package, Bogdan. If you want me to find someone else – "

"It's not a problem. Relax."

Obruchev stared at his cousin. He needed to be absolutely certain that he was making the right decision.

In the weak light, Bogdan's uncanny resemblance to himself stood out more than usual: the large head, bald except for the narrow band of closely cropped gray hair around the sides; the heavy features that conveyed only basic emotions; the bull neck and enormous shoulders; the big gut, more muscle than fat. The legs completing the image were lost in darkness but not to his mind's eye. They were short like his own, and stout as tree trunks.

Their fathers, Mikhail and Sergei, had looked much the same at fifty. The Obruchev genes were as dominant as their personalities, and their loyalty to one another had always been a given.

Stepan Mikhailovich Obruchev wondered for an instant over the source of his doubts. He was an impeccable judge of character and Bogdan hadn't given him any reason to suspect that he had changed or weakened. It was just fatigue, he supposed, just fatigue.

***

Near the center of the littered factory floor, Bogdan had arranged for the construction of a large stage. Drums of burning coal provided heat and light.

Obruchev bummed another Black Russian and watched the first group of five teenage girls mount the stairs. They were naked except for the jewelry and the stiletto heels they had been instructed to wear on their visit to the company's elegant office in Ljubljana. They were also sedated, which was too bad. He would rather have seen them scared or angry. But that was not an option. No way you could conduct an auction of 100 girls, even selling them in groups, if you invited the unpredictable.

Nikolai Petrovich, their auctioneer, began with a review of the house rules. As he spoke in a mellifluous but authoritative voice he stared unblinkingly at Obruchev. His face was round, iconic and oddly two-dimensional; his eyes blue and piercing. A goatee hung like a sword from his chin, adding to his unusual appearance. Everyone called him Rasputin behind his back – but they did so with circumspection. He was not only an auctioneer but a priest. He had restored a wing of the bombed-out church near the eastern border of company land. His earnings from the business, by no means small, were said to have gone to the purchase of the church and the sacred relics adorning its confessional.

Rasputin did not hold open services; he claimed the church was for personal use. But he did not turn away men in need of confession. Those who mocked him in the presence of their colleagues, even those who believed him to be an impostor, went to him in secret to unburden their souls. Rasputin absolved them of minor sins and convinced them that what they considered their greatest transgression was, in fact, smiled upon by their Heavenly Father. Those who knelt before him, believe what they might about their confessor, always came away renewed.

Bogdan often reported Rasputin's strange behavior to his cousin – and never received the response he expected. What the hell, Obruchev said. He couldn't stand the guy either. But if a lunatic moved product like no other employee he had ever known and improved company morale on the side, he was a keeper. Only a fool would send him packing.

Near the end of the reading of house rules, Obruchev gave his auctioneer a nod. Rasputin saw him but did not react. That's how he appeared, impervious to the world around him. That's also how he maintained silent control of a difficult process. His inscrutability was perceived as a curse. It made the most disruptive buyers uncomfortable, unsure of themselves, and thus brought order to an inherently chaotic gathering.

On those rare occasions when his holy lunacy did not work, Rasputin used his stare, two parts God and three parts Devil.

That stare carried a subconscious message no amount of greed or testosterone could negate: in this hall we partake with respect and humility of the sacrament of business. When the bills are paid and the goods are delivered you may do as you wish. But here you do as I wish.

Rasputin produced a miniature silver candelabra and inserted a small unused candle with a short burn time in each of its three arms. He held up his lighter, a hand-sized ceramic gargoyle that spewed a tongue of flaming propane from its mouth. When he lit the first candle the bidding began; when the final candle went out the highest bid on the floor prevailed.

The use of this medieval procedure was considered by many to be another of Rasputin's eccentricities, nothing more. But its advantages were obvious to those entrusted with running the business. The candles served as a fair clock, visible to all. They set the tempo of the bidding and put an end to any contentious claims that the auction results had been manipulated.

The auction system itself had been Bogdan's response to the fall in profits, a fall caused by growing competition. The business that Obruchev and his cousin started in the late Eighties had become the third largest criminal activity on earth – right up there with drug trafficking and arms smuggling. They had struck gold, no question about that. But whenever you struck gold, the copycats followed. Now the entire goddamn Slavic Mafia, from the Balkans to Siberia, was knee-deep in the Trade. To stay ahead of the pack required constant innovation.

Luckily, the crop of beautiful but penniless young girls from former East Bloc countries was inexhaustible. It didn't matter if demand abroad kept on skyrocketing and every asshole in the East got into the act: Obruchev's cash cow would never dry up. But Obruchev didn't enjoy playing second fiddle; he didn't intend to sit around while some hotshot passed him at his own game. Which is why he'd reluctantly let Bogdan give the auction system a try. It proved to be the right call: the organization thrived as never before.

The girls, selected in Ljubljana for what they believed to be lucrative positions in the West, had been chosen for their looks. They were ordered by their keepers to perform athletic stretches, to touch themselves in various ways and places, to display the sexuality they would later be forced to sell. Refusal to obey wasn't recommended. As Rasputin's house rules made clear, it would be punished by public rape – carried out on this very stage by the man or men the auctioneer designated.

When the girls had finished their ritual, they were sweating from the intense heat of the coal fires. The light from the flames touched their young bodies in a way that accentuated their virtues. Buyers, some stoked with lust, began making calculations. Rasputin sized up the crowd and the merchandise, then established a floor: ten thousand Euros for the group of girls presently on stage. After a long stare from his "pulpit" he lit the first candle.

Gentlemen, I am prepared to hear your offers.

The actual bidding never lasted more than six minutes. The time for a group of girls to mount the stage, display their marketable commodities, find a buyer, retrieve their luggage and get dressed never exceeded ten minutes. If you allowed for incidentals – setting up the stage, reading the house rules, a possible rape or two, the clean-up and disposal of unsold merchandise, the orderly parade of girls to the parking lot and waiting trucks – the result was a massive auction completed between midnight and dawn.

Efficient, orderly, lucrative beyond anyone's wildest dreams. The house take averaged more than a quarter of a million dollars a night, seven nights a week. Expenses were high, but profits were astronomical. It was an entrepreneur's paradise.

"Impressive," Obruchev said, elbowing his cousin in the ribs. "You're a major fuck-up, Bogdan, always have been. Fortunately, you're also a genius. Not many men could've had us up and running this smoothly fifty kilometers from our last home."

"It's been over a year, Stepan. The early months weren't smooth, but thanks anyway."

"Shall we go?"

"You want a girl first? I put the best aside for you."

"Maybe tomorrow. I'm tired."

They drove in silence through the rain. Obruchev was at peace with himself for most of the ride, but by the time they reached his hotel he felt uneasy. When he'd brought Kristýna to the States, she was 16 years old and naive. But girls grow up. Four years later she'd outsmarted him and escaped. She had moved far from Chicago and changed her identity so skillfully that he needed almost a decade to track her down. If she hadn't made her fatal mistake – marriage and a kid – he knew he'd still be looking.

But he'd found her. She would be going to prison for murder and Teresa would be going into the incinerator. Kristýna's knowledge that he had her daughter and that he might let her live would keep all mention of him out of her trial – if there even was a trial. It was a perfect crime.

So why did he feel uneasy? It was fatigue, he decided, the same fatigue that had caused him to doubt Bogdan . . .

In his room he poured himself a vodka – Moskovskaya straight up. Losing his concubine and with her the secrets of his business had been the worst defeat of his life; but settling the score had been one of his great pleasures.

His malaise vanished as quickly as it had come.

CHAPTER ONE

New York
October, 2003

Kristýna knew long before the Department of Corrections van approached Hastings-on-Hudson that memories could unravel her composure. She was determined not to let this happen, at least not today. Yet the moment she saw the city limits sign, she was unable to fight them off. She found herself reliving the horror of the past year; the horror and also the moments of joy before he found her.

If she could get herself under control, there was a sliver of hope. For this extraordinary bit of luck she had her sister, Michaela, to thank – and Michaela's husband, Tomas. But she still had to do her part; still had to remain calm and collected throughout the post-trial hearing. The sobs with which she filled the police van did not augur well for the coming ordeal.

One of the corrections officers noticed her distress. "Cheer up, Sondheim. I heard some idiot lawyer let you plead guilty. Sounds like something the judge might listen to."

"Yeah, right," the driver said. "Greg here thinks he understands this legal shit. You did it, and you said you did it in court. What does that mean? It means you're fucked and there ain't a damn thing that's gonna change it. You'll be on this freeway in a couple of hours, only going in the other direction. So don't let this yo-yo get your hopes up."

The crass words meant nothing. Kristýna's thoughts were elsewhere . . .

Last year Michaela had opened her Czech pastry shop in this quaint old town. It had been a glorious day for her sister and their many Slavic friends. Watching Teresa run about with jam and sugar covering half her face, watching Tomas when she flew into his arms and he didn't bother to wipe the mess off his shirt – that moment had somehow allowed her to move beyond Obruchev, beyond her ruined youth.

She looked out the van window. The woods all along the freeway burned with the gold and crimson of late autumn. The sky was full of soft white clouds. There was a time when she might have found it beautiful. No longer.

***

She had been busy at the stove, seasoning the Chicken Paprika, when Arthur returned from Beth Israel. He walked into the kitchen, jacket slung casually over his shoulder, and greeted her with an appreciative whistle. Teresa ran after him, wrapped her arms around his legs and offered a child's inimitable critique of first grade. Kristýna smiled, dried her hands on a dish towel and leaned forward to give her husband a kiss on the cheek.

She never got the chance.

Two men materialized out of nowhere. One she recognized, the other she didn't.

Obruchev ripped Teresa away from her dad, snatched a pot holder from the counter and slapped it over her mouth. Arthur froze and Kristýna swallowed a scream when they saw that the unknown man had drawn a pistol. He put the barrel to her husband's forehead.

The crack came before either of them could utter a word. Arthur collapsed on the white tile floor. Kristýna stumbled backwards while his blood pursued her, following the grout lines and trapping her in a bright rectangular grid.

Obruchev, expressionless, passed Teresa to his henchman. "Well if it isn't my lost Czech whore," he growled. "Don't move."

She tried instinctively to throw herself on Arthur. Obruchev kicked her away. "Didn't you hear me? I said, don't move. I'm in a hurry. Stand up and listen."

"Stepan – "

"Shut up. You knew this day would come. I could shoot you but I don't want you to get off that easy. The gun was in your husband's night stand. You'll go to jail for his murder."

He slapped her across the face. "For his murder and for betraying me. So don't ever start thinking you're innocent. As for the kid . . . why don't we let you decide?"

"Please. You can do as you like with me but – "

"I said you would decide. Here's your choice. She can go somewhere and have a normal life or I can fatten her up for the Trade. If you want her spared, you won't mention my name to anyone. That means friends, lawyers, priests, the press. I'm officially out of the country at the moment, so bringing me into this won't help your case. All it'll do is piss me off. So let's make sure we're clear. You keep your part of the bargain and your girl will have a pleasant childhood. You don't and she'll suffer for the rest of her short life. I think you know what I'm capable of. Don't fuck with me again, Kristýna."

She threw up in the sink. The room started to spin.

When she came to she was alone in the kitchen. The body of her husband was gone. His blood had been wiped off the tiles but the odor of a familiar cleaning solution hung heavy in the air. An open bottle of her sleeping pills lay beside her, the few remaining tablets scattered about at random.

She saw Arthur's gun and a spent shell casing near the cabinets, and screamed for Teresa. Screamed and screamed until she couldn't hear herself any longer.

***

Inside the holding cell behind the courtroom, Kristýna changed into the black suit, white blouse and black flats her attorney had brought at her request. The clothes had been searched by someone in the system – a man. She could tell from the haphazard way the skirt and blouse were draped over the hanger. But it didn't matter. There were no notes to be found, nothing a search might have revealed. The clothes themselves were the message.

She tossed her jumpsuit on the bench. That crisply pressed piece of conformity revolted her as never before. She suppressed a sudden urge to tear off her prison underwear. No time for such nonsense now. She had to use every moment to go over Allison's instructions in her mind.

The touch of female clothes on her skin filled her with a longing for freedom powerful enough to distract her. Focus! The judge, the security people, even her soft-spoken new lawyer, mustn't detect the slightest abnormality in her behavior. She must appear to them exactly as she had appeared during her trial: detached. The clock was now ticking.

Five minutes later, seven months after her incarceration for life, she was seated in the courtroom.

***

A gray late-model sedan stopped beside a tightly packed line of parked vehicles in front of the 100 Centre Street courthouse. Someone yelled, someone in uniform. So what, thought Tomas, pulling on his skull cap. This was New York, not a sleepy Czech village.

He got out of the back seat, street side, and came around to open the door for the woman he had been riding with. She wore a simple black suit, black flats and a white blouse. Her hair was ash blond, shoulder length, loosely curled.

Like many grief-stricken New Yorkers entering the Supreme Court, Criminal Term, Michaela did not remove her sunglasses as they passed inconspicuously through the metal detectors. In the lobby they joined the crowd waiting for an elevator. They got out on the tenth floor and casually parted company.

Michaela entered the women's restroom, chosen in advance, and worked on her makeup at the sink until she was alone. With a Kleenex to avoid leaving prints, she lifted one of several folded black and yellow "Out of Service" easels from the maintenance closet. Carrying it with her, she ducked into the stall nearest the main restroom entrance. That sign, when she positioned it, would point Kristýna in the right direction.

Behind the locked metal door, she took a small wallet from her purse and transferred it to her suit pocket. A second wallet with fake documents for Kristýna remained in a zippered side pocket of the same purse. She stuffed the purse, her wig and sunglasses into a plastic shopping bag she had brought along for that purpose, then buried the bag deep in the trash bin beside the commode.

She heard the main entrance open and noisily reeled toilet paper from the dispenser. The newcomer sneezed, a signal. The hearing was about to begin.

The woman who had come in left in a hurry. There was a hush in the hall as the restroom door closed slowly on its damper, interrupted only by the fading clack of heels.

Michaela used the toilet paper to unlock the stall door and pick up the "Out of Order" easel, still careful not to leave prints. On her way out she set up the sign in front of the stall, a guidepost Kristýna could not overlook no matter how frazzled she was. Then Michaela hurried back to the row of sinks.

Minutes now, if not seconds. She straightened her short chestnut hair, its cut and color, she hoped, similar enough to her sister's to deceive a stranger.

Let them come. She was ready.

***

At the defense table Kristýna glanced at the crowd. She spotted Tomas in a New York Yankees jersey wearing a baseball cap seated near the main exit. No courtroom cameras in New York, thank God; no images for forensics experts to study. If you didn't know Tomas you would not be able to identify him later. She doubted many policemen and prison guards frequented his avant-garde Czech theater on 120th Street, so this seemed a good bet.

Her brother-in-law held a handkerchief to his nose. It was the green light, the first signal on Kristýna's list. All she had to do now was follow the instructions Allison had managed to get to her inside the prison. Everything seemed simple and impossible at the same time.

Words of legalese echoed like distant thunder in her head. She tried to breathe deeply without appearing nervous, and felt she was succeeding.

An overweight man in the first row fell to the floor with a leaden thud. Convulsions wracked his body. Spectators and press people jumped to their feet, aghast, forgetting for a moment the newspaper and TV celebrity they had come to watch.

"Someone get up here!" the judge shouted.

One of the officers at the back of the courtroom plunged into the crowd, ordering everyone out of his path. Just before he reached the man he fell – almost as if someone had tripped him. The second officer rushed, as if by instinct, to his partner's aid.

"Bailiff!" the judge roared, "have you called in a medical emergency?"

"Yes, your Honor. The line's busy."

An elderly man tried to shove his way through the pandemonium as people struggled to see what was happening. "Your Honor, I'm a doctor. If I can get to him, I – "

"What?"

"DOCTOR!"

The judge threw up his arms in exasperation. "Let the man through. Let him pass, for God's sake."

Kristýna melted into the mêlée. She almost reached the exit before the officers noticed. When they did, they found themselves at the wrong end of the courtroom again, blocked by the crowd.

"Someone stop that woman!" one of them yelled.

Spectators who had hung back lunged at her as she broke free of the crush. She could see the great carved doors ahead, hear the shouts of her pursuers.

"Watch out," Tomas shouted. "She's got a gun Must've been planted in here."

The stampede of footsteps dwindled as the clear-headed abandoned the chase. But the ego-maniacs still followed. The pounding of shoes exploded in her ears.

The doors, did they open in or out? Did they open into the hall or into another chamber? Either Allison hadn't told her or she'd forgotten. She find out soon enough – if she got that far.

She heard an enormous crash. Involuntarily, she looked back. The two huge men behind her, men she would have recognized anywhere, pretended to get tangled up and went down hard. The others in pursuit fell on top of them, blocking the path to the exit with a heap of flailing and cursing humanity.

"No one leave the courtroom!" she heard one of the cops holler. From the sound of his voice she knew he was still a safe distance away, his progress slowed by the unruly crowd.

Then, suddenly, she was free.

The plan! She turned right, sprinted through an eerie silence, rounded the first corner and slipped inside the women's restroom. She saw two things: Michaela in a black suit stooped over a sink and the "Out of Service" sign marking her stall. She moved the sign with her foot, ducked inside and locked the door.

Kneeling on the toilet seat to remove her feet from view, she plunged her hand into the trash cylinder. She found the bag, took out Michaela's purse and paused to hold her breath. So far, so good.

She gave a start when she heard a dry hinge screech, realized before she panicked that it was the sound of her sister closing the "Out of Service" easel. A clack of plastic on plastic came next. The sign would be where Michaela wanted it.

Kristýna started to feel dizzy. In the name of God, she hadn't been breathing.

She let the air escape from her lungs as quietly as possible. Using a tiny mirror in the compact she adjusted the wig, slid on the sunglasses, and committed the shopping bag to the chaos in the bottom of Michaela's purse.

The preparations, simple as they were, had taken forever.

Or had they?

She'd been told she had one minute, ninety seconds with luck. She'd beat the clock. All she could hear was sound of running water as Michaela washed her face.

She glanced at her watch. The second hand had stopped. No, it hadn't. It finally moved, ticking off another unit of something.

Her life began to unfold in vivid colors in her mind's eye. Her baby being born, her father at the piano, her escape from Obruchev, her passage to America. No chronology, just a starburst of images.

Then all hell broke loose . . .

***

Michaela felt their vice-like grip on her shoulders. She didn't need to fake a scream when they twisted her arms behind her and forced her into cuffs. Her face still dripped with water she had thrown on it. They yanked her upright. One of the courtroom cops ran a paper towel roughly over her face. She kicked him in the shin.

"What d'you creeps think you're doing? This is a women's room."

"Yeah, right. A women's room, not a murderer's closet. Let's go."

"You're not taking me anywhere."

"Really?"

She spit in the other court officer's face. "Really."

They pushed her yelling and swearing into the hallway. Michaela was strong, her anger real. She landed another kick on the ankle of the guy who was still limping from her assault on his shin. He yelped and let her go. She almost managed to sink her teeth into the second officer's forearm, but he was ready. He shoved her face-first into the wall. When she made a last-ditch effort to free herself with a back kick, he yanked her other leg from under her. She nearly crashed to the floor.

"Get over here, Jake. Let's do it right this time."

The man she'd kicked used his fingers on a pressure point in her arm. She tried to scream but her lungs were empty.

"We're taking her back in."

"Bullshit. She resisted arrest. She's ours."

"Bad idea. It's politics around here, buddy. You play by the book, you lose."

The officers returned to the courtroom with their catch. The mob of reporters who had been restrained from joining the chase swarmed toward the aisle.

"Sit down," the judge ordered. "This has gone far enough. So we had an unfortunate incident, sixteenth page stuff. So what? It's over now. Sit down, I said."

Kristýna's attorney seemed to be in a daze. While the rest of courtroom sat, she stood like a marble statue at defense table. Michaela, still cuffed, kept her eyes on the floor. The officers led her to the front of the courtroom. One stayed with her, the other returned to his post at the exit.

"You heard me," the judge barked. "I said, sit down. That means you, counselor. And you, Ms. Sondheim."

"Who?"

"WHO?"

"My name isn't Sondheim and I can't sit down until someone takes these handcuffs off."

Time, use it. The longer she tied up the court, the longer Kristýna had to escape.

"Your Honor," the cop at the back of the room announced, "this woman resisted an officer. We have grounds to arrest her."

"You practically killed me in the women's room. I have grounds to sue your ass."

"Remove the petitioner." The judge whacked his gavel, furious.

"Kristýna," the attorney said, "why are you doing this? We worked so hard to – "

"Kristýna? Kristýna Sondheim? Is that who you think I am?"

The judge stood. He was about to retire to chambers. Michaela knew she had to stop him.

"Washing my face in a public john is a crime? You people here, if you're with the TV or the papers, keep an eye on these goons. They get off terrorizing random women. If they arrest me, you'll have your Rodney King story right here in New York City. You'd already have it if you'd seen what they did to me in the women's room."

"You're in contempt." The judge took a step toward chambers.

"Just a minute, officers," Kristýna's attorney said. "This is not my client."

The judge and officers stopped in their tracks.

"What are you talking about, Ms. Delaney?" the prosecuting attorney bellowed.

"This is not Kristýna Sondheim. Kristýna Sondheim has green eyes. Very striking green eyes. You must have noticed. This woman's eyes are brown."

"How about a large break?" one of the officers moaned. "Why was she leaning over the sink when we found her? Contacts maybe? As in brown contacts?"

The judge stepped back to the bench and slammed his gavel down hard enough to break it. "I will not have my courtroom turned into a circus. Not by you, you or you."

"You already got your circus," Michaela scoffed. "Who ever heard of brown contacts? Go ahead, officers. Take me down the way you did in the lady's room. Show your tough-guy stuff in front of all these witnesses and the judge. You'll have great fun until you find yourselves sitting in my place."

"Where's that doctor?" the cop shouted.

Michaela smiled. He looked ridiculous with his bulging neck and red face. "Doctor? You mean you had one waiting for me? How thoughtful."

"Shut up. I'm talking about the MD who helped the sick guy. He can exam her for contacts. Then you guys can go home and write your stories."

"Hey, the doctor left with the epileptic dude," a spectator volunteered.

The judge seemed on the verge of a stroke. When the bailiff tried to escort him out of the courtroom, he pushed him away.

One of those old authoritarian bastards, Michaela thought. This was his turf and he was going to control it, come what may. She couldn't have hoped for more.

The prosecuting attorney stepped in to rescue the deteriorating situation.

"Let's resolve this issue of identity right now. You say you're someone else. Where's your purse? A woman doesn't usually walk around in Manhattan without a purse."

"Excuse me. I didn't say I was someone else. I said I was me."

"You know what I mean. Where's your purse?"

"I didn't bring it to the courthouse. Last time I was here they searched it for fifteen minutes. Is that a crime?"

"You must have some kind of ID."

The courtroom had become so quiet Michaela could hear the judge's labored breathing. She smirked. "Of course I have identification. Why didn't your goons ask me that in the first place?"

"Where is it?"

"Don't get impatient." She started to reach into her suit pocket.

"Stop!" the officer nearest her yelled. "Jake, pat her down."

"You already patted me down in the lady's room," Michaela said.

The other officer removed her wallet with exaggerated care. "Michaela Hasek. That's what these fake IDs say."

"Can I go now?"

The officer ignored her. "Call forensics."

"What about the brown contacts?" Michaela asked. "Isn't anyone going to check?"

"I was getting to that," the officer said, taking out his pen light. He hadn't examined her for more than ten seconds when his face fell, telegraphing his discovery – or lack thereof.

The apoplectic judge had had enough. "Bailiff, phone downstairs. Have all exits to the courthouse sealed. Alert security. We may have an escaped convict in the building."

While watching his thunderous retreat from the courtroom Michaela felt a hand on her arm, the same hand that had grasped her so roughly in the corridor.

"You're under arrest," the officer said.

He read her rights while she stared at him. He sounded like an idiot auditioning for a cop show. She was about to tell him when a newcomer stole her audience. An officer she hadn't seen made a loud authoritative announcement from near the exit. "Nobody leaves this courtroom before giving ID and contact info."

"Make me a copy," Michaela sang. "I'll need it for my witness list."

Laughter in the courtroom gave voice to her jubilation.

CHAPTER TWO

Rural Slovenia
October, 2003

"When is my mother coming?" Teresa asked.

"As soon as she can," Zlatko Prlicev said, spooning out the stew. "But I told you a thousand times. It's not going to be as soon as we thought it was. You have to stop thinking about her all the time. Then she'll come faster. So think about all the nice things around here instead. Don't you like your dog? She's a fine German pointer. What about the farm and the other animals?"

"I like them, but Uncle Bogdan said he brought me here so my mother could find me. He said she would come right away."

"She couldn't. Uncle Bogdan didn't know. You just make things worse if you talk about her all the time. Guess what, Princess. I've got a surprise for you. We're going to have a fun visit tomorrow. Maybe we can even find a husband for Katja. Would you like to have some puppies?"

"I told you. I want my mother."

"Well now, " the gruff old farmer said, "it looks like I have to tell you something I didn't want to tell you. We have to be careful the bad guys don't find out where you are. You told me what they did to your father. If they find out you're here they'll hurt you in the same way. Then they'll wait here for your mother and hurt her too. So we're not going to talk about her anymore. If you get used to talking about her with me, you might make a mistake and mention to a stranger that you're from America. If you do, the bad guys will figure everything out. Now, I'll tell you about the visitors who are coming."

"I don't care about the visitors."

Zlatko took a noisy swallow of beer. He cut a few slices off the loaf of dark bread he had baked that afternoon. "Listen, you'll care when you meet them. There will be lots of kids. How long has it been since you've had playmates?"

"I have Katja. I'm making friends with Dana and her husband."

"Katja's a dog and Dana's a sheep. I mean people friends."

Teresa buttered a piece of hot bread. "My people friends are in America."

The old man sighed. "There you go again, mentioning America."

"You already know about America. What difference does it make?"

"I told you, Teresa. You've got to practice. Then you won't make a mistake when you're with other people. The visitors built your carriage."

"You said the carriage was old."

"Eat some of your stew, Princess. It will make you even prettier. You're right. The carriage is so old that the people who made it are dead now. The visitors are their children and grandchildren."

Teresa remained silent for a few minutes while she stirred her spoon in the stew. Then she shoved her bowl aside and took another piece of bread. "Okay."

"Okay what?"

"You can tell about the visitors."

"They're Gypsies. Do you know who Gypsies are?"

"No."

"Well, they're people who like to wander. They've been wandering all over the world for as long as anyone can remember. When I was a kid, they traveled in carriages like the one you found in the barn. I was keeping it for a Gypsy friend. He died before he could come for it."

"Will they bring more carriages?"

"No. They don't use them anymore. They come in cars, trucks and big vans for selling stuff at town markets. But they still live like they used to. They never settle down. If it's nice weather, they sleep outside on the ground. They like to dance and have a good time, especially when there's a celebration. The women wear bright colored clothes and sometimes their kids don't bother with shoes."

Teresa stood up. "I don't want them to come. They sound scary. Can you tell them not to come?"

"Listen, Princess, they're very nice people. They've been coming to this farm for hundreds of years. They leave messages for other Gypsy families and have their celebrations and help me with my work. They know a lot about horses and how to fit them with metal shoes."

"Can I go to bed, Grandfather? I don't want the Gypsies to come."

***

The procession pulled up at the farm around noon the next day. Teresa was surprised at how much fun she had with the other kids. Keja, Tshaya and Liliana – the girls – knew all sorts of games you played in barns and tool sheds. Gypsy hide-and-seek was the game she liked best. The girls would hide from the two boys, who were younger. The rules were, Yanko and Djivan had to hold their breath while they looked. They had to find the girls before they let out any air. If they couldn't do it, they lost.

Pretty soon Teresa was laughing with the other girls. The boys could never do it. They made funny sounds when they gave up and breathed again. Yanko was the worst. Sometimes he sounded like the whoopi cushion a friend in New York had given her.

Playing here was just like playing at home in America. But she didn't say "America." If these Gypsies really traveled around as much as Grandfather Zlatko said, they might run into the bad guys.

It was fun to stay out late and play. They didn't go back to the farmhouse until just before dark. There must have been some kind of a celebration because the older people had already started a party. The men drank beer and ate while some of the teenage boys and most of the women danced. The women wore bright clothes and long skirts, just like Grandfather Zlatko told her, and they had all sorts of necklaces and belts made out of gold coins. Teresa wondered why she had been scared. Everyone seemed happy and nice, and they played fun music with instruments she had never seen. Usually she thought America was a better place than where she was now, but she liked the dancing here more than the ballet lessons her mom and dad used to make her go to.

Suddenly the old men got up and started dancing with everyone else. The kids she had been playing with pulled her down from the counter where she was sitting. They made her clap and run around. She was tired after a while and stopped just as Grandfather Zlatko grabbed hold of his chest and fell on to the floor. Some of the women started to scream. The old Gypsy men leaned over him. One woman ran to the telephone. She must not have known it didn't work.

Teresa pushed her way between two men who didn't smell very good and knelt down beside her grandfather. She put her hand on his. It was all rough and calloused, and it felt like ice. While she watched, his face got pale and his lips started turning blue.

"Vesh," he whispered to one of the Gypsy men, "Vesh, come close."

Teresa squeezed in to hear what Zlatko was saying. It was hard to make out his words. He gurgled something about taking his girl with them, his girl wasn't registered, no one knew she was here . . . and . . . and her mother was in jail far away. He hadn't had the heart to tell her that her mother could never come. Please, it was the only favor he had ever asked. The only favor he and his father and his grandfather had ever asked. Would Vesh do it? Would he?

The Gypsy man said yes. Teresa thought she felt Grandfather Zlatko's hand trying to squeeze hers. Then he was dead, just like her father had been after the man shot him. At first she felt empty inside, then she felt scared. Big arms picked her up.

It was one of the Gypsy women. She said, "I'm Lyuba. Gather up your things. We must go fast. Otherwise the police will think we did this. Your grandfather wants you to come with us. You heard him. Your mother can never come for you. We will be your new family."

Teresa lay on the floor, sobbing uncontrollably. She felt Katja licking her face but she was too weak to pet her only friend. "Can I bring my dog?" she choked. "I won't go unless you let me bring my dog."

"Yes, of course. We have lots of dogs. Come now. Get up. See how everyone is packing. You must hurry."

"Will the bad guys find me if I stay here?"

"Yes. They will put you in a building with other kids who have lost their families. It will be like a jail for children. You will have more fun with us."

"My mother's coming for me. How will she find me?"

"Honey, she's not coming. You heard your grandfather. Something went wrong. She can't come. The crazy Gaye won't let her. That's the way they are. You'll see."

Teresa said, "I wish I would die."

Lyuba's big arms lifted her to her feet but Teresa fell down as soon as the Gypsy woman let her go. She heard someone yelling orders to the kids she had played with. She started crying again.

She was still crying when they loaded her into a van with her dog and some of the Gypsy kids. It wasn't until dawn that she finally fell asleep.

CHAPTER THREE

Kristýna felt as though her heart would beat an exit wound in her chest when the restroom door opened. It seemed like hours since Michaela had been dragged kicking and screaming to some unknown place. Clearly there had been a disaster. The ruse had been discovered. The footsteps on the invisible floor outside told the story . . .

As despair engulfed her, she heard a husky female voice unleash a stream of invective. A tube of lip balm skittered into Kristýna's stall. Through the fog of terror she recognized the "all clear" signal she was supposed to await. She stood on shaky legs, took a deep breath and forced herself out into the corridor.

Tomas approached from the direction of the courtroom, wearing a skull cap and army jacket instead of the baseball paraphernalia he'd had on before. The hall was otherwise empty, but she could still hear Michaela's distant protestations.

"Take my arm," Tomas whispered, pausing beside her. "No questions. Not a word until we're out. Hurry. You have a wallet and ID in the zippered pocket inside your purse. Your new name is Katarina Sivec."

"You – "

"Please. Not a word. Whatever I say, don't answer."

The elevator disgorged a load of passengers, uniformed officers among them. Her blood turned cold while sweat formed beneath her wig. They would notice her, she thought; everyone in the country would notice her. Why hadn't they gotten her a better disguise?

"You should have talked it over with me," Tomas said, annoyed. "Who's going to take care of a puppy?"

She tried to shrug her shoulders, didn't know if she had.

One of the officers stopped them. "Where's Judge Bremer's courtroom? You know?"

"Not a clue. Sorry."

"Around the corner to your left," a passerby offered.""

"Thanks," the cop said, not releasing Kristýna from his gaze. She felt naked. She knew she was broadcasting fear, marking herself for capture. Time had stopped again. How long had she been standing there paralyzed, as if begging to be discovered? A second? Five minutes? No idea.

Tomas gave her a slight tug to get her moving. "We'll talk about it tonight," he said. "I'm late to work as it is."

The cop turned away.

She was dizzy again. The shape of the elevator ballooned in her mind's eye, as if she were looking at it through a fish bowl. She noticed a red button beside the door. Red! Stop! She strangled a gasp. Inside the packed car was a group of cops. Tomas held her arm firmly, steering her directly in front of them. Why was he doing this? Why?

He took her hand. He must have sensed she was about to crack. He started talking – loudly enough to be overheard, softly enough to seem like he didn't want to be.

"Look, I'm sorry about earlier. I didn't mean to be a prick. If you want a puppy that bad, fine. We'll just have to find a dog sitter. I've heard they're more work than kids."

Six floors to go. Cops were everywhere. Getting on, getting off, sniffing like Nazis. It didn't dawn on her until she reached the lobby that they weren't searching for her or anyone else. Not even the first cop outside the restroom. She'd been the object of men's stares her entire life. His had been no different.

She felt better, almost clear-headed. She could see the courthouse entrance ahead. She could also see a cadre of uniformed officials with scanning devices and metal detectors. The line of people waiting to pass through the checkpoint stretched forever.

"Aren't you glad you don't have to go through that hassle again?" Tomas said matter-of-factly.

She looked straight ahead, trying to figure out what he meant. Suddenly she understood. The search was for people entering the courthouse. The exiting crowds passed freely through a massive door to the right, partly hidden by the crowd. He guided her into the rip tide of people and she surrendered to the street-bound surge.

It wasn't over yet, not yet. The great door could still slam shut, a loudspeaker could alert the security officials, cameras staring down from overhead could nail her as she passed beneath them.

But none of this happened. They simply walked out with the others. A damp raw wind, the kind of New York wind she used to hate, carried the smells of pizza and garbage and diesel exhaust.

A late-model gray sedan stopped three lanes from curbside, blocking the traffic that had already been squeezed to a trickle by double-parked cars. She cringed as Tomas guided her into the crush of irate New Yorkers, struggling not to confuse normal horns and shouts with escape sirens.

Tomas opened the rear door, slammed it shut when she was inside, continued on foot to the other side of the street and disappeared.

The sedan merged into the crawl of traffic creeping and blaring its way north on Centre Street. Her one-time internist, Dr. Jan Lenz, who had come to the aid of the stricken man in the courtroom, glanced back at her from the passenger seat. "Kristýna, is it really you?"

"I hope so."

"You'll never know how you've been missed. Keep your composure. We still have to get out of Manhattan."

"I'll try. Thank you, Doctor.

In the rearview mirror she caught the eye of fat Viktor, the baker who had inspired her sister to open her pastry shop. He'd made an impressive transition from courtroom epileptic to driver. As usual he was sweating.

"Don't worry, Kristýna," he said, turning on the radio. "You've pulled it off. The good doctor and I barely had time to fetch the car. By the way, everyone in our little group managed to leave the courtroom before they sealed it. We saw them all at one point or another during my medically assisted departure."

"They got out?"

"All but Michaela. Not to worry, though. They won't be able to hold her long."

"Well . . . that's great. I can't stop shaking."

The climax of a honking barrage silenced them. They were somewhere in the heart of Chinatown. Delivery vans stopped at will. The newest offender had blocked the only lane still open. Kristýna held her breath until the driver came out of a basement door. He flipped off the world and drove away.

They turned west on Canal Street. "Listen to the radio," Viktor said. "If we can get through the Holland Tunnel before we hear your name, we've got the tense part behind us."

"If," Kristýna said. "I haven't seen traffic this bad for a long time."

"You haven't seen anything for a long time," Viktor quipped.

She didn't hear him. "Even if we get through, they've got helicopters."

"Yes," Lenz said, "but they don't have any idea what they're looking for. All they can do is close bridges and tunnels and search inside each car. That's what Viktor meant."

"That's what I meant. But it doesn't matter. You don't look like you. Besides, Tomas put some kind of ID in your purse. The guy who does my copies makes better stuff than the real thing."

"They'll know it's me."

Dr. Lenz reached over the seat and patted her on the knee. "Not a chance. Try to relax. You've got a long day ahead."

"Where am I going? Tell me."

"Out to sea," Viktor said. "Doctor Lenz is right. You need to relax."

Up ahead near the tunnel entrance Kristýna spotted a bank of flashing red, white and yellow lights. "God in heaven."

"I've got more news of Teresa," Lenz said.

"What?" She squeezed his arm. The lights were instantly forgotten.

"She's been seen again. We think she's on her way to northern Italy with a tribe of Gypsies."

The car stopped. There was some sort of commotion at the tunnel entrance. Drivers were rolling down their windows, cops were leaning into cars. Kristýna looked away. "Not now," she whispered. "Please, not now."

"It's a construction site," Viktor said. "People are asking about the problem, that's all. I took this route yesterday with Tomas. The same thing. Listen to the radio. The press will have your escape on the airwaves before the police. Anyway, the traffic's moving. Just not as fast as we'd like."

"Please relax," Dr. Lenz said. "You need to seem relaxed if they look inside. That goes for the rest of your trip, too."

Kristýna's head started to pound. She closed her eyes. Behind her pulsing lids she saw the police checkpoint. Viktor probably fabricated his story to put her at ease . . .

They inched closer to the tunnel. When she dared open her eyes she had a better view. The cops weren't checking anything in particular. They were just directing traffic and sticking their heads near open windows to answer questions. A yellow crane towered above, swinging giant steel beams through the dust. Construction. The fat man had been telling the truth.

A cheerful cop waived them ahead. They drove into the tunnel. The radio barked static until Lenz turned down the volume.

She looked at the traffic ahead, eerie in the artificial light. "My God . . . oh, my God. Am I really out?"

Lenz was about to say something when they came up from the tunnel on the Jersey side. Instead he turned up the radio.

A fresh wave of anxiety washed over her. News of the escape was on the air. How hard could it be to identify her now that she had become an international celebrity?

***

"Listen, Kristýna," Dr. Lenz said, "I want you to pay close attention to what I'm going to explain. You see yourself from the inside. Not strangers. They see you from the outside unless you give them a reason to see more. I don't want to make you self-conscious, but it's important that you know what I mean. We're going to switch cars. We're also giving you another identity. Keep reminding yourself you are the person that your disguise says you are. Put your heart into it, Kristýna. Pretend like you're on stage."

"Yes, alright, I'll try. Is anyone going to tell me how all of this was planned? How did my writing teacher in prison know what to tell me? I feel so completely... overwhelmed."

It's probably better if you stay in the dark. There will be time to fill in the blanks when this business is finished and you have your little girl."

***

They came to the warehouse district of Newark, congested as usual with trucks and delivery vans. "Slow down," Lenz ordered. "See it?"

"That little brick office building on the left?"

"Yes. Take the entrance road and pull around back. You'll see the warehouse."

Police cars prowled the area. Kristýna had been here before. She knew this was normal. She could almost think rationally, perhaps because her internal clock was functioning again. Not a quarter of an hour had passed since they'd emerged from the tunnel. A manhunt couldn't have been organized yet.

She watched without biting her lip as a cop car approached from the other direction. It passed and Viktor made his left turn. They drove around back. A metal garage door to one of several warehouses went up long enough for them to pull inside.

"Here," Viktor said, "you get a new you and another car."

CHAPTER FOUR

"It's the bottles!" Obruchev shouted into the receiver.

He had arrived earlier than usual at his lavish office in the Sears Tower, high above the Windy City. The nine-hour time difference between Illinois and Moscow was a monumental pain in the ass. Whenever he needed to talk with his suppliers in Russia, he had to haul himself to work at an ungodly hour.

The wind howled this raw autumn morning, the building swayed like a bamboo flagpole. He wanted to wring his wife's neck. All Lydia cared about was the "prestige" of an office near the top. She'd already trashed his ninth floor office – far more functional than this one – with her modern art collection. Now she wanted to treat the faggots from the society pages to modern art with a view.

God, how he longed for the day when he could get the hell out of here and live his own life. A few more months, a year at most, and he would be free of the pig.

So she had gotten him started with her inherited millions, something she never let him forget. As if he hadn't done his part. He had married her at the ripe age of 40. No one else had been willing to do that. He couldn't count the times he had almost come out and said it.

He'd better keep his cool. When Lydia vanished and he moved on to bigger things, he didn't need a nasty divorce on his record.

"You can't be serious," Vladimir mocked. "What's happening to you, my dear Stepan Mikhailovich? Been in Coca-Cola land too long?"

"Goddammit, I'm trying to give you advice. Run the numbers. Take a look at what I've done for you. If you lose your American market, you'll be back in borscht business."

"I resent that. You know damned well we've succeeded because we offer quality."

A violent gust set the tower swaying like a ship in heavy seas. Obruchev felt nauseous. "You know something? You make me sick. You have a distributor in this country for a reason. I'm going to tell you once more what I've been trying to get through your skull for the last year. Quality over here doesn't mean shit. Americans don't care what's in the bottle. You ship me all this new pepper stuff and vanilla crap and you think that's enough. Well, it's not. The Swedes understand. The Dutch and Danes get it. Even the fucking French. Taste their stuff. It's lousy. But look at the bottles it comes in. My wife wants to put them in a goddamn art museum. You can sell horse piss here if it's bottled in art. Quit putting so much money into your product. Put it in the containers. You do that, and I promise you'll make a fortune."

"I don't know, Stepan Mikhailovich. My family's been in this business for six centuries. There are traditions to uphold."

"Okay, enough. We'll talk when I'm in Moscow. That should give you time to look at your competitors' bottles. Time to decide if you want to stay with me. Our contract expires the end of this year. I'm unloading my slow sellers at renewal time and you're at the head of the list. The decision's yours, Vladimir. If I were you, I'd think long and hard about what's really important – tradition or money."

Obruchev slammed the receiver down and hit the intercom button. "Bring me a coffee, two Dramamine tablets and yesterday's mail. Hurry."

"Yes sir, Mr. Obruchev."

He flipped through his correspondence without interest until he came to a small airmail letter without a return address. Turning the wrinkled dirty epistle over in his hands, he could see that it was postmarked Ljubljana.

What the hell was this? Nobody in Slovenia had a clue how to reach him in the States. Correspondence from that part of the world always came to him through his Moscow office.

Inside was a type-written note folded around a short newspaper article. The typewriter was the old manual kind: the blurred letters betrayed worn keys and a bad ribbon:

Stepan Mikhailovich:

A young girl of unknown origin appeared last November in Žiri. She spoke fluent English, Czech and Slovenian – a considerable achievement. After the occurrence described in the enclosed clipping, she vanished from this region without a trace. She is apparently alive and in good health. If this news is significant to you, visit me before speaking with anyone else the next time you are here.

In God's Service,

Nikolai Petrovich

Obruchev's mind swam with questions he couldn't answer. If the girl mentioned really was Teresa, why had Rasputin waited until now to inform Obruchev of her fate? The auctioneer obviously knew what was supposed to happen to her or he wouldn't have bothered to write him at all. But how could he know? Only Bogdan had been told, and Bogdan's orders were clear. How did Rasputin get Obruchev's Chicago address? And most important, what was his real motive for sending the note? This was very strange. Maybe having a holy lunatic on the payroll wasn't such a good idea after all.

He unfolded the newspaper clipping. It was an obituary torn from a provincial weekly. Obruchev read the underlined death announcement:

Last week employees of the Rural Health Administration found the body of Zlatko Prlicev in his farmhouse near Idrija. The final autopsy report is not yet on record, but police have ruled out foul play. Prlicev had a long history of heart disease. He leaves behind neither relatives nor heirs.

Obruchev searched the ragged scrap of paper for a date. There was none. He found no mention of the girl Rasputin had him written about. How was the girl's disappearance related to Prličev's death? He didn't have a clue and, actually, he didn't give a damn. He'd never heard of Prličev. Teresa, if she was still alive, would quickly fade into the great mass of orphaned East European children. And Kristýna . . . well, Kristýna was serving a life sentence, bludgeoned into silence by the threats and promises he had made on his night of triumph. Rasputin's letter didn't change any of that.

There was, however, something he couldn't get off his mind. Had his cousin betrayed him? Finding out would be high on his order of business when he returned to Ljubljana.

CHAPTER FIVE

During the drive to Point Pleasant Kristýna tried to revive herself with meditation. Instead she fell into a deep, dreamless sleep. When Dr Lenz awoke her, she saw the Omega III moored at dockside. Kristýna had been on that fishing boat several times. She remembered its maiden voyage quite clearly. The boat belonged to a Czech friend who had invited Arthur to christen it with a unique name. Arthur, always the cardiologist . . .

A load of ice was being dumped into the hold, the last step before the trawler put out to sea. The captain walked to the car and helped lift the bags from the Newark warehouse out of the trunk. Moments later Kristýna sat with him in his quarters. "Name's Miloš," he said. "I'm a friend of Tomas. No need to worry. We're not doing anything unusual."

"I'm most grateful," Kristýna said.

"Don't mention it. I got our coordinates this morning. We're meeting a freighter around one a.m. It left Newark Harbor while you were still in court, Ms. Sondheim. This was the way your friends wanted it. Damn smart idea. The authorities probably won't think to look at ships that departed before your escape, at least not at first. There's food and drink in the mini-fridge. Try and get some rest. I won't return until it's time to transfer you."

***

Ten hours later, on the bridge of an aging Albanian container ship, Kristýna experienced the first real sensation of freedom since her escape. She had boarded from a dinghy, climbing up the hull on a worn rope ladder. The sea was choppy; she had been happy for the cable and safety harness during her struggle to the top. But her ascent had been less nerve-wracking than she had expected, thanks to a bank of low clouds that had plunged the moonlit night into blackness.

Now, as the moon emerged, she looked out over an endless sea, its whitecaps touched by the soft light from above. A world without walls spread to the horizon. It was as if she had been offered a glimpse of infinity.

Hard to believe that less than 24 hours had passed since the previous night, which she had spent in a claustrophobic prison cell. She had to fight back tears as relief swept over her.

But her relief was temporary. Her little girl was somewhere in that infinity, somewhere in that illusion of freedom, terrified and alone. When her tears finally came, they were shed for Teresa.

***

Adem, the captain, was on the radio. Irina, his gregarious wife, gave Kristýna a garlic-laced hug. "Are you alright, dear?"

"Yes, thank you. I couldn't get your story off my mind. The skipper of the Omega III told me what happened on the way out here. It made me so very sad."

Irina and Adem had lost their only daughter to the Trade in 1998. After they succeeded in tracing her disappearance to New Jersey, the owner of the shipping company for which they worked let them switch to the Newark route. They had learned enough English during layovers in the States to get the police involved in a search for their child.

A year later their efforts paid off – in a sense. Their daughter, Merita, was found dead in a back alley of Hoboken, her face no longer identifiable, her arms and feet a pin-cushion of track marks. In addition to assault and heroin addiction, forensic examination showed years of sexual abuse, abuse that had left her as lacerated inside as out. Like hundreds of thousands of so-called "Natashas," she had been a sex slave, an unwilling prostitute with nowhere to turn. She was only 17 when she died.

Since that horrible day, Adem and Irina had smuggled 50 girls home to Eastern Europe. Fifty out of a million. Not many, thought Kristýna, but better than none.

"Welcome," Adem said when he got off the radio. He stood up and kissed her on both cheeks. "You must be very tired.

We talk tomorrow. I show you to sleeping quarters before Irina start up conversation. We let that happen, she still be talking when sun come up."

"Adem, he always joking. But he is right. You go now to bed. We talk tomorrow."

"Yes, that's probably a good idea."

The stowaway room was near engine compartment, just big enough for one small person.

Adem said, "No first class but safe. Extra caution we taking now because of prison thing. You understand? In case we get surprise visit by US Navy, we need being ready. They come on board when they want, like they never hear of international waters. Whole country like that now. Preaching on everyone how to act, then do whatever they want. Best you sleep in hiding room at night."

***

Kristýna awoke to the blackness of a tomb. The bone-jarring throb of diesels scrambled her thoughts. She waited for her eyes to adjust, but the blackness refused to yield.

Sitting up on the hard mattress she groped around for a wall. Only cold riveted metal, no light switch or door handle.

As she became less groggy, she relaxed. This sarcophagus was a refuge, not a cage. She wasn't in jail any longer. Sooner or later, someone would get her out. The real problem awaited her when they did. Never mind how brilliant her escape from the hearing had been; never mind how exhilarating her success. These things were meaningless unless she rescued her daughter.

Sweeping the walls once more with an open hand she finally hit a button. It wasn't long until she heard a key in the lock. When the thick steel door opened, she saw Irina's silhouette in the dirty gray light of the engine room.

"You sleep good?" the captain's wife asked.

"I'm sure I did, thanks. I don't remember a thing."

"There's a light, you know. Didn't Adem tell you?" She pointed to the switch above the call button.

"He probably did. I was pretty tired. What time is it?"

"Lunch time," Irina said. "Come out now. News is good. No US Navy in area. No word of sea search on radio. You take a shower in our cabin. We have fresh clothes waiting. No need to go back in there until night. Unless we have to hide you, of course. Come."

Kristýna climbed out of her lair, stood and stretched. She watched Irina lock up, then swing some kind of enormous metal tank on hinges in front of the door and secure it with a well-hidden U bolt.

"We do this for Merita, our daughter," Irina said. "She would be happy we taking you home."

CHAPTER SIX

When FBI Special Agent Randall Connor awoke, the southern California sun was blazing down on him through gaps in the blinds. He slept naked, not in honor of J. Edgar Hoover but because pajamas made him sweat. Wrapping his robe around his 6'3," 220 pound torso, he stepped out on the balcony and inhaled deeply of the warm dry air. For a brief moment he forgot his anger over the interruption of his hard-earned leave. He even managed a smile. It was good to be back in L.A.

No one close to him, including his ex-wife and two grown daughters, could understand how a Memphis boy who drank percolated Maxwell House and ate fish only if it was battered and deep-fried could feel anything but loathing for Los Angeles. Hell, he couldn't understand it either. His older brother, Robert, a successful attorney with a beautiful wife and family, had fallen in love with a foul-mouthed stripper from West Memphis. On the day he died, Robert was still obsessed with her, undeterred by 20 years of rejection. Connor supposed he and his brother had the same genetic flaw.

Connor was here because of a request – not an order – from the Bureau's Director. He didn't appreciate being called back to work, but what the hell could he do? Years ago, Forsythe had gotten him the job he coveted, head of the International Operations Branch of ISD, and had given him latitude to get involved in overseas investigations when he should have been assigned to a desk somewhere. His hands-on style had pissed off its share of turf-conscious "legats," bureauspeak for legal attachés abroad. Bad blood aside, the work Connor did overseas had been the highpoint of his career. He wasn't the type not to return favors.

After a shower and three cups of coffee, he met his driver downstairs. The short ride to the L.A. Field Office stirred memories both pleasant and painful. During their years in

Los Angeles, he and his wife, Betty, had made a pact to stay together until the kids left for college, come what may. Connor assumed she would extend the deadline, especially now that he was slated for a transfer to her home town of D.C. He had been wrong.

A few blocks from Wilshire Boulevard, their route dovetailed with the route he'd driven every day for the better part of a decade. First came a peaceful neighborhood of quaint villas, palm trees, red brick shops and cozy restaurants. If it weren't for the roar of traffic a hundred yards away, you might imagine yourself in a pleasant village on the Mediterranean coast. Then you turned left and ran into Wilshire, the source of the noise. The other L.A., big, grimy and loud, greeted you with all the charm of an unwanted surprise party.

In the distance, he saw the Federal Building that housed the Los Angeles Field Office. It was an architectural nightmare of whitewashed concrete surrounded by new glass office towers. With its antiquated styling and bizarre display of spheres and antennas on the roof, the place looked like it housed North Korea's secret police.

The driver turned off Wilshire for the main entrance. Concrete barriers lined the street. Tattered flags, planted like trees around the lawn, flapped in the breeze. Drunks slept on concrete benches.

The press, which wasn't supposed to know of his arrival in Los Angeles, met him en masse outside the entrance. Connor nodded politely but declined to answer questions, a task made easier by his own ignorance of why he was here. Cops held the restive band of reporters at bay long enough for him to slip inside the building.

The elevator whisked him up to the 17th floor. The dour hall with portraits of former FBI agents looked more dilapidated than before, but was otherwise unchanged. Alone, he stopped at the single window and gazed out at a field of neat green tennis courts. In the background the city and terraced hillsides shimmered in the hazy morning light.

He had stood for a time at this very spot the day Betty left him, feeling certain that some horrible fate lurked in the shadows. He experienced a similar premonition now.

To hell with it, he thought. His premonition had been wrong before; it would be wrong again.

His heart beat a little faster as he neared the dark paneled wall with the two enormous black doors at its center. The FBI seal gave him the same mixed jolt of pride and trepidation it had given him throughout his career. The predictable moment of self-doubt came on schedule: was he, at age 44, up to this new challenge?

No use dwelling on it until someone told him what that challenge was.

He entered the maze of bullet-proof glass, then passed into a labyrinth of offices and labs. Kenneth Hatcher was waiting for him in a small briefing room.

Hatcher, so chatty and personable the previous night, was all business. He reminded Connor of a middle-aged corporate executive in his nicely fitting dark suit and restrained tie. He parted his thinning hair neatly on the side, wore simple gray wire-rimmed glasses and displayed a politically correct physique: not thin, not fat; not short, not tall. Hatch was the kind of guy you honored with platitudes at retirement banquets. Not because he wasn't good at his job – he was – but because everything about him was so unobtrusive he was impossible to describe in original terms.

They sat at the conference table. "You slept okay, Randall?"

"Thanks, Hatch, as well as ever. More importantly, is anyone going to tell me why I'm here?"

"Yes. I am."

"You could have done that last night. I don't think I'm exactly a security risk."

"I could have if I'd known. Sorry, Randall."

Hatch placed a coffee pot and two cups on the table, then poured with a steady hand. Whatever the mystery assignment turned out to be, Connor hoped it included a role for his former comrade-in-arms. They worked well together. Connor was impulsive and outspoken; Hatch, cautious and quiet.

"Okay, Randall, this is what's happening. Forsythe's out here in L. A. for some big symbolic meeting with police and military leaders from South America. Normally, he would have had you come to HQ in Washington, but he didn't want to break off his trip. Not that he gives a damn about working with law enforcement in the Southern Hemisphere. He can't stand the thought of it. So he's not here for the official reasons. He's trying to dodge a bullet."

"Which one? They've been flying non-stop lately."

"He doesn't want the press and public to find out this Sondheim mess has him running scared. But it does, Randall. After Oklahoma City and Nine-Eleven, the Bureau's not enjoying the best publicity. Some guy busted into our Internet site the other day just to post a question: 'Forsythe or Hindsythe?'"

"Anyway, you get the picture. The President and Justice Department are under the gun. Forsythe knows that if he fucks up this one he's history. I can't blame the guy for not wanting to go out on a sour note. So you're here to solve the mess. The fact is, Forsythe needs you and he's going to make sure you get a little more than promised when you take the Washington job – more money, more time off."

"I'm here to solve what mess?"

"I told you. Sondheim."

"Last I heard she was comfortably ensconced in a New York state prison."

"Where the hell have you been?"

"My place in the Ozarks. I've got a phone in case my kids need to reach me. Otherwise, I'm isolated – just like I want it. No TV, no newspapers. Just bass and lures and real peaceful evenings with a book."

"So you really don't know?"

"Don't know what, Hatch?"

"That Kristýna Sondheim has escaped. Not from prison, from a Manhattan courtroom during a post-trial hearing. There's a reasonable presumption she's crossed state lines. A lot of people think she's managed to leave the country. So guess who inherits the job of running her down? You. The master at bringing home fugitives."

Connor drained his coffee and stared at the dregs. "This is absurd. I haven't been on the fugitive detail for almost two years. I'm going to tell Forsythe to pick someone else."

"Don't bother, Randall. He's desperate, there's a big PR component and the public still hasn't forgotten your Somalia coup. There are not only the long-term benefits I mentioned; there's also discretionary funding, provided by Justice with no strings attached. You succeed, and I'll guarantee that Forsythe will make it worth your while. A lump sum, Randall. Pay off your new place, get ahead on your alimony."

Connor shook his head, incredulous "Jesus."

Hatch was about to warm up the coffee when none other than FBI Director Jack Forsythe walked into the room. "Randall, nice to see you."

The men shook hands, Connor a bit reluctantly.

"I don't know if it's nice to see you or not, Jack. You're going to give me the specifics, I assume?"

"When you're in the air, you'll be briefed on what we know and given your schedule for tomorrow."

CHAPTER SEVEN

An Indian family, a whirling dervish of color, moved away in a chattering flock. A buttoned-down businessman who wanted to talk Chicago Bulls and pork bellies got the message and chose another chair. Even the bartender, trapped between the long marble bar and the wall of bottles behind it, kept his distance.

Dressed in a dark tailored suit, his Rolex and gold cuff links visible when he placed his arms on the bar, Obruchev was oblivious to the impact of his rancor. He ordered another vodka, his third – Moskovskaya straight up.

He should have shot the bitch the first time, he thought. What had he really gained by playing games? The satisfaction of tracking her down after her escape? Yes, okay. The pleasure of seeing her convicted for the murder of her family? Sure. The enjoyment of knowing that she had paid a price for her betrayal, a price she would continue to pay as long as the fate of her child remained unknown to her. Yeah, that too.

But his actions had been those of a younger man, a hothead, a soldier in the heat of battle who loses sight of his own self-interest. He should have shot her and her child when he had the chance. Alright, the kid first, the kid in front of her eyes. If he had called it even at that point he wouldn't be facing potential problems now.

Maybe he was overreacting. Maybe his cousin, Bogdan, had carried out his orders after all; maybe the cops would hunt down Kristýna and kill her for him. But he couldn't be sure. The bitch was lucky. She might end up in a position to fuck with his plans. No way he'd be taking any more chances.

His decision? Easy. If the kid was still alive, she wouldn't be for long. If Kristýna managed to evade the cops, she wouldn't escape him. A shot through her pretty head would do just fine.

When they called his flight, he managed to pull himself together. He had an image to maintain wherever he went. Weaving through the corridors of O'Hare in a drunken rage wouldn't do. He was a Chicago legend, man of old-world sophistication who had achieved the American Dream. Like plenty of his predecessors, he had gotten his start through marriage. But that didn't explain everything. He had doubled his wife's fortune in short order, then gone on to win the hearts of Chicagoans by giving more to charity than anyone in recent memory.

Maybe the vodka had helped, Obruchev thought. He was feeling almost cheerful as he strode up to first-class check-in. He would be flying Lufthansa. He always did. A stop in Frankfurt, then on to Moscow. Once a month for years he had followed the same routine – both here and in Russia. Tonight's change was insignificant. All he'd done was phone his secretary after he heard the news of Kristýna's escape and instructed her to move his scheduled departure ahead. A crisis with one of his Russian suppliers was the reason he'd given his office staff and the lie he'd fed Lydia, his socialite wife. At the other end he would make sure his alibi held.

***

"Stepan Mikhailovich!"

The greetings came from all sides as a throng of porters and assistants escorted him to his suite at the Metropol. He was a regular and welcome presence at this venerable Moscow hotel, for it was here that Obruchev had his second office. There was always legitimate business to entrust to his on-call staff, whatever the real reason for his stay. Each visit left behind a paper trail of normal entrepreneurial activity, a trail that stretched back over all the years during which he'd built and maintained his distributorship for Russian vodka in the States.

It was in the spectral world beneath this canopy of correctness that his other life unfolded, complete with "real" false papers, a name linked to a nonexistent Belorussian, and an income stream surpassing that of his considerable American revenues. Stepan Mikhailovich comprised the first and patronymic components of both of his names, the one belonging to the naturalized American citizen and the one of his Belorussian stand-in. The only difference was the surname: Obruchov instead of Obruchev.

Since Obruchov and Obruchev were pronounced identically in Russian, he could be addressed in public by either name without revealing the existence of his two identities. And since it was easy to confuse in writing one of his surnames with the other, he never worried that he might be nailed by the records of hotel clerks or reservation agents.

His passports were from different countries and bore those slightly different surnames. To be triply safe in the computer age, he had made sure the photograph on his Belorussian fake – though it resembled the real Obruchev enough to get him where he needed to go – could not be matched conclusively to the photo on his American passport. He wasn't the first man to lead an unknown second life, and knew he wouldn't be the last. But he doubted anyone before him had done a better job of it.

"Good to be back," he said to his chief secretary, Ivana Nikolaevna. "I have unpleasant family matters to deal with in Kursk. But when I return next week it will be business as usual. I want you to schedule the normal round of meetings – preferably over dinner – with the CEOs or top executives of my suppliers. Make clear that there are critical decisions to be taken. Use your tact, Ivana, to discern the entertainment preferences of these gentlemen. Kotov will assist you with the arrangements."

"Your flights, Stepan Mikhailovich? Would you like me to book those as well?"

"All taken care of. Most thoughtful of you to ask."

The next morning, Obruchov, the Belorussian, caught one of the two non-stop flight to Ljubljana. By afternoon he was a prominent guest at the Grand Hotel Union in the Slovenian capital – rested, refreshed and ready.

***

He climbed the dank staircase, illuminated only by an occasional low-wattage bulb. The walls were damp concrete, and full of cracks. On each landing were several maroon doors. The metal numbers had fallen off most, leaving faded outlines as reminders of their earlier presence. Crazy, he thought, that a guy he paid almost a million Euros a year lived like this.

No windows, no natural light, no way to know a bright autumn sun still hung above the River of Seven Names. Kids laughed somewhere, a tea kettle let out a howl, a television tuned to a foreign station played Austrian beer hall music. It sounded noisier than the international terminal at O'Hare.

Obruchev approached floor seven, pursued by the echo of his own footsteps. The smells of coal smoke and cabbage assaulted him as he stopped in front of Rasputin's door, smells that evoked long-forgotten memories of his cold and colorless youth.

A rat scurried across his English bench-made shoes. The idea of shooting it flashed through his mind. He patted his breast holster and knocked, both gestures wasted. The rat was gone and Rasputin already stood at the door, holding it open with one hand while beckoning with the other for his visitor to enter.

Obruchev felt uneasy. How could he explain the ghostly silence with which the man he had come to see had reached his door? Rasputin wore heavy leather-soled shoes. His apartment had no rugs. The tiniest step in this dreary Stalinist echo chamber reverberated several floors up and down. It didn't make any sense.

Unless, of course, Rasputin had been expecting his visit, listened to him climb the stairs and waited beside the door for him for him to knock. But that was even more far-fetched. A hundred people a day went up these stairs. Obruchev was ahead of schedule; he had also come unannounced. No one knew he was in Slovenia.

Familiar suppositions clouded his thinking, suppositions that had troubled him since the letter from this inscrutable eccentric arrived in Chicago. Could Rasputin be more than a fake priest? Could he possibly be a mystic and sorcerer, as many colleagues in the Trade believed? Did he really have the means to bring down the rich and powerful with some sort of mysterious curse? Rubbish, all of it. Obruchev was a rational businessman living in modern America. He knew what was believable and what wasn't.

But one thing irritated him no end: he was also a Slav, and the collective unconscious of every Slav bore fleeting shadows of medieval witchcraft. Try as he might, there were certain things he couldn't deny, things as strange as the letter. For example, Rasputin had just walked on air. He had never shown the slightest desire for the naked girls he auctioned night after night. And he claimed to be a holy man, yet played a major role in one of the most unholy businesses on God's earth. The list was endless.

Maybe there was a rational explanation for these things, but Obruchev didn't care to take chances at this point in his life. He knew two facts about Rasputin: the man did an incomparable service for the Trade, and he scared the hell out of everyone – even those, like himself, who tried to deny it.

"Nikolai Petrovich."

"Stepan, I was expecting you. Come inside. I'll start the samovar."

"No thanks. No tea. Put out your goddamn incense."

"It would anger God, which is not in your interest. Have a seat."

Obruchev let himself down on the tattered brown sofa. He watched in amazement as Rasputin lit more incense and started the samovar. He'd been here 30 seconds and had already been defied twice.

Rasputin handed him the cup of tea he had refused and sat down across from him. "You have problems, my friend."

"So what? Don't we all?"

"Perhaps, but not as severe as yours. Would you like me to tell you what they are, or would you prefer to tell me?" He could feel Rasputin's cobalt eyes piercing the vault of his secret life.

Obruchev was tempted to let him talk but quickly decided against it. If by some miracle Rasputin was right, it would add to the mysterious power this man exercised over him.

"Nikolai Petrovich, I entrusted a young girl to the care of my cousin last year. Is this the girl you wrote to me about?"

"None other."

"Tell me what happened?"

"Bogdan came to me and confessed. He couldn't bring himself to carry out your orders. He sold her instead to Zlatko Prlicev – quite handsomely, I understand. The old man wanted to raise a servant who would look after him and his farm when he was no longer able. The old man was willing to pay for his insurance with cash and land."

Obruchev leaned forward and forced himself to scrutinize that round two-dimensional iconic face with its other-worldly eyes and pointed goatee.

"You're absolutely certain Bogdan sold her to this Zlatko person?"

"Yes."

"And then Zlatko died?"

"You know the answer. I sent you his obituary. Drink your tea, Stepan Mikhailovich. It will help your nerves."

"My nerves are fine."

Rasputin lit some more incense. "It is the time after Zlatko's death that interests you. Let's not play cat and mouse."

"Then get to the point."

"When the police discovered his body, Zlatko had been dead for days, maybe weeks. The girl was gone. Her presence was unknown to the authorities, so her disappearance never came to light."

"What happened to her?" Obruchev said, growing more irritated by the second. "Can you or can't you tell me?"

"She was taken by Gypsies passing through the area."

"Jesus Christ, do you know where she is?"

"We will speak of that when you have resolved your family business. Every day I work with Bogdan. You are the boss, Stepan Mikhailovich, but you are rarely here. Thrusting myself into the middle of your disagreement would force me to serve two masters. This I cannot and will not do."

"Cut the crap. Tell me if you know where she is."

"Return when you have resolved your family business, not before."

"For Christ's sake, Nikolai, you've made a fortune working for me. You can do me one small favor."

"Stepan Mikhailovich, I hasten to remind you that the auction system accounts for your high profit-to-cost ratio. Both sides of the feather tickle. And we do not speak of a small favor. Come back when you have taken care of your situation."

Obruchev stormed out. Coal dust and cabbage fumes pursued him down the staircase and out into the frosty night. Smells, memories – whatever they were, he couldn't get them out of his nostrils. Like the treatment he had just received, they made him furious.

***

General Slobodan Majdak raised his bushy eyebrows when Obruchev handed him a second envelope. The large man had apparently eaten well. He belched while he rifled through the contents. "This is a lot. What do you want?"

"Heightened alert around the plant, beginning immediately. We're entering a new stage of our operation. We'll start with a review of your security arrangements. Not on paper, in the field."

"Tonight?"

"Tonight."

The General belched again and reached for his phone. "Bring a Tatra to my residence. Make arrangements for the driver to get home. Yes, you heard me. When? Now, idiot."

Obruchev nodded. The man had gotten physically flabby on his new wealth but it hadn't softened his spirit. Majdak, once a butcher for the enemy, now the Ljubljana regime's trusted ally, was indispensable to operations in Slovenia. The general arranged security for the factory and its surroundings. He used his genocidal reputation, along with an occasional ugly murder, to ensure the silence of his circle of conspirators, and he employed the heavy military equipment at his disposal to create the illusion of industrial activity.

He was also the interface between Obruchev's bogus defense company and the Slovenian government. He paid the leases on the property, provided detailed written progress reports on the factory's renovation and described in public and private meetings the jobs that would soon be available to the impoverished citizens of Žiri.

General Majdak's task was as daunting as it was critical. Obruchev remained vigilant for any sign that his chief of operations might be losing his grip. So far there had been none.

"Let's go," the general said. "They'll be here by the time the elevator gets downstairs."

Obruchev polished off his last sip of coffee and tugged on his sheepskin jacket. Outside it was sleeting. A nasty wind howled in the bare trees lining the boulevard.

Their wait was brief. The rumble of an 8-wheel drive Tatra soon eclipsed the sounds of the stormy night. A uniformed young driver let the truck idle, hopped down, saluted and held the door open for the general.

Twenty minutes later they turned onto the nearly invisible road to the abandoned plant. The first checkpoint blocked their progress at 50 meters.

While a flashlight probed the general's pockmarked face to rule out the chance of an impostor, Obruchev stared into the beam of the Tatra's headlights. The sleet had changed to heavy wet snow. For several minutes, soldiers examined every cavity of the truck.

"Thank you, General," the guard said when they had finished. "You stressed that you wanted thoroughness."

"Raise the bar."

The truck growled ahead. "Nasty night," Obruchev said.

"Normal night," General Majdak corrected. "What does your review entail?"

"Drive me to the entrance. If I know my cousin, he'll already be inside preparing for tonight. I wish to have a word with him before the auction starts. But that's not my primary objective. I'm worried about illicit entry."

"You shouldn't be."

"Describe to me the likely fate of a hiker who wanders onto our property. First by accident, then by design."

"By accident or design, he encounters a high security fence. Razor wire, no trespassing signs in several languages. He turns around if he's not drunk. If he tries to get through, he bleeds to death. So let's not waste time on an intruder. He doesn't make it. We had one last month. His body ended up in the plant incinerator."

"Then describe what awaits the trained military man who is on a mission to visit us. Let's say he manages to cross the razor wire barrier. I assume it can be done with the proper equipment."

"Perhaps, but the next barrier is more challenging. As the intruder moves closer, the defense perimeter becomes smaller. There are guard towers manned round the clock. The soldiers are well-armed, the searchlights blinding. The fences linking the towers are modeled on US prison designs. I keep dogs and soldiers on twenty-four hour patrol inside that perimeter just in case. What the hell are you expecting? The Israeli Army? If you're worried about reporters or green party martyrs, you can relax."

Three checkpoints and several muddy culverts later, they arrived at the parking lot near the main factory entrance. The only vehicle in the lot was a snow-covered Tatra. Bogdan was here, of course. He was a creature of habit, Obruchev knew, always had been. He arrived each evening at nine o'clock to do the books from the previous night's auction.

Obruchev pictured his cousin now, hard at work inside. When he finished up with the accounting, he would package the banknotes in neat bundles and return them to the massive safe, ready for dispatch early the next morning. Then, before the midnight chaos, Bogdan would have a drink or two and think about whatever he thought about.

They stopped beside the parked truck. Obruchev said, "You've done a good job, Majdak."

"Anything else, then?"

"Come in for a drink. My cousin would be honored."

***

Obruchev entered the twelve digit code he had committed to memory. The steel door opened on silent hinges. Bogdan looked just as he had imagined him, sitting on the stage at his portable table surrounded by stacks of bills. He glanced up, startled. "Stepan, General Majdak, come in."

The general walked through the metal detector with a pistol beneath his greatcoat. The alarm let out a shriek. "Jesus, turn that goddamn thing off."

Bogdan rushed to the control panel and flipped a switch. "Sorry, General."

Obruchev walked through the silenced detector to the stage and embraced his cousin. General Majdak slapped the snow off his hat, had a quick drink and left.

"Stepan, you're early," Bogdan said when they were alone. "That's good. We have a lot to discuss."

Obruchev was suddenly aware of the smell of coal smoke. He smiled at the blazing drums around the stage. Good to know there was a rational explanation; good the odor of boiling cabbage wasn't mixed in. "Discuss?"

"Yes, and it's all good. We've had a surge in profits. The girls are gorgeous, nothing new. The crew hasn't changed. It's the amount our clients are willing to pay. From what they tell me, there's been a worldwide spike in demand. They're buying like never before in Japan, the US, the Middle East. This is big, Stepan. If it keeps up, it will be very big. We'll be talking billions."

Obruchev filled their glasses. Bottoms up, like old times. "Too bad you're out."

"What? You've lost your mind."

Obruchev poured the glasses full. "It's because of your weakness, Bogdan. You know why I'm here early. Where's the kid?"

His cousin forced a smile. "Dead." He nodded toward the incinerator. "Her ashes are in there. Deep down."

"Bullshit."

"Believe what you want, Stepan. That's the truth."

"Bullshit."

"Not bullshit. She's been in there since she arrived."

"You've burned your last indulgence. I can't work with liars."

"What the fuck's your problem? You've gotten some kind of sick idea in your mind."

"I don't think so."

Obruchev jumped off the stage, nimbly for a large man, and pulled the feared black lever. The incinerator door rose slowly, exposing a flat grate above lines of burners. The conveyor belt began its metallic death march toward the oven. A thousand tiny daggers of blue flame flickered orange when air hissed into the inferno. Wind currents swirled through the hall, sending banknotes in all directions.

Bogdan laughed out loud. "So we're not talking? One of us is going in there? Wanna fight it out? Not a good idea, Stepan, because you'll lose." He glanced at his breast holster, which he'd hung over the backrest of a chair near the conveyor. "You're being ridiculous. We grew up together. We've made millions together. You've got some bad information. We don't have to take this road."

Obruchev reached into his jacket, watching his cousin's smile vanish as he drew his automatic pistol. "You're a fool, Bogdan. You shut the metal detector off before I walked in. Did you really think I wanted to have a drink with that asshole general? Go ahead. Go for your gun. I won't have to drag you as far."

Bogdan lunged. Obruchev hit him in the air with a stream of bullets.

Bogdan's momentum carried him onto the conveyor, which creaked blindly toward the incinerator.

Bogdan regained consciousness before the conveyor reached the oven. He struggled wildly to sit up. Obruchev watched him, mesmerized. What he saw was a perfect image of himself – the short stout legs, the muscular gut, the large bald head ringed by a band of closely cropped gray hair.

The image stayed with him after his cousin's screams ceased to echo in his head. It haunted him while he observed that night's auction and chose a new business manager. It accompanied him through the alleys of Žiri and the streets of Ljubljana. It followed him to Kursk and Moscow and back to Slovenia. He had witnessed his own death, and there wasn't a damn thing he could do about it.

***

He supposed he'd been uptown too long. As he joined the great human exodus from lower Manhattan at the end of the business day, he couldn't believe he'd worried about being recognized by the employees of the nearby courthouse. In his dark suit and heavy wool overcoat, he blended perfectly into the mob of accountants, lawyers, bureaucrats and executives stampeding toward taxi stands and subway stops.

At 26 Federal Plaza he dropped the letter that Tomas had given him into one of several mailboxes. Jostled from all sides by like-dressed refugees from work, he fought his way north toward home. Nothing to do now but pray.

CHAPTER EIGHT

"Get up, please," Rasputin said. "We need to talk, and we will talk outside."

Pimenko sank more deeply into the velvet armchair. Still in his heavy woolen coat, he picked up a chalice from a table and turned it over in his hands. "What's with you? I'm finally comfortable."

"Please put the chalice down. We must leave now."

"It's nice to be in a holy setting again. I want to confess, Nikolai Petrovich." A mocking smile engulfed his broad face. "Where's a hassock? I'll get down on my knees."

"Come. Otherwise the transaction will have to wait."

They were in the sanctuary of Rasputin's church, their usual meeting place. Pimenko's organization had tentacles deep inside the police and intelligence services of the Western world, enabling him to provide valuable information to those in the Trade willing to pay his exorbitant fees. He had approached Obruchev a decade ago to offer his services but Obruchev had rejected the offer and implied that he considered its bearer a charlatan. It was an insult Pimenko neither forgave nor forgot. That Pimenko would later count among his clients the corporate holy man did not occur to anyone. Yet Rasputin had by now become the Russian's biggest consumer of information in Slovenia . . .

Pimenko tossed the chalice in the air, caught it and gently returned it to the table. "So what's going on? Why the change?"

"Coincidence," Rasputin said, though this was far from the truth. It had been three days since Bogdan's murder, two since Rasputin had become the dacha's new occupant. "Workmen will arrive at four o'clock. I am selling the church. Its contents are being transported to another location."

"Jesus Christ, can't these guys wait? I finally get religion and you choose that moment to put me out in the cold."

Rasputin reached for his coat. "You may go somewhere warm when we've concluded our transaction."

"Where? That stinking apartment of yours?"

"I have given up the apartment. Answer my questions and take down my future requests. When that is done, we'll conclude our business and you can think about bodily comforts."

Pimenko stood and stretched. He was a big man, as gregarious as he was violent. "Quite a change, doing business with you. Most clients greet me with women, food , drink – and the accommodations in which to enjoy them. But, Nikolai Petrovich, I must admit that you pay me well. So well I'm willing to tolerate your austerity. Shall we?"

They left the church and walked through the winter forest on a footpath. In several hundred yards they came to a frozen river. The path forked, following the shallow banks in either direction. "I should've brought my skates," Pimenko said. "Does skating appeal to you, Nikolai Petrovich? I would someday like to see a man in a frock skate. You would be my first choice."

"Do you have my information?"

"What kind of a question is that? When have I failed you? No, I don't have it. The FBI was just brought into the hunt. But my people are already in place. You'll hear as soon as there is something of substance to report. And, Nikolai Petrovich, you might have thanked me for the information on Obruchev's early arrival. Money alone does not replace common courtesy."

"Thank you. You are saying that the American national police were just brought in? It's been days since her escape. How is this possible?"

"Rivalries, the normal barnyard. First the court cops don't want to admit she's not in the building, then the provincial cops don't want to admit they can't find her. It's as simple as that. Same the world over. I told you: when there's something to report, you'll be the first to know. You have my word. Anything else?"

"Yes. If the destination is Europe you will tell me which law enforcement agencies are on her trail, what that trail is and which rescue groups are helping her. Is this request beyond your reach?"

"Beyond my reach? Half the Russian Mafia depends on my services. I'll have the goods. And please make sure I know where your new church is. It would be distressing if I were forced to bow down before false idols."

Rasputin thrust his hand in his coat pocket and pulled out a roll of banknotes. "For your work to date. Go to Ljubljana and confess."

***

Back at his church, Rasputin removed his heavy boots and passed through the iconostasis into the sanctuary. In normal circumstances he would have been aggravated that the movers were late. But this afternoon he felt oddly relieved. These surroundings, so comforting, so reminiscent of the Sofia Cathedral in whose shadow he had come of age, would soon be gone. A part of his soul that had not yet spoken longed to say farewell.

He stretched out on the chaise longue where he often slept when it was too late to return to his flat in town. Rays from the low winter sun streamed in through the stained glass window, caressing his world with the spectral light of Eternity. It was, he knew, a sign that God wished to commune with him.

Rasputin closed his eyes and quickly drifted into a sentient rapture. Hovering between wakefulness and sleep, Heaven and Earth, he waited for the voice of the Almighty. But it was not God who called to him but, rather, his past. Feverish memories from his youth, memories long repressed, pushed their way into his awareness . . .

***

His recollections were as vivid as the events about which he dreamed. He was asleep in his bedroom in Novgorod when the Devil came to him, disguised as a girl. She smiled as she slid off her skirt and stepped out of her underwear. He screamed at her to stop. He knew her from school, she would listen. But she didn't seem to hear. Her dark eyes devoured him as she lifted her sweater above her head to expose her full breasts.

"Come, Nikolai, and I shall show you Heaven," she said. "You have been deceived by God into thinking your song honors Him. It is really for me. I am the flesh. I am bliss. The ecstasy God promises you is a pitiful imitation of the ecstasy I can give. He is death while I am life."

Breathless now, Nikolai stared at the black triangle between the girl's legs, close enough now for him to reach out and touch. His hand, ignoring the commands of his mind, began an involuntary journey toward the Gates of Hell. He was powerless. So irresistible was the urge that neither his will nor his prayers could halt the march of Evil.

God had endowed Nikolai with the voice of angels, had chosen him as His messenger on Earth. That voice sang out in protest. But his rich unwavering tenor, the God-given wonder that filled the Sofia Cathedral Sunday upon Sunday with a beauty not heard since the time of the Tsars, emerged as a hideous groan of lust.

As his hand brushed the spot and his burning desire eclipsed the stark admonitions of God, the girl vanished. Nikolai awoke the next morning to find his pajamas stuck to his genitals, glued there by some disgusting leakage of his body.

Night after night, the girl returned. Week after week, Nikolai Petrovich sang praises to the Lord. But he no longer trusted himself. God had blessed him with the only happiness he had known in 16 years on Earth, yet he felt destined to betray his Lord and Savior. The Devil would not release him until the deed was done. Such was the Power of Evil.

Near desperation he remembered a ritual Father Grigoriy had offered to perform several years ago on boys at the dawn of puberty, a ritual that would protect against the very torture Nikolai now suffered. He had refused for lack of understanding. But the ritual was timeless. A wave of hope, sweet as a blessing from the Lord, washed over him.

He prayed and fasted for a week. Then, on a frigid night shortly after New Year's, he snuck into the Sofia Cathedral. Father Grigoriy's office was open. He lit a lantern and went to the bookshelf. The medieval tome was still where it had been when the good Father had showed it to the boys in the choir. The painted case containing the surgical instruments from Renaissance Italy had not moved from the desk. Nikolai placed them carefully in a burlap bag, extinguished the lantern and slipped out into the black night.

At home he locked his bedroom door, lit 33 candles and prepared a fresh offering of incense. He opened the ancient leather-bound volume, careful not to crack its pages or scuff its cover, and read in Latin the words he knew would save his life. The Devil, he learned, entered the male in adolescence and built a bodily castle in the testes, located in a sack of skin just below the penis. Yes, yes, it must be exactly so. This was near the stain of his nightly emissions.

He studied the surgical diagrams running down the sides of the pages. Removing two olive-sized glands from their hiding place in the skin sack or scrotum deprived the Devil of a home within the male body. The process, he read, had been used for many centuries, both to prevent the voice of boys who sang their praises to God from losing its beauty and to rescue from the fires of Hell those who, like Nikolai, were torn between saintliness and sin.

It was three o'clock in the morning when he began. Inside the fine old case with the gleaming surgical instruments was a note in Father Grigoriy's hand. The two vials of solution and the special string, the note explained, were not part of the original the medieval process. Yet there was no harm in using these to lessen the pain, to stem the bleeding and ward off infection, which was a favorite weapon of the Devil. God, Himself, had given His permission.

Accompanying the note were sketches and directions, likewise in Father Grigoriy's hand. At the conclusion of these pages, the priest wrote that the procedures in the book were otherwise to be followed without deviation.

Nikolai swabbed his scrotum with some of the liquid from the vial marked for that purpose. His skin lost all sensation but his mother started walking up and down the hallway, apparently unable to sleep. She knocked twice on his door, then went back to bed. Nikolai wasted no time in pulling taut the skin beneath his penis, and in making two slits shown in the book with the indicated knife. The shallow cuts did not hurt but they bled on the towel he had placed beneath his buttocks. The lavish flow of red impeded his view of the cavity in which the Devil lurked.

He consulted the book again, then jabbed a finger through the incisions. He could feel the hard little olives he needed to remove. Miraculously, the bleeding stopped and he could see what held them each in place – a slimy cord labeled funiculus spermaticus in the book.

He used Father Grigoriy's string to tie off the spermatic cords before cutting them with a tiny scissor-like mechanism from the case. Then he tied off and sliced the veins still connected to the glands.

Just as the book said, the slightest pressure pushed the testes out through the incisions. He placed them as if they were glass eyes in a ceramic bowl and reread Father Grigoriy's instructions. The thread with which he had tied his spermatic cords would dissolve. All that remained before he closed the incisions was to spread about the orange liquid that would stave off infection . . .

When he had sewn up his scrotum with a needle from the case, he hid the bloody towel under his bed. Then he poured a little kerosene from an unlit lantern over the testes in the ceramic bowl and set fire to them with a candle.

The odor, which on another occasion might have made him gag, filled him with joy. It was the smell of his first real triumph in the fight against Evil.

When he awoke the next morning he was sick to his stomach, but the sticky emulsion that had fouled both his body and soul was absent. The girl had not come. There had been no full breasts, no raised arms as fingers played in heaps of tangled hair, no black triangle thrust toward his mouth.

It was then that he knew. He was not God, but he was a god among humans. He saw clearly the obstacles that existed on Earth to a deeper union between its male inhabitants and God, knew he had been sent by God to remove these obstacles. Men were driven by animal instinct away from their Master; women, emissaries of the Devil one and all, made sure this tragic state of affairs persisted. Yet there was a solution, and Nikolai's young mind was quick to grasp it . . .

***

When the movers knocked, Rasputin awoke with his hand on his penis. It was limp, just as it had been for decades.

CHAPTER NINE

"Okay, we're gonna freeze camera four right . . . here. I'll hold the frame while we fast forward the exit footage on camera five."

"Is there a time on the film in four?" Connor asked.

"No. The clock in the mechanism is broken. The date's right, just not the hour."

"So this could be morning or afternoon? You're telling me you've got no idea?"

"Wrong," the forensics tech said. "The security people always start the camera thirty minutes before the courthouse opens."

"Which would be?"

"Nine o'clock."

"This day was no exception? Someone's checked?"

"Special Agent Wilson interviewed the entire staff. No exception. Clock or not, we can come pretty close."

"Well?"

"The couple you're looking at entered between ten and ten fifteen. The hearing started at ten forty. That puts these two in the building at the time of the incident."

"Unless they had already exited."

The technician smiled that all-knowing geek smile Connor hated. "They hadn't. We have visual evidence."

Connor cracked the blinds in search of a more pleasant view. The grounds of the New York Field Office had never looked so good. "Let's see it."

"Nine-four-eight-four . . . just a second while I search. We're lucky someone thought to grab this tape before it recorded over itself. Okay, I'm freezing again. There you have what you might take for the same couple on the way out. Not a great image, but Ogden was able to work with it. This camera has a functioning clock. It's eleven nineteen."

"The angle's lousy."

"We've got enough to make a partial identification."

"What's a 'partial' identification? Either you know or you don't."

"We know the man is the man who entered earlier. Whether the woman is Sondheim we weren't able to determine with total certainty. She is, however, not the woman the guy came in with. If you look carefully at the first frame, the entry frame, you notice that the suit and shoes of the woman who came in don't perfectly match the suit and shoes of the exiting woman."

"Could have fooled me."

"When Ogden zoomed in, it was obvious. Seams in the jacket, button types, stitch patterns in the shoes – stuff like that. We've got the stills if you want to go over them."

"I'll take your word for it. Anything else?"

"The best – or worst – part. If you'll turn to this monitor, you'll see the first local TV news footage of the mess caused by the closing of tunnels and ports. The audio portion keeps updating the exact time each segment of helicopter film was shot. It took the Transit Authority more than an hour after these people left the courthouse to get their manhunt organized. It's been three days now. The long and short of it is, your people could still be in Manhattan – or in Tahiti. That's it. The boss wants to see you upstairs."

"I know," Connor said. He stood and stuffed the wrinkled band of shirt above his belt into his trousers. "Tell those guys at the courthouse to get the time stamp fixed on their security camera."

***

Jason Stuart, the SAC or Special-Agent-in-Charge, was one of the many field office directors who enjoyed the near universal dislike of his agents. He left Connor and Hatch standing – he was in an obvious rush – and gestured toward an open envelope on his desk. Connor put on the latex gloves Stuart's assistant handed him and read the typewritten note inside:

Kristýna Sondheim is innocent and Teresa is alive. If you wish to know who killed Arthur Sondheim, start in Chicago.

There you will find a prominent vodka distributor named Stepan Mikhailovich Obruchev. If he hasn't left for Moscow yet, he will shortly. From there he will travel with a false passport to Ljubljana, Slovenia. The escape of Sondheim forces him to eliminate her daughter, whom he kidnapped. In addition to Sondheim herself, whom he will also eliminate if you don't do it first, she is the only living witness to the murder. Why Slovenia? Go there and you will know.

Friends of Justice

The signature appeared to be in longhand, though it had the generic look of a computer font that had been traced over with a pen. "Addressed to you personally. Who else has seen it?"

"No one outside the lab, Randall. It was in my mail this morning."

Connor handed the letter to Hatch. "You've had it dusted for prints and traced?"

"Yes. There were no prints of any value. It was mailed from one of the boxes out front."

"To me, it seems like a hoax – or a ploy to point us in the wrong direction. What do you think, Hatch?"

"I think it won't hurt to have our Chicago office check this guy out. You know, just in case. It won't change anything at this end."

"Randall?"

"Sounds reasonable."

"Then that's how we'll proceed. You're due at Abbyville in an hour. A car is waiting down below."

***

"Jesus," Hatch said, "how would you like to spend the rest of your life in this place?"

They were driving through Sing Sing toward the river and the huge stone jetty on which Abbyville, the new woman's prison, was built. Connor said, "Look at the brickwork on those smokestacks, would you? Dissect their taper at any height and I bet you'll find a perfect circle. Today everything's a square or rectangle."

"The smokestacks? They remind me of Auschwitz."

"Forget the setting. The craftsmanship's impressive."

"Who gives a shit, Randall? If you're locked up, I doubt the quality of the brickwork would be on your mind."

"You're not locked up. What do we know about this Hayes guy?"

They reached the Hudson, turned north and drove along the bank. Connor glanced at Hatch who was staring, fascinated, at the river. Maybe the man had grown up someplace dry, like Arizona, where there weren't any rivers. As a kid Connor had seen the Mississippi every day. It was hard to imagine a piss-ant trickle like this could interest anyone.

He remembered something he wished he hadn't. When his daughter once asked him who his best friend was, he'd said "Hatch." Yet he'd never asked his former associate of two decades where he was from. Betty had been right He'd allowed work to consume him. Not only that; he was about to do it again. "Wake up, partner. What do we know about Hayes?"

"The usual. Hates Feds. US Marshals, ATF, FBI, all of us. Hates the fact he needs us when he fucks up. Don't expect a warm reception. Whatever you do, don't call him 'Warden.'"

"That's what he is, isn't he?"

"You're missing the point. The guys I talked to say he's a stickler for titles. Calling him 'Superintendent' might help."

"Fuck that. A warden's a warden. Why are there so many assholes in law enforcement?"

"We get all types," Hatch said, nodding toward a brick smokestack. "Probably the same in any line of work."

At the gate two officers checked their credentials and stored their weapons. Guards were waiting to escort them inside.

Hayes's office looked like a photo gallery documenting the history of incarceration. The view from his windows added its own chapter. Looking west, you saw the uniform concrete cellblocks of Abbyville. To the east, climbing the hillside, was the squalid sprawl of Sing Sing. The warden apparently had some kind of prison fetish.

"I received the request," Hayes said. "I have the material. There's not much."

"The tapes?" Hatch asked. "You told the Bureau all conversations in the instruction area had been recorded."

"They weren't. Insufficient funding forces us to skimp on audio surveillance. I told your office the conversations might have been recorded but that I wouldn't know until I checked. My people use our limited resources based on their assessment of risk."

"What about Sondheim and Allison Paget, Warden? Did you observe them together?"

Hayes stiffened at what he considered the improper use of his title. "Once or twice. Nothing out of the ordinary. She's a teacher in that new prison college program. Just what this place needs – free college for murderers. I want you to know something. Before this happened, I wrote the Department of Corrections and the Legislature at least twenty times. Any fool could see the risk posed by letting outsiders into the prison. No one listened. That's going to change."

"Don't count on it," Connor said. "Your college program doesn't strike me as the reason for this escape. There would have been other ways to communicate with the outside."

"So you're blaming me and my staff?"

"I'm not blaming anyone. My job is to bring back your prisoner, so let's focus on that. You spoke of materials. What, exactly, do you have?"

"Some writing Sondheim did for Paget's class." He handed Connor a manila envelope. "Maybe you can make sense of it."

"That's all?" Hatch asked, incredulous. "We're in the middle of a fugitive hunt where time is critical and you bring us down here to hand us something you could have faxed to the New York Field Office?"

"Everyone wants originals these days. Prints, DNA, etcetera. That, gentlemen, is the reason I avoided faxing."

Hatch, usually so restrained, couldn't hold himself back. "You had us down here to bitch about the college program. That's unconscionable."

"I beg your – "

"Shut up, Warden," Connor said. "Let's go, partner."

***

They were sitting in a makeshift dining room on the bridge while the sons – the crew – ate in the regular mess hall. The overcast had thickened. Rivulets of water from the first squall poured down the windows.

Adem glanced up from the table. "Bad weather tonight," he announced. "Maybe good you never eating much."

Kristýna had just pushed her untouched plate aside. "I'm not usually like this. I adore good food and everything Irina makes is very good. But my appetite just isn't there. I suppose it's all the stress."

Irina laughed her hearty guttural laugh. "Don't worry, you not ever offending me. You know what I think, though. I think you should be trying eat a little more, even when Adem say bad weather coming. You must make yourself stronger while you have this time. Stronger, yes, not weaker. Tomorrow, when bad weather pass, you try to eat. You try hard, okay."

"Yes, yes, of course. You're so right."

Her mind was elsewhere. She had spent most of day on deck, as usual. There had been only broken clouds until this afternoon, when the sky thickened and merged with the sullen gray sea. The weather fit her mood. She had sworn not to let her depression of the last year return yet seemed unable to fend it off. Visions assaulted her at night when she slept in the darkness of the stowaway room; premonitions of doom invaded her awareness when she lay awake.

Each morning Kristýna used light and space to construct a protective shield of optimism. But that optimism seemed artificial, a poorly contrived piece of self-delusion that abandoned her at sunset. Dinners were hell.

Adem poured a round of slivovitz. "Well, you rested enough to hear our part of plan?"

Kristýna nodded, hoping the account would delay the onset of her night terrors.

"Okay, good. Nobody say no, so I tell you now. We still have a few days at sea, but I tell you now so you get used to idea. And don't worry about tonight. Down below water line where stowaway room is, you feel high seas less."

"The plan?"

First stop, Genoa. Then we go La Spezia, Naples, Trieste. All the way down and up Italy. You know these places?"

"No," Kristýna said. "I left Prague when I was young. I never had the chance to travel."

"You speak Italian, though. Tomas tell me you speak Italian."

"Yes, pretty well. I learned it in prison."

"In prison?"

"From a friend who couldn't speak English. Also from a class in the prison."

"They teach you Italian in American prison?"

Kristýna managed a smile. "Not usually, Adem. They actually have a college program for inmates where I was held."

"I see. Very good choice of language. Very helpful in getting around. Very helpful in talking to some people not speaking English in rescue groups. And you, you are very important to all rescue groups for Natashas. Everyone hear your story and want to help. Maybe you know this, maybe no."

"I've been told only that people will be waiting to help me."

"Yes, of course they will. What you think? You think we drop you off and say to take the train? Very good rescue groups in Italy. And this Polish film man, people say he spend lots of money for making sure they have all they need. Tomas spend too. He even put big mortgage on theater."

"His theater? And your ship, of course. Having me on board is worse than taking out a mortgage. I can't believe so many people are risking so much to help me."

"Forget about these things. Tomas, Irina, me – we all do these things because we choose to. Many bad people out there, of course, but many good people too. Many good people. Now I tell you how we pass you to some more of those people, okay?"

"Yes, sure. Okay."

"You go inside container here on ship before we dock in Genoa. You think stowaway room on ship small, wait till you get in container. Hiding place smaller, darker."

"Darker? That's not possible."

"You find out many things are possible you think not possible. One girl we bring to Albania I see again. She tell me about container, and I tell you what she tell me so you get ready in your mind. There is no room for moving around. You feel like can't breathe. Maybe you feel someone bury you alive. Chemical smells from cargo nasty and don't help with breathing. Then giant crane swing you from ship onto dock. Maybe you get sick in the stomach from too much swinging. When crane put you down you think something is gone wrong. It feel strange on land after so much time on sea. Crazy noises in port. Trucks, cranes, machines. You hear inspectors looking inside. Maybe taping with poles, maybe having dogs. Lots of drugs coming to Europe on ship. So you must remember. Always remember they not looking for you. They looking for these drugs."

"Adem, enough!" Irina said. "I see in her face you are frightening her."

"I tell this once, Irina. I tell so she know. It is better to know and not freaking out."

"Please go ahead, Adem," Kristýna said. "I promise it's alright, Irina, even if it scares me. He should tell me everything. Like he says, it will help me mentally to know. Being tense is one thing. But being surprised while you are tense is much worse."

"Very smart girl. Okay, Irina, I go on. You hear what she say. You feel same like you are inside concentration camp. This is hardest part. You must find courage. You must make yourself to breathe and not think how horrible. This is like last tunnel to freedom. Dark and terrible but light at end. When truck drives away with container, you say to yourself, I am free.

"Now, look out at ocean before next squall, both of you look. Try remember while you are inside tiny space, Kristýna, try to remember that world is big and beautiful. Some of it water, some land. But all of it beautiful. You go through tunnel to get there. You want to be free, you have no choice."

CHAPTER TEN

Hatch read while Connor rested his eyes. He stopped after the third sentence of the story – the totality of their documents haul – to describe the difference between Sondheim's elegant hand and the professor's scarcely legible remarks.

Connor, still furious at Hayes, blew his stack. "Jesus Christ, read the story. All of it. No opinions, no interruptions. We'll talk about the comments later."

"If we can decipher them."

"Just read the goddamn thing."

"Okay, okay. Take it easy. I'll start again."

"You do that."

Hatch, unfazed as usual by Connor's ugly mood, began:

Natasha

by Kristýna Sondheim

When Natasha was 15 years old, her father lost his job. It seemed like everyone was losing their jobs. Since Ukraine left the Soviet Union, the factories that made bombs and rockets for Moscow had shut their doors. Her mother and two older brothers used to take the train to Kiev every day to work in one of these factories, but it had closed and they had been out of work for nearly a year. Her father was one of the last people in their village to become unemployed.

They sat around that night and tried to make a plan for how they would stay alive. They couldn't think of anything. Winter was coming, the garden they shared with their neighbors would be under a meter of snow and grandmother's savings had all been spent. They would probably get a little more money from the new government but it wouldn't be enough to live on.

One morning a few weeks later, Natasha was wadding up pages of an old newspaper to make a fire in the kitchen stove. She noticed an ad for positions abroad. The agency was looking for girls between 15 and 18 years old to work as domestic helpers in Germany and Holland and even in the United States. The jobs lasted for two years, and the pay was . . . spectacular.

Natasha started to get excited. She didn't tell a soul about the ad because she knew her father wouldn't let her apply. If she got a job she would write a long letter home, then surprise them with her first pay check from some rich country in the West.

She packed her best clothes for the interview in downtown Kiev, just as the ad said. If she got hired, she might have to leave that very day. It took her almost a week to borrow enough money for the train ticket to the big city but when she arrived in the agency's fancy office, she knew she would be able to pay it back right away. They were very kind to her. The men wore tailored suits like you see in magazines, and the women could have been fashion models. One of the women in the office even took her to a private shop owned by the agency and helped her pick out a new dress and expensive pair of shoes. That's when she knew she had gotten the job. And sure enough, they were in such a hurry for her in America – America! – that she would leave that very night. They put her in a room where she could write a long letter to her parents and mailed it for her when she finished. It was a good thing, too. She didn't have enough money for postage.

Her flight was scheduled to leave at midnight. Some nice man at the agency took her and several of the other girls they had accepted for positions in America to a private dining room. She had never experienced anything so fabulous. They drank imported wine and ate steaks from Argentina. The man said dinners like this would be normal in America. He said they might even get tired of all the delicacies and dream of dark rye spread with goose lard. Natasha didn't believe him.

After dark, all the girls hired that day were picked up by new tourist buses for the trip to the airport. The girl sitting next to Natasha was going to Amsterdam. The girl across the aisle had been chosen for a special position in Japan. They were both really pretty, but they must have been as poor as she was when they came for their interviews. Natasha guessed this because the agency had bought them the same kind of shoes it had bought her. A woman came down the aisle with pills for everyone. You had to take them in order to fly. Otherwise you might get sick and arrive at your destination in such an unattractive state your new employer wouldn't want you.

One of the buses broke down on the way to airport. They were going to have to use the other bus to tow it, so the agency arranged for trucks to take the girls the rest of the way. She must have already gotten spoiled, Natasha thought. The trucks were loud and ugly, like the trucks the Soviet Army used to drive through her village. There were only wooden benches to sit on. The girls had to carry their own luggage. Wind whipped through the canvas roof and messed up her hair. It would be good to get on the airplane. The man at dinner had told her how comfortable the seats were and how you got to watch a new American movie that wasn't showing yet in Kiev.

Then a strange thing happened. The trucks turned onto a dirt road. Branches clawed at the torn canvas as the trucks bounced up to a dark warehouse and stopped. There were no airplanes in sight, only armed men in uniforms barking orders at them to bring their luggage and follow. Some of the girls fell in the mud, ruining their new clothes. The pills they had given out on the bus might help you in airplanes, Natasha thought, but they made you feel strange on land.

Natasha tried to ask the girl beside her where the airplanes were, but one of the guards snarled at her to shut up and keep her eyes on the ground. Inside the warehouse were lots of little rooms. Seven girls accompanied Natasha into one of the rooms and the door was locked behind them. There was nothing in the room but a bed with dirty sheets – none of the beautiful paintings and fine furniture and thick carpeting that had so impressed her at the agency's main office.

A key clattered in the lock. The door flung open and a fat older man with a beard entered. He closed and locked the door behind him, then stared at each one of the girls. "Virgins," he said in some kind of foreign accent. "How many of you virgins?"

Natasha raised her hand. The man smiled. Some of his teeth were missing and the other ones were stained. He was very ugly. "Get undressed. Hurry. You cannot be virgins on arrival. Employers object."

She stood, trembling, as he moved toward her. Something was terribly wrong. She knew it now: she had been lured into some kind of a trap. She wanted to scream, wanted to fight, but the pills they had given her on the bus made her too weak. The other girls must have felt the same way. They were upset but they didn't do anything.

The man ripped the clothes from her body, shoved her onto the bed, opened his fly and had his way with her. "Rest of you, undress," he growled. "The event will take place in the main hall. Obligatory. Shoes, okay. Jewelry, okay. Everything else off."

The event was a sale of teenage girls. What began as Natasha's happiest day ended as her worst nightmare: she was bought by a trader from Albania. Several weeks, a dozen rapes and multiple beatings later, she arrived with false papers in America – the only part of her promise they kept.

Now Natasha is 20 years old. She has no papers, no identity. She works for a pimp in Newark. Every week she must provide him with $3000 to keep her room and not be turned over to the police. She is a drug addict and commits petty crimes when her earnings fall short. Every month she finds it more difficult to earn her quota. She has lost her beauty. She has lost her soul. She has been transformed into an animal. Her life is over.

She is not alone. There are now almost one million East European girls like Natasha serving as sex slaves in the West, the Middle East and Japan. This story is about all of them. It is about how they were deceived and how they will spend the rest of their short lives. It is about the Natasha Trade. Governments are doing nothing to stop it. Nobody seems to care. In America most people don't even know what it is.

Natasha knows, but it's too late.

Hatch finished just as the driver pulled into an Exxon station in Ossining. He said, "This stuff really happens, Randall. We had a briefing on it last month in L.A. I'm not sure if it means anything in this story that will help us, but it's major criminal activity and it's headed our way. We're talking about millions of teenage girls? Why don't Americans know and get pissed off? We're still horrified by Auschwitz, and that happened in East Europe too."

"I know, Hatch. We work for the same agency. I also have daughters. It's a nightmare – worse than a nightmare. But our job isn't saving the world from atrocities. If it was, I'd start with that son-of-a-bitch warden."

"Still, Randall, even if we focus on our fugitive and nothing more, we have to consider the letter Stuart got this morning. It talks about a guy with a Russian name going to Slovenia. That's over there somewhere, isn't it?"

"Slovenia used to be part of Yugoslavia. So yes, it's in Eastern Europe. Your thoughts?"

"For what it's worth, maybe our fugitive came to the States as one of these girls. Didn't you get that feeling from the story? Maybe she had some sort of connection with the Russian in the letter. If he exists and if the Sondheim kid really is alive, he might lead us to her."

"Obviously, Hatch. But that's a lot of ifs. We don't even know yet if he exists. If he does, and if he in fact makes the predicted departure from Chicago, we'll put him on our radar screen."

"Sounds reasonable."

"So let's hear those comments on the story you were so excited about."

"Good beginning. If this is meant to be fiction based on reality – which I assume it is – you need to massage the narrative so it reads a little less like a piece of journalism. We'll go over possible techniques you might wish to use at our next meeting."

"That's it?"

"Every scribbled word."

"So what do you think, Hatch? You think they talked literature at their next meeting?"

"Sure. They obviously couldn't plan an escape in that setting. I've been meaning to ask you something, Randall. Any idea why the place is called Abbyville? Sounds more like a spa to me than a prison."

Connor shook his head. "Ever hear of Abby Hopper Gibbons?"

"Who?"

"Jesus, Hatch. You need to take a year off and do some reading."

***

Connor liked bricks. He supposed it was because his great grandfather, J. Reid Connor, had made a fortune firing the bricks that paved the mud streets of Memphis. Never mind that J. Reid Connor II, his grandfather, had lost every cent on a crazy scheme to breed race horses in the syrupy heat of the Delta. The bricks you saw today in the restored quarters of old Memphis were Connor bricks. In this age of the ephemeral, a man had to look to things that endured.

Connor liked the bricks at the University of Virginia, where he had gone to college, and the bricks of nearby Monticello.

And he liked the bricks in L.A., the Mexican adobe bricks and even the universally hated blond bricks of postwar suburbia.

There was something refreshingly simple and straightforward about bricks. They didn't lie about their age or condition; they didn't betray you because you forgot to call the termite man or pamper them with overpriced sealer.

Bricks, thought Connor, were the way people should be. Too bad there was so much drywall and cheap siding around.

At this particular moment something was bothering him. As he sat in Bremer's study waiting for the judge, he found himself staring at one of most spectacular interior walls he had seen in decades. Its faded red and white bricks were pocked with age, their grout lines slightly irregular from the weight of time. Yet the bricks themselves were as strong and authentic as the products of his great grandfather. Anyone with such a wall would be a person with whom he had a lot in common, a lot that would contribute to his hunt. Or so his intellect informed him; his gut said something very different.

A half hour after the time set for the interview, Bremer finally strode into the room with a cognac in one hand and a legal journal in the other. He let himself down in an ugly armchair big enough for two, tossed his journal on the coffee table and lit a fat cigar. He offered his guests nothing, proffered no apology for his tardiness and did not ask whether his FBI visitors minded the cigar smoke. They didn't, but still . . .

Judge Bremer openly showed his displeasure at being disturbed after dinner. Hatch apologized; Connor wanted to take a swing at the surly bastard.

Bremer said, "We shouldn't be talking about the case at all, not even during business hours. I'm not Scalia. If our conversations became known, I'd have to recuse myself from any related proceedings in the future."

Hatch, sensing his partner's irritation, beat him to the word. "It's unusual, of course, to have a judge as a percipient witness. We intend to keep the meeting off the record."

"Make sure it stays off. What would you like to know?"

"We just want to ask a few questions," Connor said. "We understand you don't like the Feds paying you a post-dinner visit, but it seems to me that finding the fugitive who inexplicably escaped from your courtroom would be first on your agenda as well as ours."

"Go ahead. But drop the insinuation that the escape was in any way my fault."

"No insinuation, and we'll be brief. The newspapers detail circumstantial evidence of a conspiracy. Are they on the right track?"

"We all suspect conspiracy. Some kind of East European thing on the outside. We'll know more as the investigation progresses – but we're not going to know it overnight."

Connor said. "This woman who impersonated Sondheim – exactly what do you know about her?"

"Too goddamn little. She's Czech, like the escapee. She looks like her. My guess is, they're related. The prosecution needs a DNA test. I'll stress again that it all takes time. At present our investigators are looking into phone records. One thing we do know is this: they had different maiden names when they entered the US."

"That doesn't mean squat. They probably had fake papers like everyone else who comes here. The phone records might help, but what you really need is the DNA. Perhaps the Bureau can help you out and speed things up."

"We're quite capable of dealing with this ourselves."

"As you wish. Where is Ms. Hasek now?"

"I don't know."

"Excuse me?"

"The State held her as long as possible. Her arraignment and bail hearing were yesterday at four p.m. She pled innocent to all charges. She made bail. End of story."

"You mean, you let her go?" Hatch groaned.

"I followed the law. She hired Lou Weissner, a top criminal attorney. There was no ground to deny the defendant's bail petition. She's married and owns a business in Hastings-on-Hudson. She has no criminal record, not even a traffic ticket. The prosecution failed to convince me that Ms. Hasek posed an imminent threat to the community – or a flight risk."

"How high did you set her bail?"

"Two hundred thousand dollars."

"Jesus! We need to speak with her tonight."

"I'm sorry. I don't have her address. The court records will be available in the morning."

CHAPTER ELEVEN

Obruchev had spent the previous week in Moscow, making frequent calls to his Chicago office. Each day he waited impatiently for news of Kristýna's capture. But the bitch was wily and had made law enforcement everywhere the laughing stock of the press and public. It was beginning to seem possible they would never find her. If they did, which he considered improbable, they wouldn't be in a listening mood. She could say what she wanted about him when she was back in prison. Her words would never make it past the walls. Or would they? Why take chances? If the cops got to her first, great. If they didn't, he'd do their work for them.

For now, though, the kid it was a bigger problem. She wasn't a convicted murderer or a fugitive. The press, the public and the cops would listen to her, and they'd do it from the instant they found her. Bottom line: he couldn't leave a seven-year-old who had the potential to destroy him alive. Kristýna could wait.

This is why he had returned to Ljubljana; and why General Majdak was driving him at the moment to Rasputin's new residence.

"You want him out, I'll take care of it," Majdak said. "You're not gonna like what he's done to the dacha."

"Who gave him permission to move in?" Obruchev grumbled.

"Your new business manager. The place was assigned to Snyna but Snyna didn't want it, not after what happened to your cousin. I waited for your instructions."

"Look, we'll talk about living arrangements later. I have pressing business. Just do me a favor. Have someone leave me a jeep out front. I don't plan to spend the night."

Majdak laughed. "I'll try not to forget."

It was three o'clock in the afternoon, sunny but frigid. They turned into the secluded drive that led to Bogdan's former residence. Limbs brittle with hoarfrost clawed at the truck. Frozen potholes jarred the suspension and rattled the doors. As they came closer Obruchev noticed a white Skoda sedan, Eighties vintage, parked out front. He felt like he had been punched in the gut. His cousin wouldn't be waiting for him. Bogdan was gone. He'd killed family. He hadn't had a choice, he'd been betrayed. But the son-of-a-bitch wouldn't go away. He lived on in Obruchev's mind – as real as if he were alive.

Obruchev forgot his troubles when Rasputin opened the carved wooden door. What the fuck was this? The holy freak had turned the hunting lodge into some kind of church. He stared, speechless, as the dacha's new occupant relieved him of his fur hat and greatcoat.

"Welcome, Stepan Mikhailovich," Rasputin said. "Take off your boots before we move to the sanctuary. One does not tread like an ox into the House of God."

Obruchev, dumbstruck, exchanged his boots for the purple slippers on the edge of the foyer. He couldn't take his eyes off the wall that dissected the parlor. It was nearly as high as the vaulted ceiling. Icons – fake or real he didn't know – stretched in three horizontal rows. Patriarchs highest, prophets next, then the liturgical feasts. Below the icons was a door, rounded at the top and covered with yet more icons. He recognized all of them from his youth: the Annunciation, the Last Supper, the Church Fathers.

The memory of frigid childhood mornings at his mother's cathedral in Kursk wrapped itself like a serpent around his psyche. What was this goddamn thing doing in the middle of Bogdan's hunting lodge?

He tried to voice his disgust, but a saint whose name he couldn't recall stared at him with such reproach he was unable to utter a word.

It had been the same when he was a kid. Icons filled him with dread. They seemed to hold dark secrets about his future they refused to divulge – secrets of impending doom. Maybe that's why he liked America. No one cared about medieval bullshit. He could escape the curse of his origins. But not here. In East Europe his past stalked him with the same persistence as Bogdan's ghost.

"Let's go in the kitchen," he said.

"We will talk in the sanctuary."

"We'll talk in the kitchen."

"Stepan Mikhailovich, I erected this place of worship for my personal use. However, at this time, it is you who needs it. Without intervention of the Holy Father, you are lost."

"Jesus Christ, Nikolai Petrovich, you're talking like a lunatic. I should shoot you right here."

"You may dispose of me when and how you wish. We are all merely passing through this veil of tears. I have no fear of death. It is the portal to eternal life. However, you strike me as the type who would rather cling to earthly existence. If this is so, accept the truth: without me, your journey to the other side will soon commence."

"Stop talking voodoo. There are more important matters to discuss."

Discuss . . . discuss. Even the words came back to haunt him. Hadn't Bogdan wanted to "discuss" something before he took his trip to the incinerator?

Rasputin raised his hand. "In your case, this is wrong: there are not more important matters. God has placed me in a position to help. I do not know the reason. I do not ask His purpose. Please accompany me into the sanctuary. When you have a better understanding of the choices allotted you, it will be less difficult to choose the proper course."

Obruchev hesitated. Rasputin was an impostor. He was certain. Almost certain. But a sliver of doubt held him hostage. What if he was wrong? What if this guy really did have some kind of direct link to God? Or the devil?

They walked on slippered feet into the sanctuary. Obruchev stopped in his tracks when he saw a massive gold cross, exquisitely engraved and set with jewels, adorning the far wall.

"Where's the goddamn boar's head?" he bellowed.

"May the Holy Father forgive you your ignorance. You are blaspheming in the presence of one of His most precious gifts to mankind, the crucifix from the Sofia Cathedral in Novgorod. Where that cross is, so too is your Savior."

"Yeah, alright. But what about the boar's head?"

"Please be seated, Stepan Mikhailovich. I beg you, be respectful. It is for your own good."

Obruchev was about to erupt in fury when another set of eyes fixed their hollow gaze on him. They belonged to St. Seraphim, hand across his heart, appearing to kneel before a grave. Obruchev swallowed hard. Could it be an omen? Something was fucking with his mind. He'd better hold his tongue, he decided, and listen to what Rasputin had to say. He would find a more propitious time to break this living icon's hex. He would then confirm the guy was a lunatic and send him to a joyful reunion with the Holy Father – or wherever the hell he was going.

But not yet. What if the police found Teresa? He'd be a hunted animal, a wild boar with a trophy head. Which meant one thing: he had to find her first. Rasputin seemed to know where she was. Holy man or fake, the bastard had him by the balls.

"Look, I'm sorry," Obruchev said, "Moscow stresses me out."

"Kneel and pray."

"What?"

"Stepan Mikhailovich, I cannot help those who refuse to help themselves."

Obruchev knelt and raised his eyes to St. Seraphim. He said a silent prayer; it addressed the salvation of his body rather than his soul.

When he got to his feet, Rasputin directed him to a chair. There he quietly sat while his host lit several dozen candles. "We must hurry, Stepan Mikhailovich. The auction begins in two hours."

"I want you to find the girl. You asked me to settle my family differences before you began your search. I have done that."

Rasputin sat in the velvet throne chair beneath the cross. "Indeed this is true, Stepan Mikhailovich. Our discussions may now begin."

Obruchev kept a lid on his temper. "Are you positive you can find her?"

"Yes."

"Can you bring her to me?"

"Yes."

"How much time?"

"Two weeks, God willing."

"Two weeks!"

"I believe I pointed out that she was abducted by a passing group of Gypsies. She may not be with the same group. She may be in a land whose language I do not yet speak. I cannot determine the schedule by which miracles occur. I – "

"Alright, two weeks. What's your price?"

"You will convey to me your business and never compete with me anywhere on God's earth. The operation will of course be moved from Slovenia. Hence the "anywhere" provision. Do not look at me like that, Stepan Mikhailovich. I know you have spoken with a number of associates regarding your intent to sell in order to pursue other things. The girl will serve as my payment."

"That's outrageous. Just the people and know-how are worth millions."

"What is your life worth, Stepan Mikhailovich? What is your freedom worth? Think in those terms or we need not continue our talk."

"We'll continue with a more realistic starting point. But first you will answer a question to my satisfaction, a question I've been wanting to ask you for years."

"Yes?"

"Why would a man of God like you traffick in young girls? I could never understand your participation as auctioneer. I certainly can't understand your wish to become owner."

"That is because you believe what we do is wrong. It is not. These girls carry a stigma. They have been condemned by God for their impurity of mind and spirit. With their flesh they create much earthly treasure. When that treasure is used for good works, as in your charitable donations, the sale of their bodies constitutes nothing less than a redemption of their souls. We are their only hope."

"Well, Nikolai Petrovich, it's comforting to know I've been in the business of redemption all these years. I should have thought more highly of myself. In fact, now I do. So highly I've decided to continue my noble work. The business is not for sale. Name a reasonable price for the delivery of the girl."

"There is but one acceptable form of payment, which I have already indicated."

"Then I guess we're finished. You're fired. I'll conduct the auction tonight. Get this shit out of here by morning. And don't forget to remount the boar's head."

Rasputin smiled. His eyes seemed to hold the same dark secret with which the icons of Obruchev's youth had tormented him.

"Very well, then," Rasputin said. "I should inform you in parting, though. Bogdan came frequently to me for confession. Fedir as well – before you contrived his suicide. I know more of your present dilemma than you realize. Kristýna Sondheim is not a name unfamiliar to me. Nor is that of her husband. Having Fedir pull the trigger does not exonerate you. The fact that he is no longer alive is insignificant. The kidnapping and murder are on your hands. I suggest you accept my proposal."

Obruchev was about to get up and leave but thought better of it. Any sale of his business – whether for well-laundered cash or a girl presumed dead – would involve no written contracts. What difference did it make if he promised Rasputin the moon? When he had Teresa, he would take back what was rightly his. The holy charlatan's unexplained disappearance would not be mourned.

"I suppose, Nikolai Petrovich, that it would be pointless to ask how you know what you know?"

"On the contrary. My information comes to me in visions. It is from God. I need only ask. I have not yet asked where to find Teresa."

"Start asking."

"Then you accept my proposal?"

"Do I have a choice? Find the girl. Bring her to me. I'll work the auction block until you've met your part of the deal."

"A wise decision, Stepan Mikhailovich. Your earthly demise is not necessary. Though you have often treated me rudely, it is not what I would have wished."

In the foyer Obruchev put on his boots. Rasputin helped him into his greatcoat and handed him his sable hat. He said, "If you want me to start my search tonight, you will have to hurry. The auction is set to begin in forty-three minutes."

"I want you to start tonight" Obruchev said. "Worry about your new job. I'll worry about your old one."

Outside the stars shone with a clarity he never saw in Chicago. Obruchev was tempted to stop and look at them. He did not, however. He feared God might suddenly materialize up there somewhere.

He strode briskly to the jeep Majdak had promised, started the engine and drove toward the factory. Bogdan came along for the ride, ignoring the confines of his grave deep in the ashes of the plant incinerator.

CHAPTER TWELVE

"You're not going to believe this," Hatch said, clapping shut his cell phone.

They were being rushed in a Bureau car from their hotel to the New York Field Office. Their driver was young; the car, judging from its shocks, was old.

"What am I not going to believe?" Connor asked.

"Your favorite boss, Jason Stuart, heard from our Chicago people. The Russian named in the anonymous letter – Obruchev – left O'Hare on the evening of Sondheim's escape. Whoever wrote the letter knew something."

"Maybe."

"Maybe?"

"What was his destination?"

"Moscow."

"A scheduled trip?"

"No. This is from our agents who visited his office. There was some kind of a problem with a vodka supplier. Obruchev's employees all gave the exact same story in one-on-ones. No indication they had been prepped. True or not, it must have been what he told them."

"Is this unusual? I mean, the guy taking off on a moment's notice. Did anyone ask?"

"Of course they asked. We're talking FBI, not imbeciles like your friend at Abbyville. He makes a trip each month, booked in advance. But this trip was different. He left two weeks ahead of the reservation. His personal assistant remembers only one other time in eight years he's deviated from his schedule."

"And you find all of this significant? "

"Don't you? We have a letter saying Obruchev killed Sondheim's husband and that he'd have to leave Chicago when he found out she'd escaped. Why? Because Sondheim's kid is a living witness. I don't think we're talking coincidence."

"Let me ask you something. Did you notice when the letter was postmarked?"

"No."

"After the escape, Hatch. Which means the person who wrote it might already have known of Obruchev's departure. Whatever the case, there are still questions about the meaning and intent of the message."

"Remember what you said yesterday?"

"If he left Chicago, we'd put him on our radar. We will. We'll inform our legal attachés at every US Embassy in Europe that we want this guy found and followed. But I still have my doubts. If your objective was to slow the fugitive hunt, wouldn't it make sense to lure the FBI, Interpol and European police forces into a wild goose chase? In fact, Hatch, let's take it a step further. Maybe Obruchev is part of the escape conspiracy. It's too early to say."

"So how do we proceed?"

"I've already mentioned our legats. We're not chasing a possible decoy to Moscow or Slovenia. That will be their job. We're asking Forsythe for six teams. One to scour the City, the ground troops if you will. They'll look for Sondheim and that woman the judge let go. Then we'll want a team to cover the surrounding states and another to work airports, train and bus stations, car rental agencies, every form of transportation they could have used within a specific radius. We'll want to cast the big nets, too: a team for the rest of the North America and one for Latin America."

"That's five, Randall."

"We're Number Six and here's how we start. You and I are going to sit in a quiet room at Twenty-Six Federal Plaza with lots of coffee. Then we're going to brainstorm until lightning strikes."

"With forensics present, I hope."

"No forensics, no computers, no white coats. Not until we have a theory we like. We've got five other teams, plus our legats, to handle the evidentiary approach. While they plod, I want to sit where it's quiet and think. That's what these new agents never learned to do. That's where our break will come."

"Know something Randall?"

"What's that?"

"It's good to be working with you again. I didn't say pleasant, just good. You're better than anyone I know at bringing home the bacon. Mind telling me your secret?"

"My secret, Hatch, is that I think like the bad guys."

"That's profound."

"What are you saying, partner? If I start catching fish I should worry?"

***

"Well?" Connor asked after an agonizing session of mental gymnastics.

"I say we focus on your first theory, escape by sea."

"You're beside the phone. Give Stuart a call. Invite him to join us in the geek room."

"Shouldn't we come up with something concrete before we do that?"

"Listen, Hatch. I worked with that man a quarter century ago in Baltimore. If we don't strike oil nothing's lost. If we do he needs to be in on the first gush. Better, he needs to believe it was his idea. I'll make sure he does. That way we get everything we want."

"Stuart's one of those?"

"He's the boss in New York City, isn't he? Well-positioned to become the Bureau's next director if he accomplishes something of note. But he has lousy connections and a second-rate mind. How smart does that make him? Smart enough to know he won't be able to get to the top without riding on someone else's accomplishments. We let him ride, Hatch. For our own sake."

"If you say so."

"By the way, where did you grow up?"

"Arizona. Why?

"Just wondering," Connor said. "Use the phone."

CHAPTER THIRTEEN

Jason Stuart, seated between Hatch and Connor in the map room, made no attempt to hide his skepticism. While technical people scurried around in the penumbra, he kept repeating his litany of doubts. "Goddammit, Randall, I told you we'd been down this road before. I also told you it leads where it leads. Nowhere, remember? We don't have the luxury of exhuming investigative theories we've already buried."

"You're not listening," Connor whispered. "You were on the right track from the start. Your people gave up too early. They didn't give your theory a chance to breathe. I'm convinced we buried a live one."

"Quit speaking in tongues."

"Escape by sea, your original theory. It deserves a second look. I wanted you with us."

"Very considerate. This better not be for nothing."

"You can't lose," Connor said. "We're going to broaden the search. If it doesn't turn up anything, Hatch will take over your dues at the Westchester Country Club."

"He couldn't afford them. Get to the point."

"Matt, put up on the screen every ship departing the greater metro area in the six hours before the escape. Don't start the movement yet."

"Yes, sir, Agent Connor."

"For Christ's sake," murmured Jason Stuart, "what the hell are you doing?"

"Bear with me. I'm exhuming your theory and looking at it from another angle. We all know the NYPD alerted every dock you see an hour after Sondheim broke out of the courthouse. But wouldn't people smart enough to pull off an escape this sophisticated have also anticipated our reaction? If so, might they have tried to counter it by using a ship that had already set sail?"

"So you're saying – if they actually took the marine route – that they boarded somewhere in the harbor."

"Or even further out. Put your graphic in motion, Matt. One minute equals one hour."

"Yes, sir."

Green lines began snaking away from the New York and Jersey coast. Stuart sat up straight, suddenly interested.

"Samantha," Connor said, "did you have time to run a check on all of those ships since I phoned down?"

"I did."

"And you have her data, Matt?"

"Already loaded."

"Good. Clear the screen and put the graphic in motion again, this time only with those ships that have some sort of European connection – ownership, captain, destination. Switch to red. Let's start with the hypothesis that Ms. Sondheim is heading for the imagined protection of home."

"No problem, Agent Connor. Same speed?"

"Same speed."

What had been hundreds of green lines became a much smaller number of red lines, but there was no difference in the overall pattern of movement.

"Cliff, what did you turn up in the small boat category?"

"Not much. If they were private planes we'd have like flight plans. Well, they aren't and we don't."

"But you have ownership lists?"

"Five point three megabytes. You'd be better off with the Greater New York Yellow Pages."

Hatch whispered something to Stuart. He nodded, but his eyes never left the electronic display.

"Keep running it," Connor said. "Out seventy miles, then back in."

Someone said, "Looks like capillaries under the scope."

"That's enough. Cliff, here's what I want. Call up our database of Eastern European names. Make that Czech ships only. Run a match against your Yellow Pages."

"Why Czech?"

"We believe it's her nationality. If there was a conspiracy, her circle of compatriots in the area deserves our first look."

"Okay."

The mainframe groaned and whirred somewhere in the distance. "Two thousand sixty-four," the technician said when the powerful computer fell silent.

"Okay, good. Now let's limit ourselves to commercial craft. In fact, make that fishing boats. Commercial fishing boats."

"Ocean-going yachts?" Stuart said. "Shouldn't we include them?"

"Let's hold off. The Coast Guard was put on alert the same time as the Port Authority. That type of yacht tends to stand out."

"Why fishing boats?" Hatch asked.

"It's winter. They have the structural and navigational attributes that would allow them to operate on high seas . . . How many now?"

"Twelve."

"Okay. We're going to leave you alone for a while. Here's what I'd like you to do. Find out if any of those boats set sail in the twenty-four hours after the escape. Be sure you don't let on that the Bureau's involved. If we get lucky, we'll need to keep our fugitive in the dark."

"You want us to send out undercover people?"

"Too slow. Use the phones that transmit fake numbers. You're a concerned relative, a job seeker, a fish monger. Samantha, you're good at this stuff. Teach these guys something."

"Don't ask the impossible, Agent Connor. We'll have your results in an hour."

"Excellent."

***

It was mid-afternoon when they reconvened in the geek room. Stuart, now convinced they were following his keen insight, took up where Connor had left off. "Samantha, go ahead please."

She stood in front of the giant electronic map, her wiry figure and long blond hair touched by the monster's pale glow. She was young, attractive, smart as hell. About time, Connor thought, that the Bureau started tapping the enormous reservoir of female talent out there.

"A commercial fishing boat left Point Pleasant, New Jersey, the afternoon of the escape. We don't have the exact time but it was around three. You're going to like this part. The boat belongs to a Newark company owned by Josef Topol – place of birth, Prague. Now get this: it's named the Omega III."

Stuart said, "Who gives a shit what it's named?"

"Jason," Connor said, "wasn't Sondheim a cardiologist?"

"That's hardly a compelling link."

"The devil is in the details. Didn't you used to say that in Wichita?"

"The relevant details."

"Gentlemen," Samantha interjected, "may I continue?"

Connor and Stuart nodded their assent.

"Matt, put everything in motion, the likely path of the Omega III in blue. Include the estimated departure times of the larger ships and everyone's projected speed. Factor in the tides, please."

The worms started snaking again, dozens in red, one in blue. The Omega III intersected the projected path of two ships, allowing a margin of error of 40 minutes and 10 nautical miles.

"Kind of tight parameters but let's check these two," Stuart said. "Owner, type of ship, the usual."

"We already have, sir. The first is a cruise ship going home to Norway for repairs. The second is an Albanian freighter hauling agricultural chemicals to several Mediterranean ports."

"Nice, Samantha," Hatch said. "Have you had time to research the captain and crew?"

"Yes. This is interesting. The captain and his wife have been sailing the same vessel – I can't pronounce its name but we have it written down – to Newark since the late-Nineties. The home port is Durrës, Albania. Here's something you might be able to make sense of. We ran the captain's name – can't pronounce that either – against criminal records and police complaints in New Jersey and New York. Their daughter went missing around the same time the couple took over the

Durrës-Newark route. The police found the girl in Hoboken, age seventeen. She was dead in an alley. The parents enlisted the help of a Czech who spoke perfect English, a guy who runs an avant-garde theater uptown. He tried to interest the media in the fate East European girls in this area sold into prostitution. The name of that man is Tomas Hasek – "

"Excuse me, Samantha," Connor said. "Hatch, did your messenger pick up the court file of the woman Judge Bremer released on bail?"

"First thing this morning."

"Have you looked at it yet?"

"No."

"Do you have it with you."

Hatch patted his briefcase.

"Wasn't the last name of our Sondheim look-alike Hasek?"

Hatch leafed through the file. "Hasek, Michaela. I thought it sounded familiar."

"Is there mention of a spouse?"

"Give me a second . . . yes. Randall, you're not going to believe this. It's Tomas Hasek."

"Alright. Our first real break. Samantha, back to you. What did the coroner find to be the cause of the girl's death?"

"Heroin overdose, battery, multiple rapes."

"Was the case ever solved?"

"Never solved. There's a note here that says Tomas Hasek went ballistic at the cops."

"Over what?"

"He accused them of ignoring something called the Natasha Trade. I've heard of it. What exactly is it?"

"I don't know," Connor said.

"Randall, don't you remember the story – "

"No. Neither do you. Thank you, all of you, for your thorough work. Every detail discussed here will remain strictly confidential. That includes spouses, relatives, shrinks and pets. Clear?"

He went around the room to confirm that each person had gotten the message. When he was convinced they had, he turned to Jason Stuart. "We need to talk in private," he said.

***

"Tell it now, Hatch," Connor said. "Describe to Jason the content of that thing we got at Abbyville."

"It was a story Sondheim wrote for the college program. It dealt with the trafficking in teenage girls from Eastern Europe – the so-called Natasha Trade. That was what Hasek blew up at the Newark Police about, the fact that they were ignoring it."

Stuart said, "It's mainly a foreign thing. The cops have a lot more serious problems on their agenda, especially in Newark."

Connor helped himself to a fresh cup of coffee. "That may be, Jason. But the point I believe Hatch wanted to make is this: the husband of the woman we suspect of impersonating Sondheim – as well as Sondheim herself – had an obvious emotional reaction to this Natasha stuff. Which leads me to believe Sondheim, Michaela Hasek, Tomas Hasek and of course the parents of that Albanian girl all have something major to do with the escape. Have your City teams reported yet?"

"They're still in the field."

"Maybe they've looked in by now on the Hasek woman's business. Why not make a call and find out?"

"I'll have Carter do it."

"Please, Jason. You heard me downstairs. The fewer people who know what we're doing, the better."

"Probably true."

As Jason Stuart listened to the preliminary findings of his agents, his face went through an unusual range of expressions. At one point he reminded Connor of a math student trying to calculate a cube root in his head. At another he resembled the student after he had come up with the correct answer.

Keep this guy thinking he's the genius, Connor reminded himself again. Fighting crime entailed a lot of things, most importantly the art of bureaucratic massage.

"She's on vacation," Stuart said when he hung up. "With her husband. No one knows where they went. According to employees and friends, they left last night to celebrate Michaela Hasek's release."

"By car?"

"Apparently. We'll order a five points bulletin."

"I'd rather not, Jason. The woman already has a court date and she's represented by Lou Weissner. She's not going to talk to us. We gain nothing and lose our element of surprise. Find them. Watch them. Just make sure they don't know we're looking. These aren't dumb people. If we treat them like they are, we'll be transmitting information through them to the fugitive. If that happens, our chances of bringing Ms. Sondheim home will start to look like a goose egg."

"Point well taken. How do you suggest we proceed from here?"

"You make the call, Jason. You've earned the right."

"Where's that ship scheduled to dock?"

Connor consulted the paper Samantha had handed him on the way out. "Genoa, La Spezia, Naples – "

"Organize an undercover sting in Genoa. Italians talk too much – unless they understand the consequences. We have to find someone over there who can get them to see this as a kind of omertà for cops: break your oath, lose your job. Get started. Make travel arrangements yourself. We'll keep this quiet at my end. When Forsythe asks for progress reports I'll clarify the need for secrecy. I'd like both of you out of here tonight. You know the drill."

"Thanks, Jason," Connor said. "You're a prince."

***

"Prince?" Hatch groaned in the elevator. "More like princely asshole."

"Sometimes you sacrifice for the public good."

"Well, Randall, my compliments. Jesus Christ couldn't have made him believe this was his idea."

They were still laughing when they walked into room 1732, where the world's best-equipped document forgers plied their trade.

CHAPTER FOURTEEN

Northern Italy

Castelfranco is a walled medieval city at the foot of the Dolomites. Its stone towers, elegant porticos and cobbled squares make it a natural tourist attraction. But few tourists come to Castelfranco. They are claimed by the proximity of Venice.

For Vesh's tribe of Gypsies, Castelfranco provided an ideal spot to settle down in the winter and spring. The climate, harshly Alpine to the north and west, was tempered by the Adriatic. And even though tourists were in short supply, the nearness of Venice put them within easy reach.

Good relations between Vesh's tribe and the town's elders dated to the nineteenth century. This unusual compact of nomads and bourgeois involved a substantial transfer of cash. It required as well that the Gypsies conduct their business outside the walls of the city. In exchange, the tribe was allowed to camp on the banks of the outlying river. Here they lived in peace, free from vigilante intrusions and permit requirements.

Vesh was the Rom-Barro, the tribal leader of the extended family that pitched camp each year on the outskirts of this very proper town. His seven children ranged in age from newborn to young adult. It was into this loud, happy group that Teresa was adopted. What had begun as a death-bed favor to the farmer Zlatko quickly grew into a warm familial relationship. Everyone loved the moody little Gaye girl who spent hours hiding alone with her dog – then suddenly emerged in high spirits to join a raucous game. She could speak three languages when they found her and she learned Romany, the Gypsy tongue, so effortlessly it was easy to forget she came from the other side. In fact there was a rumor among Vesh's brood that she was a lost member of their tribe.

Over dinner the night after their camp had been readied, Vesh explained to his new daughter how they would spend the next months. It was, he said, a lot of fun – especially for kids and women. They got to go into Venice on the train each day and compete to see who could "harvest" the most money and valuables. The winner earned a special prize. The tricks for getting the items were easy. Old Lyuba would show her everything she needed to know in the time it took to travel on the train from Castelfranco to Santa Lucia Station.

Vesh told Teresa she had a big advantage over the other kids: she spoke better English than they did. This would help a lot with American tourists, the Gaye with the biggest hearts and smallest brains. If she just concentrated on them, she would come home every night with a bag of coins that would do the family proud. When they went to Venice the first time, they would show her how to pick an American out of the crowd.

By now Teresa spoke English with an accent of indeterminate origin. She looked like a street urchin. Vesh promised her that no one would recognize her. It didn't matter anymore who she had been before she found her real family. Now she was safe.

But Teresa was still very frightened of the big city. She knew from Grandfather Zlatko that the bad guys would be looking for her everywhere. She hadn't told anyone she came from America. Even Vesh, when he inquired after her origins, got nothing in return but a blank stare.

Vesh never insisted she tell him more than she wanted to. It wasn't a matter of great concern. A Gypsy child from another family, who would have been about the same age as Teresa, had died last spring. She had been born in Kosovo and her birth was registered with the authorities. Her parents hadn't bothered to report her death. Vesh bought the girl's papers for a penance. They gave Teresa a bureaucratic identity. This was all the Gaye cared about.

***

"Why can't I stay at the camp?" Teresa asked. "I don't want to leave Katja all alone."

She and Vesh were walking hand-in-hand to the train station. He always took her hand when they left camp, sensing that she was afraid. It was an overcast December morning, bleak with the promise of rain. Thick clouds hung motionless over the city. The smoke that rose in vertical columns from a thousand hearths seemed to support the sky.

Teresa's brothers and sisters ran ahead, playing one of their rowdy games. Peals of laughter shattered the morning quiet. Old Lyuba, who walked behind with the other women, shouted at them to settle down. Her voice was louder than all of their voices combined, maybe even loud enough to carry to the camp alongside the river. Teresa wondered if Katja might be listening . . .

"We all have to work," Vesh said after a long silence. His hand was big, its folds and creases filled with something that looked like dirt but wasn't. "The kids and women go into the city each day. They come home in the evening with money so we can eat. The older boys and men get called to the farms outside the city to shod horses and sharpen tools."

"That's not what Djivan said. He said he got sick last year and came home early. He said all of the men were at that tavern near our camp getting drunk."

"Well, he must have come home later than he remembers. Sometimes the men go have a drink after a hard day's work. The Gayo who owns the tavern has been our friend ever since I was a boy. He treats us fairly and we reward him. Sometimes, when other families come to visit and it's time for a young man and a young woman to get married, we have a feast there. It's important to keep the owner happy."

"Djivan said you would tell me that. He said when he's grown-up he'll spend the whole day at the tavern drinking like the other men."

"You shouldn't listen to everything Djivan says. Look at me today. Am I at the tavern? No. I'm coming into the city to help you get started."

"Will you come every day?"

"I told you. The men have work on the farms. But the women and kids will always be with you. They won't ever leave you alone. You mustn't be frightened."

In the train, Lyuba sat beside Teresa on the vinyl bench. She picked up the newspaper that someone had left on the seat and opened it in the middle. "Now watch," she said, poking Teresa with her elbow. "Look at Vesh over there across from us. Pretend he's one of the Gaye we'll see at the station."

She shoved the open paper into Vesh's torso just above the belt. "Now, if you imagine he is standing up, you could stick the paper a little higher. The tall men are good because you have to hold your arms up. When they see you holding your arms up, they feel sorry for you. The women are even better. They almost always feel sorry. Even if they don't, they think just like the men. They think the paper is there for a reason. The Gaye have to have a reason for everything. So they throw coins onto the newspaper because they think that's the reason it's there. You'll see. It rains money. But you must always be careful that you don't take away the newspaper too soon. If you do, you might get Djivan and the other boys in trouble."

"Why, Grandmother Lyuba?"

"Because they will be searching the Gaye. Sometimes the men keep their wallets in unbuttoned back pockets. Sometimes the women leave their purses open like bags of treats. This is how God takes care of us. These things we find are His offerings. Without them we could not live."

"My mother said that's stealing."

"Don't be silly. Taking from the Gaye isn't stealing. You can only steal from other Roma. Anything the Gaye have is also ours. This is the law of Heaven. You must never forget it."

The train stopped inside a big station. Teresa hadn't seen such huge crowds since her dad took her to New York City. That was a long time ago. She could hardly remember it. She could hardly even remember what her dad looked like. Sometimes at night she would dream about her beautiful mother, but she was starting to forget her too.

***

Vesh lifted Teresa down onto the platform. She was glad he took her hand. If she lost him in the bustling station she didn't know what she would do. They gathered where all the people were coming in. At the bottom of broad steps was dirty water. There were speedboats and ferries like in America. But there were also strange boats, pointed at both ends. Men in funny clothes with poles stood at the back and pushed.

Teresa didn't like these boats. They were scary, especially the ones with animals sticking out the front. It would be these boats that brought the bad guys. She didn't like the city either. It was old and had all sorts of ugly buildings that sank down into the filthy water. She started to cry. At almost the same moment it began to rain.

Lyuba pulled her back under the cover of the station roof while Vesh went off to have a word with the boys. "See all these Gaye coming from the trains," she said. "If you can't hear them talking, watch for the ones who are smiling all the time. If they wear light-colored clothing and pants that are too short and have teeth that are too white, they are Americans. You step in front of them. You stick a newspaper in their bellies like I showed you on the train. Try it. Take my paper. I'll watch from here. You'll be surprised." Lyuba gave her a pat on the rear. "Go."

"I'm scared, Grandmother Lyuba."

"I'll stay until you see how easy it is. The other kids, the ones Vesh is talking to now, will be working with you all day. I have a special place across town where I tell people what is going to happen in their lives. A lot of these Gaye come back to me every year. They like what I say so they give me lots of money."

"How do you know what's going to happen?"

Lyuba laughed. "I don't, child. I tell them what they want to hear. If I told them what was really going to happen, they wouldn't pay me. See that tall man over there? Take my paper and meet him when he comes toward us."

"I told you. I'm scared."

"You have to try. I'll be right here."

Teresa ran toward the man, opened the newspaper and pushed it into his stomach. At first he looked confused. Then he smiled, reached into his pocket and dropped a few coins onto the paper. It was just like Grandmother Lyuba said.

As the coins fell, Teresa noticed her brothers behind the man. She couldn't see for sure what they were doing but she remembered not to take the paper away too soon. The man smiled again and reached for his back pocket. All of a sudden his mouth dropped open. His hands went everywhere like fluttering birds, to his pants pockets, his coat pockets, his suit jacket underneath his coat. Then he spun around and, shouting loudly, plunged into the crowd.

Teresa stood like a statue, staring at the assortment of coins on her paper. When she heard Lyuba's sharp command, she folded the paper in half, let the coins slide into her hand and hurried toward the voice.

Lyuba picked her up and hugged her. "See how easy it is?"

"Yes. He was nice. Why did he run away?"

"Djivan got his wallet. We'll eat well tonight."

CHAPTER FIFTEEN

Vesh stood at a kiosk drinking a coffee and watching the newest addition to his family make haul after haul. She was a natural. Americans all gave to her, the same Americans that chased off his other daughters. Sometimes they even gave her banknotes. This wasn't good because they had to take their wallets and purses from his boys' reach. But it wouldn't be a problem for long. He would teach Teresa to stay put and thank the Americans and talk a little English while they put their valuables away. Then his boys wouldn't have to search. Pickpockets usually got caught because they had to search for valuables before they could snatch them. That's when the Gaye felt something and got suspicious. It also made the kids rush and take risks after they found what they were looking for. Getting his operators out of jail cost him half the family take. He could see right now this was going to change.

It was mid-afternoon. Rain dimpled the Grand Canal. Vesh decided he should catch an early train home and check on his men. Teresa didn't need him, and the others in his family knew the city well. His men . . . his men. They could work and they could be taught not to do things like littering and burning tires, things that made the people of Castelfranco mad. But the men had to be reminded. This way of thinking that included what the Gaye thought was foreign to them. They needed a leader. That's what his father had been, and his grandfather before him. That's what Vesh was now, a leader. Times were changing. If his people were going to preserve their way of life, he would have to guide them with a balance of force and wisdom.

He was turning to leave when he noticed a man leaning against a marble column with his arms folded in front of him. The man was watching Teresa run around with her newspaper. He wore a wide-brimmed black hat and a matching black frock. Around his neck hung a large silver cross studded with jewels.

At first Vesh thought he was a Gaye holy man. But something didn't add up. In his wanderings Vesh had been to Moscow and Paris, Budapest and Rome. He had seen every kind of priest. There were different breeds, just like with horses, but they all belonged to the same cult. He knew the man watching his daughter was not a priest. Maybe he was a Gaye devil or sorcerer. Maybe he was one of those perverts Vesh had heard about who tried to have sex with children.

Slowly, the man turned until he was looking at Vesh. He was pale, even for a Gayo. His eyes were bluer than the bluest water. Their gaze cut like a dagger. His face was flat and round, as if it had been painted on a wall. From his chin hung a narrow beard, its tip pointing at the jeweled cross on his chest. He stared until Vesh looked away.

There would be no early train trip home this evening – not with an evil spirit hovering so close to his family.

***

Teresa's newspaper was growing limp. Some rain must have gotten inside the station, she thought. Perhaps it came on the hands of the Americans, or on the coins they shoveled her way. She glanced around and saw a man getting up from a bench. He had just put down a brand-new paper. When he walked away, Teresa went over and exchanged it for her old one. She was tired. The coins in the pouches beneath her dress felt heavier by the minute. Sure, this was a fun game, getting the Americans to give her money. But she was hungry and missed her dog.

Djivan and his brothers were buying hot chocolate at the kiosk. She hoped they would bring her some, but they seemed to have forgotten her. She sat until she got bored, then opened the paper in the middle and prepared to go back to work. Before she stood up, she noticed a picture looking up at her out of a frame of newsprint. It took her breath away. It was her mother! She squinted at the words. It had been a long time since she had read anything. But if she concentrated hard enough, she thought, maybe she could still figure out what the article said.

She couldn't. The words were too big. All she could read was her mother's name: Kristýna Sondheim. Was she dead? Teresa had to find out. She ran to an old lady who shooed her away like an insect. She spun around and found herself in front a man who looked like an American.

"Mister," she begged, tugging at his sleeve. "Mister, you can help me please?"

The man smiled. "I'll try. What is it?"

"Please read," she said, holding up the paper.

The man glanced at it. "Oh, yes. The Herald Tribune. This article?"

Teresa jabbed with her finger. "Here This one here with picture."

"I already read the whole paper this morning. It says the woman escaped from jail in America and everyone is talking about her. The police are looking for her because she did something very bad, but they can't find her. Some people say she is trying to come back to Europe where she was born." He looked at her like a mind reader. "Why do you ask? Do you know her?"

Teresa shook her head no. "I think she is pretty."

"Are you trying to learn English?"

"Yes. Thank you, Mister. You're nice. I have to go now."

Teresa folded the paper and disappeared in the crowd. She hadn't gone far when she bumped into Lyuba. The fat woman laughed and picked her up. Teresa clutched her newspaper like a toy. She was trying not to cry.

"We're going home now," Lyuba said. "You must have done well. You're heavy. Come on. We'll get your brothers. The train leaves soon. Throw your newspaper in that trash container."

"No! It's lucky. I want to keep it"

Lyuba said, "Maybe you are Roma. Some people in your family think you are. Do you know?"

Teresa stared at the folded newspaper, wondering if she should answer.

***

Trattoria Giorgione, which the Gypsies called simply "the Tavern," was near the center of a tiny village a kilometer from the campground. Though no one admitted it, the economy of the village during the long barren winters depended on the Gypsies, whose earnings in Venice and the countryside – despite their proclamations to the contrary – made them as flush as many rural noblemen.

Paolo Giorgione, wishing to give both the villagers and his nomadic benefactors exactly what they wanted, built an addition to the Trattoria in the 1980s. The original building remained what it had been for three centuries: a modest Italian restaurant where the locals came with their children. The addition proved a great success. It was furnished in the style of a German Kneipe, and served as a drinking establishment capable of hosting everything from nightly card games to loud festivities. Giorgione thus managed to please both groups – and to double his income in the process.

After dinner on the night of Teresa's introduction to Venice, Vesh and a dozen of his colleagues set off on their first annual trip to the Tavern. As always, they walked. The rain had passed shortly after nightfall and the stars shone brightly in a moonless sky.

Giorgione greeted them by name as they flocked into his addition. They hung their coats, sat down at the heavy wooden tables, called out orders for beer, grappa, playing cards – and for Fabrizio.

Fabrizio was an old tailor with crooked wire glasses who always met them at the Tavern on the first night of their return. Tonight was no exception. He came out of the back room and made his rounds, following closely behind the waiter, taking orders for the suits the men bought each year and wore until they disintegrated. He had the men's measurements on file. But bodies change like the seasons. With his keen eye he discerned who had gained or lost weight, who had become more stooped or more muscular. He measured the men anew each year while they stood proudly, drink in hand, anticipating the fine figures they would cut in their new clothes.

Vesh had put on a few kilos. When his turn came, he stood and sucked in his gut for a waist measurement. Amid general merriment, the tailor made some quick notations in his little notebook. Vesh heard what his buddies were saying about his vanity and the gastric distress it would cause him when he tried to squeeze into his new silk tuxedo. He laughed along with the others. There would be no gastric distress, no flying buttons or exploding zippers. Italians were unique among the Gaye. They had a rare understanding of human nature. The tailor, he knew, would add back the centimeters he'd removed from the tape measure with his stomach sucking. If anything, he would need suspenders to keep his pants up. In fact, Fabrizio would probably include a fine red pair. That's what he'd done last year.

As Vesh turned around and stretched out his arms for a behind-the-back measurement, he noticed the presence of a shadowy figure seated at a corner table. It was the man who had stared him down at the train station, the man who had been watching his daughter. As soon as the tailor finished, he walked over to the stranger and sat down. When their stares locked this time, Vesh did not look away. Instead he slid a hand into his pocket and laid a stiletto with a carved ebony handle beside the man's cup of tea.

"What the hell are you doing here?" he asked in a low threatening voice.

The man's eerie blue eyes and plaster-like face cut through the shadows. "It is I who should be asking such questions. You have a young girl who is not one of your own. You abducted her and took her across a national border. There are numerous rural people in Slovenia who know this. They willingly volunteered the information which led me to your camp. In the civilized world, what you have done is known as kidnapping and is punished by life in prison. I am the priest of Teresa Sondheim's family. I am here to fetch the girl so she may be returned to them."

Vesh, still staring into those otherworldly blue eyes, those windows on the world of evil spirits, put a finger on the button of his knife. A slender blade leaped out, hitting the man's tea cup and causing it to ring like a crystal wine glass. "Get out of here. Don't let me see you again. You'll end up with your testicles severed by this blade and stuffed down your throat. You'll end up as spring garbage in the Lagoon."

The man stood, put on his black frock and wide-brimmed hat and gave a slight bow. "Good evening," he said. Vesh jumped to his feet and ran the dull end of the blade across the man's crotch. His action produced a smile as eerie as any he'd ever seen. Then, suddenly, he understood. This was not a man. This was an evil spirit, and evil spirits did not have testicles.

CHAPTER SIXTEEN

For Connor it was a triumph of international organization. In five days he had been able to assemble a massive undercover team of FBI agents and Italian police. The problems he had anticipated – lousy equipment, turf battles, language barrier – had never surfaced. The patrol boats and helicopters were new, the Italians of higher rank all seemed remarkably proficient in English, and the government had put at his disposal an elite corps of intelligence officers. But whether Italy had made incredible advances in law enforcement or whether he'd bought a seat to some post-Mussolini pageant he wasn't yet sure.

"What's the name of the goddamn ship?" he barked into helicopter's HF radio. "This time I'll write it down."

"Elez Jusufi," crackled the mildly accented response. "Want me to spell it?"

"Thanks. I'll manage. But who the hell is Elez Jusufi?"

"The kind of Albanian they name ships after. Tonino, can you see the ocean yet?"

"Are you kidding, Marshall? There's a thick blanket of fog hugging the water. Up above we have a clear night. Bad luck."

Connor had just taken off from a military base near Genoa. He was speaking with the newly appointed head of Italian maritime security, Marshall Carlo Giotti, whom he had left in charge of their joint headquarters in the customs bureau of the container port. Several other law enforcement agents, FBI and Italian, were in the rear of the chopper. More were positioned in larger groups at several points around the city.

Connor and Giotti had agreed on the decentralization of their people. A few hundred undercover cops in the port area would alert every criminal from Naples to Marseilles. The

Elez Jusufi might be transporting more in the way of contraband than the fugitive. Just his luck, he thought, to have a thug tip off the captain for reasons unrelated to the sting.

Giotti said, "Doppler indicates a break in the fog southeast of San Remo. You'll see it soon. If the Elez Jusufi stays in her shipping lane, she'll enter the clearing in several minutes."

"Where are the patrol boats right now?" Connor asked. "I don't want any last-minute fuck-ups."

"They're unobtrusively plowing the shipping lanes in both directions. On my orders, they've adjusted their speed to arrive near the freighter around the same time you do."

"Good, Carlo. You and your people are doing a first-rate job."

"We try."

"There's your hole in the blanket," Tonino, the pilot, announced over the HF. "I see boat lights."

"Excellent," Giotti responded. "We've cleared you to climb another thousand meters. I prefer that the people on that ship don't hear you until the noose is in place."

"They won't, Marshall. I'll corkscrew up and around."

***

Someone shouting her name yanked open the door of her stowaway. When Kristýna was awake enough to focus, she recognized Adem outside. The captain, usually relaxed and jovial, looked like a man with a gun held to his head.

"Hurry! Five minutes you must be in water. I give instructions. I talk, you listen."

"What's going – "

"Shhh. I intercept message. They know. They coming already to board my ship. Not yet midnight. I follow exactly contingent plan Genoa group give me."

"How did they – "

"No talk. Hurry. Come with."

They ran up the metal stairs to the main deck while Kristýna pulled on the clothes she was carrying. "Adem, you must – "

"Please. No talk, just listening. You go down ladder to ocean in two minute, no time for harness. Irina putting out rubber dinghy right now. Life jacket, boots, stuff you need all in there. Take this."

Breathing hard, he handed her a small plastic bag that looked like a zippered bank deposit pouch. "Do not lose. Money inside. Compass. Also passport and address Genoa group say you go to if something screw up. Put in pocket. I give you more."

"Yes, alright," Kristýna said, still dazed. Adem showed her something that looked like a kid's lunch box.

"This, this most important thing. We strap on you when you go down ladder. You lose this, you probably get caught. Now you watch how it works." He opened the box and took out some sort of radio with a short antenna.

"Adem – "

"Silent. You watching now." He held the device beneath her eyes and flipped a toggle switch. A pale green light flashed. He immediately switched it off. "Don't turn on right away. Try in one hour. When light start to blink, you steer boat this way and that way. Steer boat until light stay on all the time. Understand?

"Not exactly. What is it?"

"FM homing thing genius make for Tomas. I forget to mention. Hard for police track signal. Contact man on shore soon sending signal. Just like it say in contingent plan, he going down there now. He look like fishing man. He wait in truck to take you where Genoa peoples tell him. They coordinating everything now. You keep steering boat so green light stay on, this thing taking you right to rescue man on shore. Now turn around. I strap thing on you. When Irina come up, you go down ladder. Fog thick. Good for escape. Listen for ships. You can't make light or they see you for sure. So you must look out for them or you get smashed. If fog clear, bad fortune. Still, ocean is big. Not easy find little boat. I forget, compass setting you follow until man with signal get in place. You go three hundred four degree, you be pretty much right on course. One hour, understand? In one hour you start trying like I show you."

"How long is the trip? How many hours?"

"Don't know. Depend on tides, wind, if you getting lost. You travel twenty, twenty-five kilometers from here to shore. Boat have tiny engine for quiet. Part gasoline, part electric, slow like hell. Fishing thing. Electric charge when running on gasoline. Electric leave no trail. Best use electric much as possible."

"Is it easy to operate? The compass I can handle, but we didn't go over – "

"Smart girl. Instructions on tape recorder Irina put in dinghy. No time to explain. Irina coming up now. Dinghy ready. Time for you to go. Remember. We just doing what they give me in contingent plan. But I know waters around here. Not usually rough. You be okay."

After hugs and hurried good-byes, Kristýna started down the same rope ladder she had climbed up an eternity ago, this time without the safety harness. Fog and darkness hid the sea.

When she was seated and the boat was steady, Kristýna untied the mooring rope. Irina had already started the motor. It idled silently in electric mode. Nothing to do but stay on the compass course for now, she thought. Thank God she was familiar with boats. The changeover to gas she would figure out later.

Grabbing the handle, she rotated it a quarter turn and gradually increased the throttle until the dinghy started to move. It bounced over the freighter's wake, then onto the gentle swells of the Mediterranean. Kristýna concentrated on the faintly glowing face of the compass. After a few jerky turns and over-corrections, she settled onto the northwesterly heading Adem had given her and watched the freighter that had brought her so far vanish in the fog.

The sea grew calm, the air near the water was cold. Kristýna put on the wool sweater and rain slicker Irina had placed in the dinghy. Water splashed rhythmically against the rubber sides of the boat. The motor hummed as if it would run forever, but a tiny red light soon indicated that the battery was low.

She was listening to the recorded instructions that explained how to switch the engine from electric to petrol when a deafening roar shook the night. Powerful boats sped by several yards away, nearly swamping her. She held her breath, terrified that she had been seen. When would she know? When could she be sure they wouldn't come back for her?

No time to think. Almost instantly another angry noise replaced the roar of the speed boats. A helicopter, flying low, clattered somewhere in the fog. She tensed.

The reason she was alone on this vast expanse of the Mediterranean and not aboard the freighter had been clear to her but the urgency of her debarkation had not. Now she understood, understood in a visceral and sickening way. She found herself worrying less about herself and more about the nightmare awaiting Adem and Irina. Those two supremely generous souls had risked everything for her . . . everything . . . and she had not even properly thanked them.

***

"Hatch! How's the reception?"

"Can't tell. I've got ten Italians around me talking at the same time. These guys are crazy. Non-stop chatter, no one paying attention, the captain flying balls out, zero visibility."

"They're being directed by AWACS."

"Directed where?"

"To a clearing in the fog. Our fugitive boat just sailed into it. You don't know this, but you'll be there any second."

"Holy shit, we're there now. I see the freighter. It's all lit up like they're throwing a welcome party. I'm looking at four other PT boats as we speak. Searchlights everywhere. I've changed my mind. These guys are good. Reckless but good."

"Look up. You'll see something else."

"Jesus! You're landing on the containers?"

"We've got a dog on the chopper. The handler doesn't want her lowered in a cage."

"What? You're letting a dog determine procedure?"

"A hound, Hatch. You wanna search those containers yourself?"

"Okay, Randall. But maybe you should consider waiting in the helicopter. From here it looks like a nasty climb down and you – well you're not exactly a kid anymore."

"Thanks for your concern, partnero. See you on the bridge."

***

Italian maritime police, customs officials and FBI agents, all wearing black wind breakers with the identifying letters of their various organizations on the back, scaled the freighter's sides on cable ladders. As they went up, Connor climbed down from the stack of containers on which the chopper had deposited him, trying to get Hatch's comment out of his head. Descending with him were some of the men who had been in the back of the chopper – three FBI boys, a couple carabinieri with their ridiculous white chest belts and the dog handler, his beagle tucked against his chest in a front-facing baby tote.

The helicopter contingent reached the ship's bridge first and burst inside, weapons drawn. The captain, in rumpled khakis and a plaid shirt, was sitting at the wheel. He yawned, shut down the engines and returned to his dinner. Equally unperturbed, the woman beside him picked up a platter of baklava and helped herself to a sticky square. Connor felt like blowing out the bridge windows with his 9 mm.

"Parlate italiano?" one of the carabinieri shouted. The captain and his wife shrugged their shoulders in unison.

"They damn well speak English," Connor growled. "We know it from their police depos in Newark."

The captain turned slowly in his chair. "Now police care about what we say in Newark. A little late, no?"

"Where's the woman you're hiding? Come clean NOW or you'll do serious time in a US prison."

"Where is who? No hanky panky here. Only sons and wife on ship. My wife over there."

Hatch spun into the bridge with two FBI agents. "Any luck, Randall?"

"We're being stonewalled. Get off your ass, Captain. Take me to your sons. Massimo, bring your dog."

In the above-deck sleeping cabins were two young men who spoke broken English. They had nothing to say. "The woman?" Connor roared. "Where's the woman?"

"Woman. Like woman but have to wait on Albania for having one."

"Who the fuck do you think you're lying to? Out with it. Where is she?"

Hatch took his friend by the arm. "Randall, cool it. Let me talk to these people."

"Not yet." Connor turned to the dog handler, struggling to control himself, and scratched the beagle behind the ears. "Massimo, what did you say you called this beauty?"

"Dolce, Agent Connor. She'll find your fugitive. Don't worry about these idiots."

They went out on deck, where the rip in the fog had repaired itself, then back inside and down a riveted metal staircase to the engine room. A tangle of pipes gurgled overhead.

"Where's the hiding place, Captain? Where do you keep her?"

Adem said, "Bullshit question. Like asking when do I stop beating my wife. Don't stop beating my wife cause I never start. Can't tell you where I keep mystery woman because I never have her. Ship have tiny room down here like most ship, sure. No one in there."

"Where the fuck is it?"

Adem, who had left the fake boiler that hid the entrance to Kristýna's room in its daytime position, pointed toward the steel door.

"Open it," Connor snapped.

"Cannot do, Mr. Late Police. Never use room, don't have key."

"Jesus Christ. HENRY! How long to pick the lock?"

The FBI specialist studied the key hole with a halogen flashlight. "Longer than you want to know."

"Okay. Maybe we can use some Italian expertise. You Italians, any of you know about this sort of thing?"

A thin-hipped stud with longish hair walked the door without uttering a word and shined a pen light into the lock aperture. "Andrea, per favore passami l'uncinetto numero seidici."

Ten seconds with a crochet hook and the man the Italians called Il Napolitano stepped to the side. He gestured toward the door with a slight bow. "Allora, chi la apre? Agente Cònoro?"

"Connor," said Connor. "You're telling me it's open?"

"Opened, yes."

"Many garcias. Let me through."

Connor cracked the door and immediately leaped back, slamming it shut. "Goddammit. They've dumped TCE in there. That would be Trichloroethylene in Italian. Old timers used it to degrease engines. The fumes'll put you on your ass faster than sodium pentothal."

"Maybe why door locked. Ever thinking that, Mr. Late Police? Maybe ship maintaining company in Durrës use for cleaning engines. Plenty of old timers in Albania."

"Asshole. You could have exposed one of my men to that stuff."

"Me? Not me picking lock. Safe down here till you go picking lock."

Connor ignored the captain. "Massimo, this guy's not going to volunteer anything. We'll let your dog move in the opposite direction of the escape. We find the places on deck where our fugitive might have gone over. Your dog picks up the scent follows it back to its point of origin. Hatch, take a couple of guys upstairs and start looking for any 'where' possibilities. I'll secure the area around the door and join you in a minute. Captain and wife, stay down here. Greenlee, make sure they do."

"Agent Connor," Massimo said, "a scent will not last very long out in the salt air, not with salt water all over the place."

"Good."

"Which is signifying?"

"That only recent scents will remain. We need to get them NOW, before the ocean does. Give your dog a good sniff of the captain."

"But – "

"Explanations later."

"One moment, Agent Connor," an FBI colleague blurted out. "What if we find nothing? What then?"

"Then we've got her. She's in a container or stashed somewhere else in this miserable rust bucket. Easy work for the hound. Let's move!"

***

Connor said, "The rope that came up last was the rope that went down first. That means the top layer on the reel will have been contaminated with salt water. We'll check the part of the ladder that stayed near the deck."

"Clear," Hatch said. Reading Connor's mind he hit the button on the winch control panel that lowered the ladder. When the reel was several turns from the end, he stopped it. The beagle and her trainer moved in quickly. A few seconds later Dolce, nose to wet metal and tail wagging in delight, started to traverse the deck. The hound went straight to the riveted stairs the police had just come up and continued through the engine room until a cop stopped her at the cordoned-off area in front of the tiny chamber filled with TCE.

"She went overboard," Connor said. "Finding her will be like fishing in a tank. Thank you, Massimo. The expected results are now confirmed. Remind me to send you a pound of bully sticks from the States. We have the world's best."

The captain was livid. "What that dog proves? I go from deck to engine room all day. I come down here from deck with you before dog doing bullshit search."

"Right, buddy. But do you always lower the ladder first? You had a some kind of a boat down there. You had your wife stock it with baklava while went down and hauled Sondheim out of her cubby hole."

"No proof of nothing. I lower ladder lots for checking things down there. Ship old and water line always need checking for rust."

"Shut up. I've heard enough lies."

"I'm only person hearing lies. From you. From police in Newark. Always same lies so no one have to do any work. Your law bigger bullshit than Albanian justice under communism."

"Yeah it is, and you haven't seen the worst part of it yet. I'm gonna make you a civilized offer. You help me bring in this murderer and we'll recommend leniency at your trial."

"Can't help you. Don't know about any murderer. I want lawyer. I see every show on American TV cops don't like when innocent person ask for lawyer. So you get me lawyer. Then I decide if to talk. Or maybe you rather beat me first. I see that on American TV, too."

"Shut up. All of you, listen. We're finished being stalled by this clown. Italians friends! I want every officer, agent and customs official from Livorno to the French border mobilized at once. This doesn't mean by lunch time; it means NOW. One minute, yes? Yes. I want every little harbor and every yard of shoreline covered with men and dogs. I want every unit of your Maritime Police patrolling the water, and every available chopper in the air waiting for the fog to lift. Claro? Someone call Giotti."

"I'll do it," Massimo said.

"Good. Tell him I want this goddamn piece of junk towed into Genoa port, quarantined and searched – just in case. Tell him I want every safety violation written up, even if you don't have safety regulations. I already have enough to lock these people up for a year. I want enough to lock them up for life. Maybe they'll come to their senses then and join the good guys – right, Captain? You don't cooperate, you go down for life. I wanna make sure you understand that. Abetting the escape of a convicted murder is as bad as doing the murder yourself. That's for life, Captain. A life sentence. You know what happens inside an American prison. You've seen that on American TV too. So think about yourself, your wife and my offer. Think real hard."

***

Kristýna, shivering uncontrollably now, glanced at the tiny engine to see if it had finished charging. Not yet. What was taking it so long, she wondered? She would need the electricity's silent push soon. The fog, which she expected to thicken toward morning, had not cooperated. Instead it was disintegrating like a windblown shroud. She could see for miles. The eastern sky already glowed with the gray light of dawn. The calm sea, a blanket of tarnished silver, stretched to the horizon. She would soon be exposed, easy prey for a search from the sky. Her best hope was to leave no wake and no rainbow trail of gasoline residue on the mirror-like water.

She stared at the pudgy receiver Adem had given her. The green light glowed steadily, indicating she was on course. Just to be sure, she steered the dinghy a few degrees to the north. The light blinked furiously: no technical malfunction, but it took her five minutes to reestablish her course.

Why was she still on the water? Adem had said a journey of 25 kilometers lay ahead. She had certainly gone that far.

A few banks of fog still lay on the water ahead, great sleeping beasts that would offer refuge now and again. But they too would vanish with the sunrise, leaving her dinghy the focal point of what she imagined to be a thousand watchful eyes.

The green light flickered, less visible now that morning was about to break. She made a slight course correction and entered a bank of fog. She hadn't finished breathing a sigh of relief when the boat hit a gravel beach, hurling Kristýna onto the pebbles. A man, a ghost in the fog, rushed toward her, waving one hand while he placed the other over his mouth to signal silence. He helped her to her feet and pointed to a van with its rear door open.

"Hurry," he whispered. "Not a word. The police, they're everywhere."

Kristýna was still dazed. The man, noticing, took her arm and led her to the van. With hand signals, he instructed her lay down in the storage area and disappeared. Seconds later he returned and buried her under a heap of dripping nets that reeked of brine and fish.

"It's a short ride," the man said. "Try not to move or you'll tip over a cooler full of fish I'm putting on top of these things."

"Where's the dinghy?" Kristýna mumbled beneath the soaking nets. "Won't they find it?"

"Shhh. The motor was still turning after you ran aground. I went back there just now and sent it out to sea. It'll end up on the shore, maybe nearby, maybe not. But it won't matter. You'll be long gone. Take a deep breath while you've got a chance. There's a roadblock up ahead."

The driver greeted the cops cheerfully. When Kristýna heard them discussing a manhunt that stretched from France to Livorno, her heart felt as if it would stop.

She listened best she could through the sodden nets, listened through the pounding of her heart and the rushing of blood in her ears . . . a fugitive from America . . . a woman . . . either in a lifeboat or raft, not sure which . . .

"Long way to come on a raft," the driver said. "Not a trip I'd like to make this time of year."

Both carabinieri laughed. "You've got it wrong, cretino. She got off a ship somewhere nearby. She's a murderer. Looks good but kills. I don't suppose you saw her, did you, Luigi?"

"Pietro's fishing over on the other side of the point. They say he stabbed his wife. Other than him, no murderers yet this morning."

"Sorry, but we gotta take a look in back. Orders from above."

"Just don't knock over my cooler. Mario likes 'em swimming."

Kristýna heard the rear door go up and tensed. She tried to breathe softly but imagined she sounded like a steam engine. Her leg knotted in an excruciating cramp.

"Take this cooler out, Giovanni. Put it over there."

She felt hands digging through the soggy nets, digging deeper . . .

"Madonna, Roberto, get your ass over here and look at this."

The digging stopped; the muffled sound of heavy boots on gravel reached her ears.

"Sea bass. Who would have thought? Fish must not know when it's foggy. Put the cooler back and shut the gate. We're having lunch at Mario's today."

They pulled away from the roadblock. "Good work," the driver said. "Mario owns a seafood restaurant in the town center. He and his wife know you're coming. They're in charge of getting you to your next hideout. You okay, Signora?"

"I am," Kristýna said. "Just cold."

"Don't worry. Not much longer. You'll get out in the restaurant garage. A hot shower, dry clothes and several new identities. We've had a week to prepare the contingency. You're going to like the plan. You'll be in the Bristol Palace Hotel in a couple of hours. A guy brings Mario cheese and ham from Parma every Thursday. He doesn't know it yet but he'll be giving you a ride to a boat insurance agency in Genoa on his way home. You'll take a cab driven by one of ours from there. Mario and Anezka have the details – like who you're supposed to be, why you need the ride and why you're going to a fancy hotel. You'll be in good hands."

She heard the garage door go up, felt the van inch forward and stop, heard the door clank down. The driver and another man pulled the nets away and helped her out. Then came a torrent of heartrending words in Czech. The beautiful woman who spoke took Kristýna in her arms and held her for a long time.

CHAPTER SEVENTEEN

"Coffee?" Marshall Carlo Giotti asked.

Connor and Hatch both accepted. They had just entered joint operation headquarters at the Genoa container port. Computers hummed and telephones rang. Men and women hurried from one work station to another amid a frenzied cacophony of laughter and multilingual chatter. Cultural differences, Connor reminded himself. In the States, this scene would have been taken for an office party. Yet statistics seemed to support the way these people went about their job. If the stats weren't fake the Italian Criminal Police were enforcing the law far more effectively than the FBI. Not that he believed it: no American did.

"Maria, tre cafè."

"Subito Maresciallo."

"Sounds like they're singing," Hatch quipped. "I hope all the good cheer doesn't degrade the quality of their work."

The girl named Maria arrived with a silver tray. On it were long slender cookies, a sugar bowl big enough for oranges and three tiny cups of liquid the color of crude oil. God forbid, it was espresso! Connor should have seen this coming; he should have asked for American coffee. How could anyone function on this stuff?

While Marshall Giotti heaped spoonful's of sugar into his cup and downed it in one quick contented gulp, Connor searched the human chaos around him for an American with a pint-sized mug. No luck, no one to lead him to a secret oasis of real coffee. His compatriots had all been ruined by this strange country. They drank from the same microscopic cups as Marshall Giotti. Worse, they pretended it wasn't a problem.

Well, it was a problem. It impeded his ability to function. In the old days, the top-ranked FBI agent at the Embassy would have sent a tanker of Maxwell House up here with his people. Anything less would have been dereliction of duty. Some things, Connor thought, should never change.

But change they did. America, for one, no longer ran the world. You had to adapt, had to be "sensitive." He drank his bitter ounce and grimaced at Hatch, who grimaced back.

A man dressed like a model for Giorgio Armani stopped beside their table and handed Giotti a print-out. "Marshall, sir, we just received a call from the police in Bordighera. They found a rubber boat on the beach. No information on when it landed, but there were still things aboard."

"Such as?"

"You are holding the comprehensive list. A life jacket, blankets, boots and food are the most prominent items. They are being flown here now. We should be able to determine whether they came from the Elez Jusufi."

"Va bene, va bene. The freighter is in Dock Seven. Get the forensics people out there."

"Yes, sir, Marshall."

"Hold on," Giotti ordered. "Did they mention whether the boat has a motor?"

"It does, sir. An American gadget."

The Marshall raised his eyebrows. "Gadget?"

"A fishing motor that runs on battery or petrol. The capo seems to know something about it. He says it could propel a small boat from any Mediterranean shipping lane to his beach."

"It could," Connor said. "I happen to own one. And it's a serious piece of machinery, Lieutenant, not a gadget. Remember that, please. Where the hell is that town they telephoned from?"

"Near the French border, sir."

Connor glanced at his watch: 8:14 a.m. "Isn't there any way to determine when the boat came ashore?"

Marshall Giotti shook his well-coifed head. "Relax, Randall. Europe isn't wide open like the US. She won't go far. The items from the boat will arrive shortly. Once we've made positive ID, we'll initiate our manhunt."

"We should start now. We know the ID is going to be positive."

"We do not, Randall. There's a good possibility your woman is still on the ship and that the rubber boat was a decoy. We will wait until the items arrive – or at least until the container search is finished."

"Look, Giotti, I – "

A woman from military intelligence rushed to their table, cutting off Connor without a word of apology.

"Marshall Giotti – "

"Can't you see I'm talking?"

"Marshall, I think this merits an interruption."

"Make it quick."

"A call from police HQ in Parma. The assistant director's brother reports that he drove a woman from Ventimiglia to Genoa. She was young, dressed to kill, a knock-out as he put it. He didn't become suspicious until he read an article on the fugitive in today's Corriere."

"What about luggage," Connor said. "Did she have any luggage?"

"Yes. Two suitcases and a bag. According to the driver they were somewhat gaudy but looked expensive."

"Was she hitchhiking?" Giotti asked. "She hardly fits the profile of a hitchhiker."

"No. The brother delivers specialties from Parma. On Thursdays he stops at a restaurant in Ventimiglia. According to the restaurant owner, the woman was going to Genoa to file police reports and insurance claims. She told him this at the counter where she was taking a cappuccio. Her husband's yacht allegedly collided with a ship and sank. She was planning to take the train. Since Genoa is on the way to Parma, the restaurateur claims that he asked the delivery man if he could make room for the woman."

"What about the husband?"

"In the hospital in Monte Carlo. Allegedly."

"Most interesting," Giotti said. "Thank you."

"It's certainly possible she's the one," Connor said. "Excuse my non-existent geography. How far is the place with the restaurant from the place where the boat was found?"

Giotti stabbed a finger at the map spread on the table in front of them. "Close, Randall. From here to here. A few kilometers."

"Jesus! She's right under our noses?"

"Under our noses? Whether she's still in town is anyone's guess."

***

Kristýna waited for the cabby to deposit her bags with the bellhop out front, then walked purposefully through the lobby of the Bristol Palace, Genoa's most prominent fin de siècle hotel. She stopped at the reception and summoned the clerk but did not remove her sunglasses.

"You're expecting me," she said. "Josef Kamiński will have informed you."

"Yes, certainly. One moment, please. We're in the middle of a shift change."

Kristýna pushed back a strand of long dark hair that had fallen in front of her face. It was genuine hair . . . but not her own. While the clerk checked for messages from Kamiński, the film director, she gazed with apparent indifference at the broad marble staircases, crystal chandeliers, oriental rugs and Renaissance paintings.

"Ms. Ellison-Morley, yes?"

"That's right."

"Your passport, please. A formality."

He glanced at an antique grandfather clock snuggled into a marble nook. "Almost nine o'clock. Very good. Mr. Kamiński did indeed leave word at the desk that you were to join him when you arrived. He has, of course, booked the Garibaldi suite. The rest of the film crew, if you will allow me to comment, did not fare as well. But . . . but one can't have everything, and the Garibaldi suite is unique in all of Italy."

"A bit talkative, aren't we? Have your boy show me to Josef's suite."

"Yes, Signora, at once. But I still need so see your passport. We have had some trouble in Genoa this morning, what I do not know. We are required by the police to check the papers of everyone entering or leaving the hotel, no exceptions."

"I'm not a guest of your hotel. I'm a guest of Josef Kamiński. Now, instruct your porter to show me to the suite."

"I am sorry. I cannot, at my age, risk my employ – though I certainly understand your irritation. I must see your document."

Kristýna dug in her purse and slapped a worn British passport onto the counter.

"Ellison-Morley, Veronica. Satisfied?

Yes, quite. However, since you are not officially a guest of the hotel I must make a copy for my own protection."

"Hurry, please."

On her way to the top floor, almost all of it occupied by the Garibaldi suite, she ignored the exquisite interior of the hotel's original elevator, ignored the bellhop in his splendid uniform, ignored his fine gold-barred cart carrying her Louis Vuitton luggage. But while her attitude and bearing emanated haughty indifference, her head spun with vivid images of the last hours: soggy nets, police blockades, exhaustion and revival; following Anezka up creaking wooden stairs to a bedroom above the restaurant; a hot shower and a rush to transform her into the mistress of Josef Kamiński; quick explanations about the celebrated film director's role in financing much of the fight against the Trade; the silent ride in a van to a shipping insurance agency in Genoa; hailing a cab to the Bristol Palace as soon as the van drove off. What awaited her she did not know. Nor did Mario, Anezka or the man who had brought her to them. The European rescue operation was divided into hundreds of cells, each with very limited knowledge of what the others were doing. It sounded sinister, thought Kristýna, built as it was on the model of terrorist movements. But she understood the need to protect the living whole from death, should any of its organs fall into unfriendly hands.

"Signora," the bellhop said as the elevator slowed, "do you per chance play a role in the film Signor Kamiński is shooting in our city."

Kristýna, feeling more comfortable in her disguise, ventured a tiny smile. "Really, you should not ask such things. Josef Kamiński, for all you know, could be my lover."

"Oh, well yes, I'm so sorry. I just assumed – "

The elevator stopped. The horrified boy reached for the lever to open the door. "I'm so ashamed. Please, Signora, please don't tell anyone or I'll lose my job. I wanted to ask for your autograph. It was an unforgiveable breech of etiquette."

She glanced at his brass name plate. "It's quite alright, Matteo. Of course I'm part of the cast and I'll be glad to give you my autograph. Come to an outdoor shooting one day – we have many scheduled. Find me when I'm not working and remind me who you are. Now, however, I must hurry. So, please – "

***

Kristýna fell into Josef Kamiński's outstretched arms. He hugged her tightly but quickly released her. "We have no time to talk. There are already things going on in the street that tell me we need to move you along at once. Are you physically and mentally able?"

"Yes."

"Good. Leave the British woman with me, suitcases, handbag, wig, clothes, documents, everything. I have arranged for the immediate disposal of everything we don't want to be found. Go into the bedroom to your right and dress for your new role."

"Which is?"

"A nun. Hurry. One of ours disguised as a priest is coming for you. He will lead you to the hotel chapel and show you an unobtrusive exit. There will be commotion below, plenty of it. The priest will tell you where to go – and although he will no longer be with you, you will know from the commotion when to leave."

***

It was mid-morning when the last of the transcribed and translated interviews reached Connor's desk. A flashlight from the dinghy bore Kristýna's fingerprints. Food left behind in aluminum foil matched scraps found in the ship's galley. They had enough. It was time to close the noose.

Giotti said, "I've ordered the city sealed off." He looked at his gold wristwatch, ignoring the railway-style clock in front of him. "That means all roads out, airports, train stations, docks and – "

"I get the picture," Connor snapped. "We'll visit hotels and parks first. I don't know if this woman has money but I know she's tired. You'll remember how we caught the Washington sniper?"

"Asleep in his car," Hatch volunteered.

"I know," Giotti said. "That was a coup. I hate to bring this up again, Randall, but we might not be so fortunate. It's possible your fugitive left Genoa before we even knew she was here. Europol is keeping an eye on points beyond the city."

Connor smiled. "That's unnecessary, Carlo. She's still here. I can smell the perfume she's not wearing."

"Cosa?"

"Forget it. You had the last call. This one's mine. I want us to think like she thinks we won't think. I want us to begin with the most exclusive hotels in Genoa."

"Randall, that's idiotic. She's not going to climb dripping wet out of a – "

"Listen, Carlo, we wasted forty minutes waiting on your goddamn proof. Let's do it my way. I take the blame if I'm wrong."

"Va bene, va bene. I'm starting not to understand you. Capisci, Randall? I start out with a sane partner and end up with a malatto di mente."

"Do me a favor, Marshall. Stop pelting me with Italian words and get your people off their de-rears."

CHAPTER EIGHTEEN

Police cars screeched to a stop in front of the hotel, disgorging hordes of carabinieri and FBI agents. Giotti, backed by an army of police officers and special agents, directed a stream of Italian at the desk clerk. Connor nudged him aside. "Carlo, please. This was my idea. Let me handle it."

The clerk pulled down the tails of his jacket. "If you're worried about my English – "

"Did I say that?" Connor barked. "A woman checked into your hotel around nine o'clock this morning. Is she still here?"

"Yes, Signore. And since she was not an official guest of the hotel, I made a photocopy of her passport. I hope I have behaved in a manner consistent with – "

"Where is she? In which room?"

The clerk looked away from Connor's ferocious stare. "It is a delicate matter, Signore."

"Special Agent," corrected Giotti. "He's with us."

"I don't care you call me," Connor rasped. "Out with it NOW. Which room is she in?"

"There are things I must consider, Special Agent, before I divulge such sensitive personal information. I shall telephone the Director of the Bristol Palace."

Connor slammed his palm onto the counter. "What the fuck are you talking about? You have a murderer on the loose in your hotel, you see who you're dealing with and you are going to tell me this second where she is."

"Maresciallo, Signore, con tutto rispetto, this woman is not some piece of Southern trash. She is a very elegant and very rich person from abroad who . . . please, this must remain between us . . . who appears to be the mistress of Josef Kamiński."

"I don't care if she's banging the entire film crew. Where is she?"

Giotti said, "Please. It is a matter of urgency."

"Very well, then. If you will assure the direction that I did not give up this information on a whim. I was ordered to do so by the – "

"WHERE IS SHE?"

The Garibaldi suite, sir."

"Which is located – "

"On the sixth floor, the top one."

"Have that passport copy sent up with one of my men." Connor glanced at the bank of ornate elevators and the great winding staircase. "Hatch, we'll take the stairs. FBI agents, use the elevators. Carlo, I want three of your men in the lobby, the rest guarding the outside of the hotel. Move!"

***

Connor, Hatch, Giotti and two dozen agents burst into the suite, their weapons drawn and steadied. Joseph Kamiński stood beside the French doors that opened onto the balcony. He was talking softly on the phone, glancing at the phalanx of armed agents as if they were members of the cleaning crew. He cupped a hand over the receiver. "One moment, gentlemen. I believe it is customary in the civilized world to talk before you shoot. I would like to see the paperwork that gives you the right to invade my privacy like a pack of Nazis. We in Poland know something of Nazis – something that you people, those of you from the FBI, obviously don't. Now please, one moment while I finish my call. Then we'll summon my attorneys and discuss your concerns in a manner that does not transform the Garibaldi suite into a CIA black site."

Connor, already seething from the delay at the hotel reception, blew his stack. He almost stumbled over two elegant Louis Vuitton suitcases as he leaped at the Polish director and ripped the receiver from his grasp. He put his ear to the phone and hurled it to the ground when he was met with the sound of a dead line. He grabbed Kamiński by the necktie and slung him down in an overstuffed armchair. "You arrogant son of a bitch. You're harboring a fugitive here, which gives us the right of pursuit. Where is she? I can smell her perfume. Those are her bags. You stall me and I'll turn this place upside down. And you . . . you'll wish you were in a black site."

Kamiński asked for a glass of water which Marshall Giotti, horrified by his American colleague's treatment of one of Europe's most respected artists, immediately handed to him. "Signore, allow me to apologize – "

"Apologize, my ass." Connor grabbed the glass from Kamiński, threw the water in his face and hurled it at the wall. "Where is she? You don't want what's waiting for you, buddy, if you try to stall me again."

The director laughed while water still ran in rivulets from his hair down his nose and into his eyes. "Such a circus over a simple affair. You people haven't changed since the Mayflower landed. Ms. Veronica Ellison-Morley, more correctly Lady Ellison-Morley, dropped off her bags here before her appointment with her Genoa masseuse. She was late and left in a rush. She'll be back, though. We really have become quite fond of each other over the last months, especially in the exchange of pleasure. Of course you Americans wouldn't know anything about that."

"You're goddamn right we don't," Connor snarled. "But we know a lot about pain and it's gonna be my pleasure to teach you."

"That's it," Giotti said. "You're done treating Mr. Kamiński like this. Signor Kamiński, I beg you to forgive my colleague. He's not usually like this. The stress of the fugitive hunt has obviously taken a toll on his nerves. So let's reach a reasonable agreement. You let us search the suite and ask you several questions. I'm sure there will be nothing more."

"Fuck you, Giotti."

"Thank you, Maresciallo," Kamiński interjected. I would be pleased to help you catch your fugitive. If ruling out my friend is of assistance, then go ahead. And tell your American boor that he would have received the same response from me, had he not conducted himself like an Al Qaeda operative."

"I resent that. Your pleasure lady is my fugitive, and you're going down with her."

"Please," Kaminski said. He made a sweeping gesture of the suite, signaling that the search could begin.

Connor ignored the others thrusting his face an inch from Kamiński's. "Who were you on the phone with."

"Room service. I ordered breakfast. Perhaps your nerves are frayed because you have not eaten. If you would like to join me – "

"Yeah, right," Connor said. "That breakfast better show up or you'll be on the table in place of the toast."

At that moment, an employee of the kitchen knocked. Kamiński told him the door was open and he wheeled an ornate cart with coffee and several chafing dishes atop it into the room. Connor flung open the French doors and stormed out onto the balcony overlooking Genoa. He did not know about the earlier call Kamiński had made to the parking garage.

***

The roar of a mighty twelve cylinder engine on the street below shook Connor's head. Vibration penetrated to his bone marrow. Below he watched a sleek yellow Italian car stop at a light. The driver hit the accelerator every few seconds, making sure the engine – and the noise –did not die. The Italian cops burst onto the balcony with a sense of purpose they hadn't shown when they burst into Kamiński's suite, rushed to the wall and elbowed each other aside to get a look at the car.

"What the hell is going on?" Connor shouted.

"The new Murciélago," one of the Italians who spoke English yelled into Connor's ear. "They say it's the best Lamborghini yet."

When Connor looked down again, the entire contingent of carabinieri assigned to guard the hotel's exits were crowded around the car.

Kamiński strolled out onto the balcony. "Beautiful, isn't she?"

"I'll take a Ford pickup," Connor said. "Is that thing yours?"

"Yes indeed. Murciélago number three from Mr. Lamborghini's plant. The Countach in its day attracted similar attention. But I forget. Your love is for that most pedestrian of all autos, the Ford – the beginning of the mass-produced mediocrity that transformed your country into an aesthetic nightmare."

"Shut up. Who's the driver?"

"My Genoa mechanic from the garage around the corner. He was nice enough to come for the car, a big help as this is a busy day for our film company."

"Oh, yeah. Who else is in the car? Kristýna Sondheim?"

"Sadly, no. From her photos in the paper, she seems to be quite an attractive woman."

"Until she cuts your balls off. Hey, you, the cop that speaks English, radio down there and tell someone to impound that garish piece of crap."

At that instant, an army of police cars, sirens screaming, announced their presence to the world. Connor watched in disbelief as a wall of honking traffic coagulated behind them. In the States, he thought, they would call this place a fugitive's paradise.

"Idiots," Connor shouted. "What the fuck are they doing? Who's on the hotel exits?"

No one looked up. No one heard. Christ, he couldn't even hear his own words. What was wrong with this country? It made rush-hour Manhattan sound like a designated meditation area.

Furious, he rushed back into the suite to find his FBI people huddled together, as clueless as he was about the most promising next step. Not one to hesitate in the midst of a crisis, Connor gave an impulsive order: "Don't just stand there, agents. I want every room, every broom closet, every nook and cranny of this place searched. I don't like this movie prick's story. She might be in the building, and if she is she's not getting away."

Giotti approached Connor, looking angry. "Randall, the entire city is closed off. No one is leaving by train, plane, boat, car or donkey. Look at this room. Look at it! She went out for a while. Everything points to her coming back. We're going to wait."

Connor ignored him. "Agents, search the building. Someone get those men down below back to the exits. They're bunched in the middle of the road like sheep."

"Randall," Giotti interrupted firmly, "we are not going to tear this hotel apart. If she is here, we'll make sure she doesn't leave. But we'll do it Italian style – discreetly. May I suggest an early lunch?"

"Lunch! You're out of your mind. We're not waiting on undercooked meat and a mini-thimble of coffee. Not this shit again, not when there's every indication we have her trapped."

"Then, Randall, I'm sorry to say we've come to an impasse. I will not allow a general search of the Bristol Palace. It is the pride of Genoa and deserves to be treated with respect."

"I'll use my people," Connor growled. "This is totally ridiculous."

"Sorry again, Randall, but you're not in Texas. You're in my country. If you wish to proceed on your own, you'll need my permission – just as I would need yours in the United States. We're colleagues, Randall. We have the same goals. I certainly don't want cultural differences to damage our relations. So please reconsider my lunch offer. You, as well, Agent Hatcher. While you're waiting on your raw meat and thimble of coffee, the woman you wrongly suspect of being your fugitive will return."

"She's an American fugitive," Connor scoffed. "She doesn't go by the pansy playbook of European criminals. If you're going to insist we wait, I'm sure as hell going to insist that you get me a real cup of coffee."

***

When the Bristol Palace was built, the architect insisted on a secret passage that would link the Garibaldi Suite to the tiny hotel chapel, six stories below. In future decades this proved to be one of the establishment's great drawing cards among royalty, image-conscious politicians, dictators and visiting dignitaries. The indiscretions of the rich and powerful could be confessed and forgiven at all hours of the night without threat of detection by a porter or lurking newspaper columnist. This morning, however, the passageway served a very different purpose: it allowed Kristýna, in full habit and thick glasses, to descend to the chapel with Josef Kamiński's priestly impostor, and to do so with a same guarantee of privacy enjoyed by some of the past century's great philanderers. Her instructions were simple: when any kind of commotion erupted outside the hotel, she was to exit calmly through a door at the rear of the chapel and walk to the nearby Piazza della Vittoria. The walkways under the porticos would be crowded and no one would be less obtrusive than a nun. At 11:09 exactly she would be picked up by a taxi while walking in the direction of the traffic in front of the Andrea d'Oria school for classical studies.

Easy enough, she thought, as the priest said a short prayer and left the chapel. He would be alright, thank God, long gone by the time her steps were traced. Kneeling in front of the altar with bowed head, she tried to pray. But it was Obruchev who answered her silent call, not the Holy Father. Memories of that dreadful night overwhelmed her again and sucked her into a vortex of terror . . .

***

The blaring of police sirens and the frantic honking of cars jolted her back to the present. She glanced at her watch: 10:56. If she left at once, she would arrive at her appointed destination on time. But where was the commotion outside in relation to her route of escape? The last thing she needed was to walk into a nest of cops . . .

At the rear exit of the chapel, she hesitated to open and bowed her head. She could hear the voices and footsteps of service people outside, all moving in the same direction. What had the priest said? That the incident would take place at the front of the hotel; that her exit was at the rear, close to the service doors for maids, bellhops, waiters and cooks.

She was in the right place at the right time, which also struck her as some sort of dream. Pushing the door open, her heart in her throat, she saw waves of traffic speeding past under the fierce Genoa sun. Suddenly, the cars and delivery vans screeched to a stop. Her first thought was that she had caused this to happen, but she quickly saw that the light at the intersection in front of her had turned red. A crosswalk with a green miniature pedestrian attached to pole on the other side of the busy street invited her to cross. The sea had parted in biblical likeness, making her feel more comfortable in her habit.

Minutes later she entered the noisy crowds beneath the porticos. Fighting back a mixture of fear and joy, she began to walk toward the Piazza della Vittoria and her scheduled rendezvous with the cab. The light changed, the din of traffic filled the avenue she had crossed. The Bristol Palace was now behind her; the sea that had parted to allow her escape was once more whole.

She arrived at the Piazza slightly out of breath but on time. As she strolled the cobbled walkway in front of the Andrea d'Oria school a cab cut across two lanes of traffic and screeched to a stop. The cabbie flung open the back door and she climbed inside.

"I'm Lucio," he said, glancing at her in the rearview mirror. He squealed into the traffic, setting off a cacophony of horns, brakes and curses. "Welcome to Genoa. You probably haven't heard the latest."

"The latest?"

"They know you're here. The entire city has been sealed off."

"My God."

"Don't worry. Everything's going to be fine. We'll just have to hide you for a while."

"How long? This blockade could last for weeks."

"You're mistaken. We have these dramas all the time. It's just opera. The carabinieri stage a production worthy of Verona. It's always brief, the law enforcement equivalent of a one-night stand. Then something terrible happens and they have to leave. It's their version of stage fright. They screw up, they can't handle the bad reviews in the morning press. When the show's over, I'll drive you to your next contact."

Kristýna touched his shoulder. "Thank you, thank you from the bottom of my heart."

Lucio looked at her in the mirror, smiling broadly. "Don't thank me," he said. "Thank opera. It was invented for people like you."

CHAPTER NINETEEN

Being auctioneer wasn't as easy as it looked. During his first week, Obruchev pushed himself to the edge. Fatigue made him irritable, irritability made him impatient and impatience made him hotheaded. He flew round-trip from Ljubljana to Moscow whenever he got nervous, which was often. The flight always seemed full; the seat beside him always occupied by some loud mouth who wouldn't let him nap.

While in the Russian capital, he touched base with his staff, lunched lavishly with his suppliers and bombarded his Chicago office with calls. His mother in Kursk was dying: his explanation to Chicago for why he would be overseas so long; and to Moscow for why he looked like hell. Miserable trips, but they shielded him from unwanted questions and provided him with a future alibi . . . just in case.

In Slovenia he was staying at his dead cousin's place. He'd nailed up a tarp to avoid having to look at the makeshift church. When he got back from his fourth lightning visit to Moscow, it was already 10:00 p.m. Delays on the ground, delays in the air, a telephone fight with his wife that had caused him to miss the early flight. He should have been at the factory an hour ago, setting up for another round of lucrative chaos.

He longed to eat something and go to bed. That was a joke. Once he gave in to temptation, he wouldn't move for days. This was about survival, and if life had taught him anything, it was that the weak didn't survive. He exchanged his business suit and dress shoes for khakis, a sweater and heavy boots, grabbed a sausage from the refrigerator and left.

By 10:30 he was in the factory. He lit the coal fires in the drums around the stage and opened the safe. Three days he'd put off doing the books, three days he'd let banknotes pile up like garbage. Fuck it. He slammed the heavy steel door shut and spun the dial. He couldn't deal with accounting. Not now. He couldn't stomach anything, not even the prospect of gorgeous young females parading naked before him.

Jesus, he'd been a fool to let Kristýna and her daughter live. Lucky his mistakes hadn't come back to haunt him. Lucky he was well on his way to burying them forever. All he needed was a little breathing room.

"Breathing room" meant the disposal of the kid and a trip to the incinerator for the charlatan he'd employed to find her. It meant recruiting a new auctioneer. And if the cops didn't do their job soon, it meant taking care of the escaped bitch.

He heard trucks outside. The girls had arrived. Their handlers would take them to the boiler room down below to prepare them for auction. A full hour until show time, and all that remained for him to do was check on a few things. He'd be able to squeeze in a much-needed rest.

He took a shot of vodka, something he was doing more often lately. After making certain his supply of virgin candles was adequate, he set up Rasputin's miniature candelabra and gave the trigger of his ceramic gargoyle a pull. It produced a wavering yellow flame. He adjusted it to a sharp blue arrow, extinguished it, then loaded the candelabra with the first three candles.

He looked into the incinerator. A nice even burn and strong suck of air. Bogdan's ghost rose from the ashes to greet him. No surprise, not anymore.

Almost finished. He switched on the metal detector for its nightly test, walked through it with his 9 mm. and thought his head would burst when it unleashed an earsplitting shriek. Done, though his ears still rang. Fifty minutes of paradise awaited him, 50 minutes of sweet oblivion before all hell broke loose.

Stepan Mikhailovich Obruchev stretched out on a bench. But the peace he craved eluded him. A group of saints from the icons of his youth materialized behind his eyelids and knelt before his open grave. One of them looked up, jeering. The face belonged to Rasputin.

**

"Hey, pretty swank," Hatch said. "You've never been big on fancy stuff. You sure we can justify the expense?"

Connor smiled as he draped his jacket over the back of a chair. "I've changed. No one said anything to me about per diems. If they raise hell later, I'll remind them who delivered the bacon."

"And your buddy over here, as in me?"

"You didn't have a choice. I'm your boss. You saw the place in Genoa. We're not going to be outdone by the people we're chasing. It's psychologically unhealthy."

"Psychologically unhealthy? You're already ruined. Want a drink?"

"Take a guess."

They had flown from Genoa to Vienna two days after the fiasco at the Bristol Palace. Connor already felt better. It wasn't the luxury suite he'd booked at the Sacher that explained his improved mood: he was a Maxwell House guy who didn't give a hoot about such things. Rather, it was his new base of operations in a country that took police work seriously.

Hatch handed him his usual double scotch on the rocks. He downed it before tipping glasses with his colleague.

"That drink, Randall, is gonna cost more than a night at the Holiday Inn."

"If you don't mind," Connor said, "I would like you to stop obsessing about money. From now on we're spending. The Bureau dragged me away from my vacation. The incentive pay was an insult. Careers are on the line. They want me to save their asses but they don't want to pay for it. Well, it doesn't work that way. Not anymore, it doesn't. So, partner, let's you and me worry about the hunt and let them worry about the cost."

"Jesus, man, the Italians really sent you over the deep end."

"I'm on my way back up. We're in a good place. We'll be in a better one soon. You were right about the note."

"I never said I was sure. I just wanted it included among other possible leads."

"Backing off, are we?"

"It's not my position that's changed. It was 'maybe' from the start. We followed your theory and missed them by a few seconds. You were on the right track. It's not your fault the Italians are . . . Italians. Who the hell knows if things are any different in Slovenia. Do you have any idea where the place is?"

"Next door, Hatch. Right across the border. The note said, 'Go there and you will understand.' So we'll do just that. If it doesn't pan out, I'll blame you. Then we'll come up with something else."

"Very generous. What makes you think the Slovaks will be any more cooperative than the Italians?"

"Slovenians, Hatch. It's not going to be up to them to determine such things."

"What?"

"It's not going to be up to them because they won't know we're there."

"But – "

"No 'buts.' I'm not risking another disaster."

"But, Randall, we can't just walk into someone else's country and take over."

"Why not? Our president does."

"I hope you're kidding."

"Hardly. Relax, please. Make yourself another twenty dollar drink. We'll use those Canadian passports they gave us in New York. We'll visit as tourists and have a look around. Nothing illegal about that. By the way, we're meeting Drexler downstairs in fifteen minutes."

"The Embassy legat?"

"You remembered. I'm impressed. I called him from Genoa to check out the options for our Slovenian tour."

"I hope you know what you're doing."

Connor smiled. "I'm fishing, Hatch. With your bait."

***

Drexler was waiting in the hotel bar. He was a big bald guy Connor's age, handsome in a rugged sort of way. After cursory introductions and handshakes he said a word to the bartender, who held up his hand and snapped his fingers.

"I've booked us a private dining room," Drexler announced, tossing a banknote onto the bar. "I hope you guys are hungry."

"Starving," Connor said. "I've been too pissed off to eat since those dago clowns let our fugitive escape."

"Listen, Randall, Giotti's a good cop. I've worked with him before. If you had a serial killer on the loose, it would be different. But the man's got bigger problems than catching a girl who looks like Sophia Loren in her prime. To tell you the truth, I'm surprised he committed any resources at all. Give it a rest, okay? You can't expect him to grasp the symbolic importance of this mess for our criminal justice system. I do."

Hatch said, "Our legal attaché in Rome understood."

"It's a different situation. We're not looking for her in Austria. This gives us a lot more latitude."

"I'm not sure I follow."

"You will. It involves a commonality of interest."

The maître d' led them to a small room with a gilded baroque ceiling, oil paintings and linens on the table. Hatcher picked up one of the elegant plates and studied the bottom.

"What the hell are you doing?" Connor blurted out.

"I don't know. My wife got me in the habit. Everything in the States says Made in China. She'd like this. Real Dresden stuff."

"You could try taking her somewhere nice," Connor said. "You'd have better luck on both sides of the plate."

"Thanks, friend. My partner's had an epiphany. He's become a big spender. Twenty years of frugality wiped out by a week in Italy."

"Good to hear," Drexler said. "It was something he needed to work on."

They ate and drank as if they were trying to bankrupt the Bureau, then began planning over kirschwasser and a cup of what Connor happily proclaimed real coffee. "Jerry, I hope you've had a chance to look into the stuff I faxed you."

Drexler lit a Cuban cigar. "This is the only thing Castro does right," he said, watching whorls of bluish smoke make a slow journey toward the angels on the ceiling. "So that's what we boycott. Anyway, Randall, I got on your request immediately – with good results. There's someone named Obruchev selling girls near Ljubljana."

"How many?" Hatch asked.

"Somewhere in the neighborhood of thirty thousand a year."

"I heard there are two million teen prostitutes from East Europe working out there right now. I guess he's not the kingpin."

"In the girl trade there's no such thing as a kingpin. That's pop culture stuff. You don't have five families or a CEO. The racket is totally decentralized. To understand how it works you've got to see it as thousands of separate organizations – some big, some small. We don't know exactly how many sellers there are. What we do know is this: for every creep we put out of commission, two more show up out of nowhere. The smart ones like Obruchev move their place of business every couple of years. He's worked out of Russia, Bulgaria, Albania and at least a dozen other countries. And he's bigger than you think, Hatch, even if his sales numbers compared to the total don't give that impression. In fact he's the largest single operator we're aware of. He's been mentioned as a pioneer by some of our informants – the first guy to see the opportunity presented by the fall of the East Bloc and to make a fortune off it. America won the Cold War, right? A lot of people over here would say the Slavic criminal element won."

Connor frowned. "So tell me something, Jerry. How is it possible there are two million kids working as sex slaves, most of them right here in Europe, and no one does a goddamn thing about it? Sounds to me like pretty lax law enforcement."

"Let me ask you something, Randall? How well have we done in the States stopping the flow of narcotics? The problems are similar. Thousands of sellers, huge demand, astronomical profits and plenty of product. A lot of these girls end up with small-time pimps who run between two to five girls. You make a few busts and the effect is zero.

"There are other problems. One: you can't torch the crop because it's human. Two: the girls, once they get where they're going, end up with no papers and often no knowledge of the country or its language. Three: you can't peddle influence to the House Majority Leader or any other politician if you're an illegal alien with no money and no constituency. Four: a lot of these sleaze balls have now figured out it's a lot safer to keep the girls locked up in the former East Bloc countries and to import the clients. We've got no jurisdiction there, and the profits are so huge the police can usually be bought."

"Wait a second," Hatch said. "How can they make big money staying where everyone's poor."

Drexler took a sip of scotch. "You didn't hear what I said about importing johns. The answer is, they don't pimp their girls to penniless natives. Sex tours to 'exotic' places like Kiev are advertised all over the Net. 'More bang for your buck,' that sort of thing. You want to be picked up by a limo at the airport with a couple of beautiful young blondes in back waiting to give you the time of your life, you just ask. It won't cost you any more than doing the same at home, even if you figure in airfare. Maybe less. And there's almost no possibility you'll get your ass busted. So they still make their money off the male citizens of rich countries – but with less risk to themselves and their clients.

"I'm sorry to say American men have made sure this new approach thrives. I wonder if most of them would give up what they're doing if they realized they were helping to keep young girls in bondage. Two million of them if we accept Hatch's figures. Think about it. The number is almost five times greater than the number of men we lost in World War II. I'm talking about both theaters. Okay, maybe these kids aren't physically dead – but they might as well be."

Connor shook his head. "You can educate till you're blue in the face, Jerry. Guys who do this sort of thing don't give a rat's ass about others. If they did, they wouldn't be doing it."

"I'm not sure I agree," Drexler said. "But I'm taking us away from more immediate concerns. Let's get back to work.

Wiesel's got Obruchev pegged as owner of the Slovenian operation, even though he's away most of the time. As the founder of a trade that's about to become the third largest criminal activity on earth, he'd be a catch. Wiesel's intent on hauling him in. He knows it's just a start but still. For him it would be like bringing in Escobar was for us."

Connor seemed distracted. He raised his eyebrows. "Did you say Weasel?"

"Inspektor Doktor Lutz Wiesel of the Austrian Staatspolizei. That's the secret service branch of their Federal Police. He's the chief undercover man on human trafficking. This guy's good. I mean, really good. He's got the nose and the training to run down the sleaze. Speaks enough East European languages to revive the Austro-Hungarian Empire. A German father, Romanian mother, something like that. He knows the US and the Bureau. Did his graduate school in criminology at Duke, then came back a few years later for some liaison training at Quantico. We've been working with him on busting up the sex trade for the last several years, which is what I meant by commonality of interest."

Connor ordered another round of after-dinner drinks. "Obruchev, that's a pretty common last name over there. How do you know we've got the right guy?"

"We checked on your Stepan Mikhailovich of Chicago. He's in Moscow as we speak. Wiesel called his US office, introduced himself as an old friend. He was told your man would be away for a while because his mother was dying in Kursk. The Austrians did some further checking. His mother is alive and well in Odessa. Which gave Wiesel an idea. If he was in Moscow and claimed his mother was sick, he must be traveling somewhere pretty often. He was – at least we think he was. Interpol ran down the records of a Stepan Mikhailovich Obruchov – pronounced the same as Obruchev – who is more or less commuting between Moscow and Ljubljana. His papers are Belorussian, but everyone's convinced he's the Chicago guy. I think your pigeon's come home to roost."

"Hatch's pigeon," Connor said, lifting his glass.

Drexler carefully folded his napkin and laid it aside. "And you're certain he'll lead you to your fugitive?"

"Certain, no. But if we don't scare him off I think the odds are good. How hard will it be to shadow him."

"Right now, very hard. Whenever he arrives he's picked up at the airport by his security director – a Slovenian general named Majdak – along with the general's army entourage. I don't mean in the terminal, either. I mean on the tarmac, like a head of state. When he leaves it's the same thing."

"How can he get away with the VIP shit? Seems to me that would create suspicion, more than a little suspicion."

"It doesn't. He's posing as a Western defense contractor who's converting a defunct factory into a labor-intensive operation. The area is poor and unemployment is high, so it's a politically popular project. Everyone's behind it: the government, locals, the press. They don't have a clue what's really going on."

"So the military escorts Obruchev like a head of state to his place of business?"

"Yes, at least since Wiesel's had him watched."

"I take it the premises are heavily guarded."

"More heavily than Three Mile Island. In addition, Randall, Obruchev only ventures out when he's going to the airport – with official military protection, as I said. He doesn't just stroll around the countryside. I can't see how he's going to lead you to anyone."

"I can't either" Connor said. "Maybe he's got people out scavenging for him. I won't know until I get inside the place. Don't tell me it's impossible."

Drexler smiled. "I know you better than that, Randall. There's a way. Wiesel's just as anxious to bust this ring as you are to catch your fugitive. You'll make a good team. He can get you past security if you're willing to go along with his plan."

"Of course we're willing," Connor said impatiently.

Hatch had been fidgeting through the entire conversation. Now he cleared his throat, rested his arms on the table and leaned forward. "Before we commit, Jerry, I think we should know exactly what this 'plan' involves."

"Wiesel's got the details." Drexler said. "The US government is willing to help in some very tepid ways. But guys it basically boils down to this: you go in as clients and buy yourself a busload of girls."

CHAPTER TWENTY

Teresa was growing tired of the game at the Venice train station. It seemed to her a lot more people were being mean, even Americans. But most of all she hated what she had to do every night after dinner. When the evening meal was over, the men went off to the Tavern and the women gathered in a couple of the big vans to rest and tell stories. By now it was always dark and cold. Sometimes it was raining too. It didn't seem fair she and the other kids had to do the dishes. She wondered why the others never said anything.

Feeding leftovers to the dogs was okay. But washing all those heavy metal pots with burnt stuff stuck to the bottom was awful. Whenever that time of night came, she couldn't help thinking of home in America. Her mother used to let her help with the dishes and she didn't mind at all. She climbed up on her own pink and white steeping stool and put her hands in the warm soapy water. Everything smelled good and there were special kinds of scrubbers to get the big skillets clean. It was easy. All the other things went in the dishwasher. Then you put in the special soap and pushed a button. When it started making noise, you were finished. All except for the last part, the part she liked best. That was when you got to rub some special lotion on your hands.

She and her mother rubbed all four of their hands together. It felt sort of funny, but she liked it. Afterwards they went into their library. She wasn't allowed to watch television. Her dad made her do homework instead. But it was nice. He would always stay nearby, reading things that helped him be a good doctor. He called it his homework.

Sometimes her mother curled up on the big sofa with an afghan and read a book. That was good because all three of them were together. On nights like this, Teresa was even allowed to ask questions as long as she kept her voice down and didn't disturb her dad.

The evenings she liked best of all were when it was cold outside, like tonight. Her mother always played the piano when it was cold and her dad didn't mind. If it was snowing, he would make a fire in hearth. Sometimes he even looked up from his work and talked to them. She remembered how she would feel all warm inside and start to go to sleep, and how either her mom or dad would carry her up to bed. She had a big soft bed in America, with stuffed animals and ruffled pillows and a down comforter that kept her toasty warm.

Here she was cold all the time. Sleeping in her clothes on a hard cot wasn't the worst part. It was doing the stupid dishes in the river. She begged Vesh to let her stay with Lyuba but he said that wouldn't be fair. His other little girl, who was even younger than Teresa, had to go down there too and she didn't complain.

When Teresa cried and held onto his leg, he said she could break one of the rules and take Katja with her. Vesh made all the other dogs stay in the camp after dinner because they barked a lot and disturbed some of the people living nearby. But Katja was different. She was a good dog. Sometimes she went off on her own for a little bit while Teresa was doing her job and sometimes she jumped in the river, but she never barked or bothered anyone. Having Katja come with her helped, but she wished the other kids wouldn't tease her about being afraid of the dark.

The river didn't scare her during the day. It wasn't a big river like the one by Aunt Michaela's pastry shop. Before they started playing their newspaper game in Venice, she used to go down these same paths with Lyuba to get water. She used to love the river. The ducks and geese came to float on the water and some other animals she had never seen in America played with each other along the banks.

The only problem was the path. There were just a few spots where you could go down to the water. When they first got to their camp, each kid picked out a spot for the nightly chores. Teresa had the worst spot because she got last choice. It was muddy, making it like a slippery slide. Everywhere else the bank went straight down as if it had been cut with a cookie cutter. There weren't any other places. She had to be careful she didn't go sliding into the water. You wouldn't drown if you did. The water wasn't real deep and the current was only strong enough to make little dimples on the top. But if you got all wet, it made you even colder.

That's what had happened to her last night. She was carrying a big pot on a loop handle. It was full of knives and forks and spoons. Katja ran off where she liked to go lately, and Teresa lost her grip on the skinny tree she used to help her down. The pot was heavy. She slipped, fell on her bottom and went all the way up to her neck in the black water. The silverware spilled out. She was too scared to hold her breath and put her head under the water to look for it.

Everyone seemed mad at her when she got back to the camp. They said one of the men would have to miss work in the morning to go and find the things she had spilled. It cost a lot of money when one of the men missed work.

Tonight, as the big group of noisy kids walked to the river to do their chores, Teresa lagged behind. She didn't feel like talking to anyone. All she wanted was to go back to her mother's kitchen in America, and after that to the library with the piano and big fire in the hearth. She knew her dad wouldn't be there anymore. The bad guys had killed him. But her mother was out of jail now. The newspaper she kept under her cot proved it. So at least her mother would be there.

Djivan and the others hadn't noticed she was behind them. She turned off her flashlight so they wouldn't come back for her and listened to their voices fade in the distance.

All of a sudden Katja started to whimper and run ahead.

"Katja, come back here. You can't go play until we get to the river. Bad dog."

She turned on her flashlight, just for a second. Katja stopped, pointed her tail like she was hunting, then came back and licked Teresa's face. She wasn't really a bad dog.

There was a moon in the sky. When the clouds moved away you didn't need a flashlight. But as soon as you turned it off, the clouds came back. You could see them swirling all around, trying to cover up the moon. They were strange clouds. Sometimes they turned into animals or dragons. The sky was moving fast. If she stood still and looked up, she felt the ground under her feet start to move too.

She decided not to look up anymore and to leave her flashlight on all the time. Vesh told her that batteries cost a lot of money and she shouldn't use the flashlight if she could find her way without it. Usually she did the things Vesh told her, but tonight was different. She was cold and she didn't like the way the ground moved. She tried to think of something else that wasn't so scary . . .

Her new family was sort of nice, even if they teased her a lot. They had given her a small pot and just a couple of metal plates tonight, not any silverware. The man who had climbed into the water and found all the stuff she lost came by to show her and tell her it wasn't so bad. He'd even given her a hug.

For a while she felt better.

She came to the baby tree she used to help her climb down to the water. She grabbed the limb she always grabbed. It bent like a bow while she took tiny careful steps in the mud. Katja went off into the woods before she reached the water. She wished she knew what her dog did, but she never had a chance to find out. By the time she finished her washing, Katja was always waiting for her up above on the path.

Not tonight.

Well, that was okay. The pot had been easy to clean because they hadn't made the kind of stew in it that stuck to the bottom. The plates were easy, and she didn't have to worry about silverware. It took a lot less time than usual. Katja was smart. She knew how long it usually took. She would be back soon.

Only she didn't come.

Teresa turned on her flashlight and saw a smaller path through the trees that branched off the big path along the river. So that's where her dog went every night! If it hadn't been so scary she would have followed the path to find out Katja's secret.

The wind came up and made the trees talk because they still had a few shriveled-up leaves on their branches. She shivered. The pot and dishes started to feel heavy. She found a grassy place where there wasn't any mud and put them down.

"Katja," she called. "Katja, come! It's time to go back."

Teresa thought she heard her dog whimper somewhere deep in the woods but she wasn't sure. That was because the other kids were coming, pushing and shoving and laughing loud like they always did. If they found her before Katja came, they'd make her go back to camp without her dog. She had never spent a single night since being dropped off at Uncle Bogdan's without Katja. She had to have Katja with her, especially tonight.

She grabbed her pot and plates and went a little way down the small path. She would hide and let the other kids pass, then she could wait for her dog.

A few minutes later the kids trampled by. Then the night grew still.

"Katja! Come here now! We have to go home!"

This time she heard it for sure, a whimpering far off in the woods, then a bark no other dog knew how to make. All of a sudden she realized what had happened. Katja had stepped into one of those terrible traps the hunters set. Last week one of the old dogs came home all bloody and without a front leg. Everyone tried to help him but he'd just laid down and died. Vesh had told her then about the traps. He said even people had to be careful. The hunters didn't care if they caught a deer or a little girl. That's how the Gaye were.

She could feel her heart beating. The wind blew some more and a few crinkly leaves brushed across her face. It was dark. She turned on her flashlight. She had to go find Katja. She left her dishes and took off running along the narrow path, calling her dog's name and squeezing the light so she didn't drop it. The whimpering grew louder. She had guessed right! It was a hunter's trap. Maybe she could do something while there was still time. Maybe Katja wouldn't die if she found her right away!

The closer she came to the noise, the more she forgot about the scary night. She fell twice on roots that lay like snakes across the path. She was lucky. Even though her flashlight crashed to the ground, it didn't stop working.

She came to a clearing with a white car parked in it. She shined her light past the car. There was a dirt road, a hunter's road!

She called for Katja. Nothing. Her dog had been whimpering just a few seconds ago. She looked around the clearing but she couldn't see much. The batteries were wearing out, the light was getting dim. She would be alone in the black night if she didn't find Katja soon.

Just then the moon broke through the clouds, lighting up the whole place. She turned off the flashlight right away. Vesh had shown her how you could turn it off when the light started to get dim and it would work better when you turned it on again. It was like a person, he said. You had to give it time to rest.

The trees were like giants and shook their bony arms in the wind. They made her feel small. She saw bushes near the hunter's car. Katja must be in there, she thought. She hoped the hunter hadn't come back yet.

She crept closer, helped by the light from the moon. She was afraid to call out. She didn't know if she should go any closer to the car so she stopped and tried to think. While she was standing there, the clouds came back to cover the moon.

Something rustled in the fallen leaves. She turned on her flashlight and aimed it at the noise. Katja! She wasn't in a trap at all. She was eating a big piece of meat the hunter must have put near his trap to catch an animal.

"Bad dog!" she cried. "Bad dog! Come here right now."

She started to run, then realized Katja might take the meat and play tag. One of them might step into the trap. She had to be careful so her dog didn't think she was playing. She stopped and held her breath. The flashlight started to go dim. She turned it off so it could rest. She didn't think she was crying but felt warm tears on her cheeks.

This was really scary. Maybe she should sit on the ground in the black night and wait until Katja finished the meat. That way her dog wouldn't play a game.

But what if the hunter came back to his car and saw that a dog had eaten the bait for his trap? Would he shoot her dog? What about her? What would he do to her?

There was something else, something worse. Vesh had sat all the kids down and told them to be careful, especially Teresa. He said there was an evil spirit lurking around the family. The spirit could only catch you if you were alone so it was super important for the kids to stay together. Teresa had forgotten. Now she had gone off alone, just what Vesh told her not to do. She felt a chill go up her back that was different from being cold. She finally understood why the ground had moved. The evil spirit had been following her and whenever he took a step the ground moved. He was here too, not only the hunter but the evil spirit. Maybe the spirit was afraid of Katja. Maybe the spirit wouldn't think she was alone if her dog was with her. She had to make Katja understand.

Shaking and crying, she turned on the flashlight. It had rested, it worked. That was good but what it lit up wasn't. The piece of meat was big and had a thick bone sticking out of one end. Katja loved bones. She never got enough to eat at the camp so she never got full. It would take her half the night to finish.

Katja didn't even look up. Maybe that was lucky, Teresa thought. Maybe she would be able to tiptoe close enough to grab the piece of meat. Then she would run back down the path where she knew there weren't any traps and her dog would come running after her, and together they would scare the evil spirit away.

The clouds parted and swirled around the moon. She turned off her light and tried not to look too long. That's when the ground moved, that's when the evil spirit came closer. She crept toward Katja on her hands and knees. She was already muddy and badly scraped up from falling so she didn't care that she was getting dirtier and hurting herself more. She had to get her dog to help her. If she didn't, the hunter and the evil spirit would do terrible things.

She had never been so scared, not even when the bad guys killed her dad and took her away. That had happened so fast she hadn't had time to get scared. The bad guys gave her a shot right away and she didn't remember anything until she got to Uncle Bogdan's. But this was different. It was sort of like time had stopped. Her whole body was shaking. She wanted to cry out loud. She wanted to scream at her dog. But Katja didn't understand anything when she was eating.

The clouds must have gone away from the moon completely, because for a moment it was light as day. What she saw made Teresa gasp. Katja was tied to a tree! The evil spirit had tricked her dog. She hoped the spirit wasn't so strong that she couldn't get the knots in the rope undone. Katja hadn't been able to scare him off. But maybe the two of them together could do it if she could only untie the knots.

She stood up. Now she could run to her dog. Katja was on a rope. She couldn't run off and play games and get caught in the hunter's trap.

Lightning flashed. The bumper and windows of the white car flashed too, like mirrors in the sun. She saw a wall of grayish black clouds with ragged bottoms rushing at the moon. Katja finally quit eating and barked. It wasn't supposed to lightning in winter. When thunder cracked and echoed all around her, Teresa knew it was the evil spirit.

She had to hurry. She put one arm around Katja's neck and pushed the meat out of reach. But when she started to work on untying the rope she heard footsteps behind her. She also heard something scarier. It sounded like someone was breathing.

She spun around and there he was, the evil spirit, dressed in black with a big cross on his chest. She tried to scream but nothing came out.

The spirit knew her name. He said, "Teresa, don't be frightened. I'm taking you to your mother."

The moon went out and the spirit grabbed her. He was rough. He covered her mouth with something heavy and wet. Then she felt it, the same bee sting in her arm she had felt after they killed her father. It was a shot, she knew it was. She started to fall asleep while the spirit carried her to the car. He put her inside the trunk and slammed it shut. She could hear the rain hammering on the car metal. It sounded far away. Then her head started to spin. She tried to stay awake as the car bounced over the dirt road, but she was too tired. Her mind drifted back to evenings in America. There was a fire in the hearth. She felt warm and sleepy. The last thing she remembered was her mother folding her in her arms and carrying her up the stairs to bed.

CHAPTER TWENTY-ONE

Lucio drove slowly for the first time since their departure from Genoa, an eye fixed on the road signs. "Get down on the floor please," he said, interrupting his own story. "Get down as far as possible so no one outside the car can see you."

"Now?" Kristýna asked.

"Yes, immediately. Hurry. We're coming to the intersection I was telling you about."

"Okay." When she had scrunched down low, Lucio turned onto a narrow two-lane road with little traffic. He lit a cigarette, coughed, exhaled and waited several minutes to speak again. When he began, she sensed a nervousness in his voice she hadn't noticed before.

"You'll have to stay down there until we reach your drop-off point. I'm going to tell you several more things while we cover these last few kilometers. There's a big box of photography supplies in the trunk. The guy at the gas station in Vicenza is one of ours. He loaded it while we were filling up."

"Yes, I saw. And I take it this box is related to what we are doing?"

"Yes and no. The man who lives in the villa where I'm going to leave you placed the order. It's addressed and sealed, and there's a real order with a receipt inside. Every few weeks these orders are delivered to him by taxi. It must be important stuff because he has it transported like a passenger. It's good this way because coming in a taxi to drop off a package won't appear unusual. Like I said, yes and no."

"This sounds rather strange."

"Yeah. William Hewitt, the guy you're going to meet, isn't exactly your normal type. At least not in Italy. I can't say if he's weird in his own country 'cause I've never been to England. Maybe it's just how these people are. You can decide for yourself when you meet him. I should give you your instructions now."

Kristýna squirmed around on the floor to get more comfortable. "I'm listening.'

"Good. When I come to the villa, I'm going to stop at the end of the long drive, get out and take the package from the trunk. I'll carry it up the steps to the main entrance and ring the bell. No one will answer, so the package gets left behind a clay planter near the door. It will be hidden from view and protected from the elements by the entrance awning. Bottom line is that the supplies were delivered but no one was home. Capito?"

"Fine. But I still don't understand who you think is watching us."

"Maybe no one, like I said. But William and his wife think otherwise. They have reason to believe their group has been compromised."

"Lucio, listen. If that's true, I have a right to know who these spies are."

"Maybe. But I can't tell you because I don't know. I was told only that you must not be seen anywhere near Castelfranco and that it's critical you get where you're going without anyone knowing. Listen, none of us in the rescue movement has much information about what members of the other cells know. That's how we work – in tiny cells. You will have noticed."

"I've noticed, but – "

"Good. Then you understand. The Englishman and his wife will tell you."

"This is awful. I thought we would be safe for a while."

"We all did, but nothing is for sure in this business. Get ready. We're almost there now. While I am carrying the box to the door, you get out your door and disappear in the bushes along the right side of the house. No one will be looking in your direction for a few seconds. They'll be watching me – unless we have bad luck. But we won't. You, Signora, don't have bad luck or you wouldn't have gotten this far. Wait in the bushes until a woman opens the front door for the package. She will tell you how to enter the villa unobserved. The only bad thing is that you will have to wait for dark. The Englishman doesn't think the people spying have had enough time to get night vision equipment. In the dark you can probably go undetected."

"I'm used to waiting. You learn in jail. Lucio, you know how grateful I – "

"Sorry. We can't talk anymore. I have to hurry. Farewell for now."

The car came to an abrupt stop, and he got out before she could say a word.

A moment later, Kristýna heard the trunk open and close. She waited a few seconds, then slid out the passenger door on her belly and cut across the unprotected swath of gravel separating her from the bushes.

***

The cold rain that had come up in a sudden tempest drummed on the canvas awning not three meters away. Water gushed off the villa's roof and splattered on the lawn just beyond the spot where Kristýna hid. She shivered as she watched puddles form on the cypress-lined drive, the same drive down which Lucio's cab had disappeared.

The hours passed slowly. No one came to let her in, nor was there any indication that anyone ever would. She knew she was being irrational; she knew the plan, but for the first time since her escape Kristýna felt abandoned . . .

***

The storm abated with the arrival of night, but the calm did not last. A bolt of lightning cleaved the sky, followed by a deafening crack of thunder. The lights of the villa and of all the surrounding farmhouses flickered and went out. Blackness reminiscent of those claustrophobic nights in the ship's stowaway room swallowed her up, a welcome curse.

She heard the front door open. "Quickly," a woman whispered. "Come up on the porch where the package was left. Quickly."

The woman closed the heavy door as soon as Kristýna was inside. "I'm Gabriella. Here, take my arm. Watch that you don't trip. We must be in the cellar before the electricity returns."

"I can't see a thing."

"Hold on tight. It isn't far. I was going to wait until our usual bedtime to make the villa dark before I came for you. The power outage saved us a few hours. We, my companion and I, think we have found your daughter."

"What? You have found my daughter?"

"We think so, but we aren't sure. You will be the one who tells us. Come now. Watch your step. Careful here. There's an area rug two meters ahead."

"Yes, okay, but . . ."

"Please. First things first. We must get below in case the windows are being watched. I left the shutters open to avoid the look of hiding someone. Left here. Careful."

"But Teresa, do you possibly have her here in this villa?"

"No. Please, you must be calm. We have photographs only. This way. Around the sofa. You will tell us if the photos are of Teresa. If they are, we will decide what to do. Stop here."

A door open on squeaky hinges.

"I am going down first. You come one step behind me. Put your hands on my shoulders. Come now. Slide your toes ahead to feel where there is a step. They are very old and uneven. I have placed a strap on the door to close it when we are both in the stairwell."

Kristýna carefully navigated the first step down, her hands tightly grasping the shoulders of the woman whose silhouette she was finally beginning to see. But her concentration dissolved as wild hopes of finding Teresa pulled her into a world of enchantment, a world gentle, intimate and safe. She heard the door squeak shut, felt a leather strap brush across her cheek and tripped.

Gabriella spun around and caught her. "I know it's hard," she scolded, "but you have to empty your mind of thoughts and focus on making it to the bottom in one piece. If you could see the steps you would understand. It's a long steep descent, very medieval. Please. Listen to me. Supposing the girl in the pictures is Teresa. This does not mean we have her, only that we have found her. Getting her back won't be easy. William's contacts should help, but they are no good without the mother. If you twist an ankle or a knee, you will hurt our chances."

"Then we should use a flashlight," Kristýna said. "Don't you have a flashlight?"

"Yes, darling. Right here in my smock. We cannot use it because the old door up top no longer has a good seal. It leaks light as well as cold. I know this too well. Often I am reading in the parlor when William forgets to extinguish in the stairwell. Mind you, we cannot chance even a candle flicker. No one is supposed to be in the villa. All the way down with no more mishaps. Hold onto me and count your steps. You have eighteen to go."

"I'll try. What happens at the bottom?"

"We pass through another door, a new door that's hermetically sealed. William has his studio in the cellar. He keeps it climate controlled. All very modern, too far down for windows. Careful, careful of this next step. It has a chunk missing. So, we can use light as soon as we are in William's sanctum sanctorum. Light, a hot bath for you, dry clothes and then . . . then we are going to see if the girl is Teresa."

"We should see about her first."

"I'm sorry, darling. You were out in the rain and cold a long time. We need you healthy for reasons I explained before. One more step. Careful. It's almost twice as high as the others. Medieval by day is magnificent; by night, less so.

***

Kristýna took a deep breath and glanced at the ceiling, then flung open the bathroom door. Gabriella was waiting in the corridor. "This way, please. William is waiting for you."

They had only gone a short distance when a man stepped in front of them. He looked to be in his late thirties, slight of build with longish blond hair parted in the middle. "Hewitt," he said, extending his hand, "William Hewitt. It's an honor to meet you."

"Yes, William, likewise. I'm grateful for everything . . . everything you and the others have done for me. I'm sorry if I seem preoccupied."

"It's quite understandable. Just a few words in here and then I'll show you what I have." He gestured to the room whose door he held open. Inside she could see a grand piano, a writing desk and a sofa.

"I can't concentrate. No words – not now, please. I need to see the pictures. I can tell you right off if it's her. Then we can talk."

"Come inside. I understand how you feel. However, after I show you the girl, it's going to be a very emotional time for you. We might need to act quickly and, whatever the outcome, good or bad, we'll need to think straight. It won't take but a second."

Kristýna sighed in exasperation and let herself down in a corner of the sofa. Gabriella sat beside her and held her hand. William stood at the piano, his wire-rimmed glasses reflecting the overhead light. He wore jeans, hiking boots and an army jacket. His accent, when he spoke, was very pronounced, very British.

"First, a word on all the secrecy. We, Gabriella and I, are leaders of the cell in this area. Given our proximity to the Adriatic, we're kept very busy. Girls from the East are often brought across the narrow body of water to the Italian shoreline at night. Some do not leave Italy, but for most this is merely the first stop on a journey elsewhere.

"Of late, under pressure from the European Union, Italian authorities have launched an offensive to shut down this critical first stop on the Trade's major smuggling routes. The Trade has countered with vast sums of capital – bribery money. One of our cell members is a member of the Italian police – very committed, we thought. Apparently not. He was arrested a few days ago with almost a million Euros in cash in the boot of his undercover car. We, the remaining cell members, have to assume that we have been exposed, in which case we are most certainly under surveillance. Whether it is because of our groups central role in this province or because of your girl, we don't yet know. "

"William – "

"One more item you should be aware of. As a professional photographer, with ITN and now as an independent, I've been places one would rather forget – Rwanda, Somalia, Bosnia, Kosovo. It was in the latter that I met Gabriella, who was the director of a an NGO that dealt exclusively with human trafficking.

"I won't go into detail at this point. But I needed you to know that she introduced me to the full extent of the Trade, something which few in the West would believe, and that I've been a changed person ever since. We took risks, we got evidentiary photographs, we were able to use them in obtaining several convictions. We are not doing what we are doing out of the goodness of our hearts: there is a personal story you will hear later. You see, Kristýna, your situation and ours bear many painful similarities. Our commitment to you and Teresa is total, as it is also our commitment to ourselves. Gabriella and I wanted to tell you this before you saw the pictures. If we have not found your girl this time, we will be with you until we have. Now, come. Let's have a look."

***

The recently developed photos had been laid out on a rectangular table. Kristýna put her hand over her mouth the instant she saw them. Teresa, dirty and ragged, occupied center stage in each frame. She was with Gypsies; you could tell from the market caravans in the background, the half-wild dogs, the facial structure and dress of the people caught by the lens . . .

William spread out the next set of photos. "These I shot yesterday early in the morning at the train station in Castelfranco. You don't look well. It's her, isn't it?"

Kristýna took a deep breath and somehow managed to pull herself together. "Yes, that is Teresa. Where is this Gypsy camp?"

"About five kilometers from here."

"That's all?"

"That's all. I know several of the men, including the head of the family. I spoke with him last night."

Kristýna was incredulous. "You know them?"

"I do. This particular group has been wintering here for decades. Gabriella's father is their tailor. He makes suits for them each Fall. They're good people, just different. Anyway, I made certain that the subject of the new little girl came up. The head of the family – Vesh is his name – says the girl is his. You'll have to convince him otherwise. Knowing Vesh, I can assure you it won't be easy."

"You were in that camp last night?"

William consulted his watch. "Not exactly. The men spend their evenings at a tavern in a nearby village. That's where I met then many years ago. Vesh could be there as we speak."

"Then we must go NOW. We must hide my daughter before something terrible happens. The men who want me dead are also trying to kill Teresa. Now I understand everything. They are also the men watching for me, the men who bribed the policeman in your cell. We must go before they learn that I am here!"

"Agreed. We'll use a back door and pass through the vineyard. I'll telephone Fabrizio and ask him to pick us up on the other side of the estate. He's expecting my call. Fabrizio is Gabriella's father, the tailor I was telling you about."

CHAPTER TWENTY-TWO

Kristýna and William sat with Vesh at a pub table, its polished wooden surface pocked and scarred from years of major abuse. Vesh flipped through the newspapers and photographs again, showing as little interest as before. Suddenly, almost violently, he pushed everything to the side and stared at Kristýna. "You are the woman in the newspapers and these are pictures of my girl. If I show you a picture of a mare and then a picture of a colt, does this tell you that they share each other's blood?"

Kristýna, in an effort to break the icy wall between them, took his hand in hers, turned it palm up and studied the deep grooves. They were colored with something that looked like dirt but wasn't. When she lifted her gaze to his face, he did not avert his eyes.

They were, she thought, the eyes of an honorable man. But they were also the eyes of a man who loved a little girl he honestly considered to be his daughter. She couldn't fault him for not wanting to give her away to a stranger.

She was certain he would do the right thing once he realized who Teresa was. But she had no proof that she was the mother, and she would continue to have no proof as long as he refused to let her meet with Teresa in his presence. The negotiations, conducted in Czech, had reached an impasse.

No, he said, Kristýna could not come to the camp. Gaye were not allowed. It was an old tradition, a law of the family, respected by everyone except police and vigilantes. His father and his father's father and their ancestors, going all the way to the beginning of time, had maintained the family by insisting on this rule. They had survived the Ottoman Turks and Nazis and today's enslavement of the Gaye to meaningless work. As the head of his family, the Rom-Barro, he had inherited the solemn responsibility of ensuring their future survival. He would not ever break the rule.

On this point he remained unyielding. Kristýna was near hysteria. She could no longer think clearly. William finally intervened.

"Vesh, my friend, you know I can't understand Czech. I should like to be included in the discussion. This woman and this child are very important to me as well."

"Where is Gabriella?" Vesh said in heavily accented English. "What are you doing here with this woman? Also your woman, this one with the green eyes." He tapped a knuckle on the photographs. "Your little girl? Your little girl with this woman? If no, you have no business." "Vesh, you know that I am devoted to Gabriella and Fabrizio. You should not say such things, even if you know they are untrue."

"Then you, William, you will tell me why you bring this woman here."

"Vesh, she is here because she is the girl's mother."

"He won't let me into his camp" Kristýna blurted out. "He says it's against his rules but the real reason is that he's afraid. He's afraid my daughter will recognized me. William, I have to convince him to make an exception. You must help me. I don't know what to do."

"One thing I'll say is this: you cannot ask him to break his rules." William took a quick sip of beer. "Vesh, listen to me. We could walk with you to the outskirts of your camp and you could bring her out to meet us. We would quickly have our answer."

The room smelled of unwashed men. It echoed with bursts of laughter and loud shouts in Romany.

Vesh remained silent but Kristýna noticed a change in his demeanor. His eyes softened and his jaw was no longer set in cement.

Encouraged, Kristýna jumped back into the conversation. "Vesh, as William suggested, you could bring Teresa to a place outside the camp. Perhaps I gave you the wrong impression. I understand and respect your traditions. I also understand that you care about my little girl. I'm grateful to you for having watched after her. But she is my daughter. We can't undo the work of Nature."

"Your daughter in blood? Where is her father? William says he is not her father."

"Her father is dead. That cannot be changed. But she can be reunited with her mother. You are a good man, I know you are. You love my daughter, one can see that. In spite of your love, I can't imagine you would want to keep a child that is not yours."

"Go to the Gaye police if you are so sure. They take everything from us. They will take her too."

Kristýna averted her eyes. "I can't go to the police," she whispered. "If you could read these newspapers, they would tell you why. The police think I killed my husband and my child. They put me in jail but I escaped. They are looking for me right now. I came for my daughter. Why won't you let me walk with you to the outskirts of your camp? Are you worried she will recognize her mother?

"I am not worried. I do not want someone else's child. But I have a duty to protect her. We believe she is a lost Roma girl who found her true family."

William said, "Yes, I understand what you believe. But how did she come to you? How did she find her true family?"

"They say in Italy destino. They do not ask how.

"Italians are Gaye."

Vesh shrugged his shoulders. "Maybe, maybe not. Since this woman with the green eyes accuses me of a very bad thing, I will tell you the story of how destino returned our little girl to her family. I will tell you how, but I cannot tell you why."

"Thank you, Vesh. You are not Gaye, not even Italian, but you are what we call a most reasonable man."

"Maybe this is not a compliment, William. Maybe it has to do with thinking backwards and is a bad thing. But I know you do not want to say a bad thing to me. Teresa was living with a man she called 'grandfather' on a farm in Slovenia. His real name was Zlatko, and he was also a good man. We stayed on his farm every year for a few days, did some chores for him and even showed him how to dance. He died while I was at his side. With his last breath he begged me to take Teresa and watch after her. That is how she came back to her people. But she has been too long in the Gaye world. She has attracted an evil spirit. I have been protecting her from this evil spirit. But this spirit, when he comes to me, tells a story like the woman with the green eyes. He says he has been sent by her family to bring her home. So, I am thinking the whole time you are here, maybe this woman is just another evil spirit."

"Vesh, no!" Kristýna reached across the table and grasped his arm. "This was not what you think. This was not an evil spirit."

"Yes. Maybe you will see. He dresses like a priest, but he is a priest of no religion."

"Vesh, listen to me. Please listen. There is a man looking all over the world for Teresa. He is the same man who killed my husband. Teresa knows. She saw him do it. If he finds her he will kill her. Your evil spirit, he has short legs like tree trunks and a big stomach of muscle, does he not?"

"No. He is tall and white as a Gayo near death. He has a round face and pointed beard and eyes bluer than the bluest water. He is not of this world. He is not who you describe."

"Then the man who is trying to kill my daughter sent him."

"No. The devil sent him. Your devil. We will walk to the camp now, yes?"

***

Vesh met them on the muddy river path. With him were three mangy dogs and his son, Djivan. "If you are the mother, you have come too late. She is gone."

"That's not true! How could it be true? You never let anyone into your camp. Vesh, are you going back on your word? Is this how you plan to keep me from her?"

"She is gone, I said. But you have told the truth. We found an old newspaper where she sleeps. It showed your picture. Djivan, tell this woman where is Teresa."

The boy threw a rock in the river. Its splash was muffled by the steady drumbeat of rain. Djivan kicked the mud. "We wash the dishes after eat. We see when we get home that she is not with us. Katja, her dog, is not with us too."

Vesh was furious. "How could you come back without her?" He snatched Djivan's cap from his head and slapped him across the cheek with it. "How? You will tell me. You will tell this woman."

The boy hung his head.

"We will find her," Vesh said. "I promise you we will find her. Djivan, where does she go to wash her pots?"

"You want that I show you, Father."

"Yes, I want. Take us there. Fast."

A few hundred meters along the river path was a muddy chute going down to the water. A small tree on one side of the chute was bent.

"It is here, Father."

"She must have drowned!" Kristýna cried. "God in heaven."

"Not drowning," Djivan said. "No current and water only this deep." The boy held his hand to his chest. "Only this deep with feet touching bottom."

"Over here," William called. "Some cooking stuff." He had wandered a few meters up a side path and was shining his light on a dented pot half full of rainwater.

They gathered around his find. "Djivan," Vesh asked, "Did Katja come home later?"

As if in answer, a bark pierced the sodden night. The mangy dogs took off down the path.

"That was Katja," Vesh said. "Come. We will find Teresa. The storm must have scared her. She is with Katja. She is always with her dog."

When they reached the clearing they found Katja tied to a rope. The dog was frantic. Vesh ignored her, examining instead the border of the clearing. The beam of his light settled on a mud road. There were tire tracks but they were filled with water, making it impossible to tell if they were new or old.

"Here, quick, look over here!" Djivan shouted. He was pointing at some kind of a plastic pouch that hung from the dog's collar.

Vesh shrugged his shoulders. "That thing, I've never seen it. Not collar either. Our dogs don't wear collars."

"Undo it, William," Kristýna cried out. "Take off the whole collar."

"I'm trying. The dog's wild."

Djivan had found the piece of meat with the bone sticking out. He tried to offer it to Katja, but she was too worked up to eat. The boy touched William's hands. "I do it. She know me."

Djivan brought the pouch to Kristýna.

William stretched his slicker over her head. Vesh ducked underneath with a flashlight. Inside was a rolled-up sheet of paper, tied like a scroll with a scrap of colored twine.

Kristýna froze. The tie was the frayed remains of Teresa's friendship bracelet – the bracelet she had been wearing the night Obruchev took her.

CHAPTER TWENTY-THREE

"It probably doesn't mean 'weasel' in German," Hatch said, trying to calm his partner. "Anyway, it's just a name."

"Thanks for your linguistic expertise. I checked at the hotel reception. It does mean weasel: Das Wiesel. I have a bad feeling about this guy. He's going to be one of those know-it-all academic types with titles up the wazoo. Thinks Americans are dumb and he's God's gift to law enforcement. Like that German asshole they sent over to work on the Zwick case. Nose in everything that didn't concern him. Now they give us another one."

"Another what?"

"Weasel."

"You haven't even met this Wiesel yet. Besides, he's Austrian, not German. Drexler swears he's good. You respect Drexler. I don't understand your misgivings."

"Neither do I," Connor said. "Another thing. That damned Sacher torte is overrated. You'd think eight hundred bucks a night would buy you the best. Betty Crocker is better."

"Randall, that's bullshit. The staff warned you. No one orders chocolate cake for breakfast. We'll try it again tonight. Like they said, you got the stale leftovers from yesterday."

"Yesterday? That thing had been in a kiln since Franz Josef kicked the bucket. Where the hell is our ride?"

"You probably scared it off. Do me a favor. Don't drink so much tonight. You're always a prick in the morning, but this is off the scale. You've got to put Italy behind you and start looking ahead."

"It's not Italy. It's the goddamn Sacher torte. Eight hundred bucks a night for a stale camel turd."

"I thought it was Wiesel."

"If you would listen, maybe – "

"Hey, the boys are here. I hope we can get you some medication."

The car, as Drexler had alerted them, was an ambulance. It stopped beside the door to the parking garage. Level B was deserted, conveniently closed for repairs. Connor and Hatch climbed into the back and stretched out on beds.

"Might not hurt to strap yourself down," Hatch suggested. Connor flashed him an irritated glance.

Sirens blaring, the ambulance wove a gut-churning course through rush-hour traffic. Special Agent Randall Connor threw up in a bed pan. Like bathroom freshener, the perfume of abused brakes added another layer to the stench.

Connor apologized when they go out in the courtyard of the Vienna-Simmering police station. "I haven't been this hung over since college," he confessed.

"Forget it, Randall. It's tough to come as close as we did. Maybe you needed to tie one on. Maybe it'll clear your head for the future."

"Let's not talk about my head."

The medics, cops in undercover, led them through the jail to a steel door painted with German words. Connor understood VERBOTEN. He wanted to ask his escorts what the other words meant but they disappeared before he had the chance. Just as well, he thought. Nothing was going to cheer him up this morning, let alone a list of prohibitions in a language whose written and spoken forms grated equally on his nerves.

The door opened on well-oiled hinges. A man in civilian dress ushered them inside with a stiff bow, then walked off down the long dank corridor. A bad omen. Connor had good reason to trust his premonitions. Hung over or not, they rarely missed their mark.

What he heard next caught him off guard. From somewhere inside the weasel's hole issued a good-natured voice in American English. The man was talking on the telephone. He hung up and emerged from his cubicle. "Agents Connor and Hatcher, welcome." He shook hands firmly, like an American. Only the slightest trace of an accent belied his foreign origins. He said, "I'm Lutz Wiesel of the Stapo, State Secret Police. It used to be called Gestapo. These days we leave off the first two letters."

"Probably a good idea," Hatch said.

"I think we can all agree on that."

Connor stared at Wiesel in shock. This guy was about as far as you could get from the weasel of his imagination. Dark hair, a pockmarked face, a broad smile that Hatch's impolitic remark had failed to extinguish. In his worn jeans and black leather jacket, he could have passed for a middle-aged street thug in South Philly. Or a pimp.

A gift from above, a Kraut Inspektor Doktor without the usual Teutonic arrogance. This Wiesel looked like a cop who concentrated on his job instead of his image, something you didn't find much these days. Connor's cleansed stomach relaxed, and his headache began to subside.

Good news seemed to flow from all directions, like the kirschwasser and scotch the night before.

On a messy desk near a brick wall, Connor noticed one of the few remaining symbols of the culture in which he had made his career: a five-pound can of Maxwell House. Never mind that it was stuffed with wire nuts, plastic ties and color-coded copper leads. It had gotten here somehow. Just the sight of it relieved him of his sense of isolation, his growing fear the youthful world of chic at any cost had rendered his breed extinct. The old Connor, 220 pounds of grit and determination, rose from the cinders of self-doubt. His fugitive was toast.

"You drink that stuff?" he asked Wiesel, flicking his wrist toward the can.

"You bet. Got addicted while I was at Quantico. My American military friends keep me supplied through the PX."

"No shit?"

"I'm not a big fan of all the fancy European crap. It's overrated and overpriced – similar to Sacher torte."

"I think we're gonna make an okay team," Connor said.

***

They moved to an austere conference room across the hall.

"We're in the middle of remodeling," Wiesel explained. "Excuse the lack of amenities. If we had time I'd take you to the Interior Ministry." He passed legal pads and ballpoint pens around the folding table. "But we don't"

"Don't what?" Connor grumbled.

"Have time for running around. The sightseeing's nice, the Ministry's comfortable, but Mack the Knife is fifty meters from where we sit."

Hatch said, "That nightclub owner Drexler told us about?"

"Right. He's the biggest buyer of Natashas in Austria, and Obruchev's biggest single client. We're on a tight schedule. I want him back at his club before he's missed."

"Which is when?" Connor asked.

"Eight o'clock tonight."

"Eight o'clock?" Hatch was always wary of rushing. "Sounds a little arbitrary."

"It's not. These guys have a network that stretches from Warsaw to Belgrade. If anything the least bit unusual takes place, word hits the street. It travels from Vienna to Ljubljana at the speed of light."

"Word of – "

"A possible rat. We can't let that happen if we plan to penetrate the ring. So, meine Herren, we have ten hours to write a perfect play, rehearse it until it's art and stage a flawless performance."

Connor adjusted his butt in the uncomfortable wooden chair. For the first and only time he could remember, he looked around for something of color. A painting, flowers, a piece of kitsch, a little ethnic diversity. There was nothing here but four recently whitewashed walls and a rickety table. His attempt to live extravagantly seemed to have led him to the birthplace of monasticism.

Well what the fuck, he thought. This suited him better anyway – as long as the focus was on work. From all indications, it was.

He said, "You mean to tell me it takes a Broadway production to get inside?"

"I'm afraid so. The more serious we've gotten about busting them, the more adept they've become at eluding us. These days the big fish deal almost exclusively with clients they know – and they check out newcomers with the assumption they're working for somebody's undercover police. Stepan Obruchev has always been several steps ahead of the competition in guarding his operation from outsiders. There's another more serious problem: he doesn't deal with Americans. He doesn't know you and you're Americans. You've already met two of the main criteria for rejection. We have a problem."

"Not promising," Hatch said.

"There's a brighter side. We also have an opening. We grabbed Mack early this morning on his way home from work. If anyone was watching, it didn't look like an arrest. A female agent lured him into her car. Anyway, this Arschloch is the key to our success. It's not a very comforting prospect, as you'll soon see. But he's got motive to make sure our play doesn't flop. If he blows it, he goes up for life."

"And if he's Richard Burton?" Connor asked.

"We turn him loose."

"He just walks out of here and keeps on managing that meat market?"

Wiesel smiled, running his finger along the scar beneath his lip. "Just until we wrap up our work in Slovenia. Then we put the missing letters back in Stapo and let news of his work with us reach the streets. Believe me, there'll be competition to eliminate him."

Hatch looked surprised. "You guys do that kind of stuff too?"

"Don't tell anyone."

Connor said, "Okay, let's run through the details once more. This Mack is Obruchev's biggest client. He puts the girls to work in the back of his otherwise legitimate nightclub, does all the usual stuff, keeps them under lock and key. Some have died under his tutelage, some have been mutilated. You have the proof to lock him up and he knows it. All that's clear. What I don't understand is how Mack gets the girls from Point A to Point B and how he conducts his monetary transactions."

"Subcontractors."

"What?"

"He uses smuggling rings that specialize in human trafficking so he doesn't have to involve himself in acquisition. Most

Europeans who pimp Natashas do the same. But Mack's operation is different in one significant way. It's this difference that gives us our opening."

"Don't make me guess."

"He never uses the same ring twice. Evidently he believes this practice immunizes him against corroborating testimony, which in a way it does. But there's an advantage here for us: Obruchev and his security people expect to deal with an unknown buyer whenever Mack needs girls."

"Yeah, okay," Hatch said. "But how does Obruchev vet these new guys? You just told us his secret was not dealing with anyone he doesn't know. He's doing it here, so he must have a pretty failsafe system for checking up on them."

"Before I answer, I should fill you in on why Mack gets the special treatment he does. His way of doing business, as you say in the States, was 'grandfathered in.' Mack's been with Obruchev from the start. He was his first big client – and will hopefully be his last. As for your security-related question: the Knife makes a telephone call to vouch for his runners. This time he's going to vouch for us in order to save his ass."

Connor took another four aspirin. "Okay, Wiesel, I get it. But all of these people have a tendency to sing when they get nailed. How does Obruchev know that Mack isn't doing what we hope he'll be doing tonight?"

"A return call to the Casa Blanca."

"To where?"

"Mack's club here in Vienna. Obruchev or one of his security goons call a private number. There's a verbal code Mack uses if he thinks anything's suspect. Otherwise it's all clear."

"I take it you know this verbal code?"

"A long story, but yes. Believe me, he won't be using it tonight. I'm more worried about the refusal to deal with Americans."

"We're Canadians."

"You're North Americans."

Hatch whacked the table with his palm. "We get discriminated against everywhere, even when we fake our identity. I'm getting sick of it. You're telling me can't even buy girls because we're North American. This is wrong."

Nobody laughed. Wiesel said, "If we do our job that will change – at least in Ljubljana. For a start you'll be the Canadians on those passports you brought. The Interior Ministry will create a paper trail of your pasts, two guys seedy enough to be credible. Minor convictions for trafficking at home; long-time residency without incident in Austria."

"But," Wiesel continued, "these measures alone won't suffice. Obruchev's been at this game a long time. He's wary and wily. His cardinal rule is keeping his own American identity squeaky clean. Being Canadian is better than being American – but it still puts you too close to his lair.

"So, meine Herren, we're going to need a reason for him to break his cardinal rule. Why not start brainstorming now? What will be Mack's argument when he calls? What makes two Canadians worthy of an exemption? Why is Mack intent on working with them? Why can they be trusted? Since you're the Canadians in question, why don't you begin?"

Wiesel lit an unfiltered Camel and put his feet on the table. Connor saw he was wearing cowboy boots. Refreshing, he thought, to bump into someone who still appreciated the US of A.

Hatch went first. "The two of us, we can't go back to Canada or the States. Criminal charges aren't the reason. We've crossed a big-time Mafia drug runner in, say, Chicago. Word is, we're dead if we show up anywhere in North America. In fact, that's why we're here in the first place. Could your people at Interior include something like this in our fictitious pasts?"

"Yes, we could. Good idea. Let's have more."

Connor said, "There's a strange thing going on in the States. I'm sure you're as aware of it as we are. I'm talking about the religious revival. Look at that Jesus film. Maybe ten people went to see it in Europe, a hundred million in America. Don't get me wrong. I've got nothing against belief when it's real. But a lot of these newborns are phonies. So what have we got? An army of fake saints who can't risk getting laid out of wedlock.

"Hatch and I have been through studies by State, Justice and private groups on both sides of the Atlantic. You've read about the problem in Israel – Orthodox Jews frequenting Natashas because their beliefs won't let them 'dirty' nice girls of their own faith. This creates exactly the kind of demand that fuels the Trade. We have that kind of demand, only a hundred times more of it than the Israelis. But this huge American demand can't be satisfied at home. Too many of our TV evangelists and 'family values' gurus have demonstrated the risk – "

"Connor, I – "

"Hang on, Lutz. You'll see where I'm going in a second. These horny hordes of repressed 'believers' are coming to godless Europe for sex. A door closes, another opens. So we've now got a huge new group of Americans making the pussy pilgrimage. Drexler knows about it, so I imagine you do as well. These men fear two things above all – getting caught and catching something. When they arrive here in Gomorrah they need reassurance. Who better to give it than a fellow North American? That is why Mack wants these Canadians. He's a good businessman. He adapts to a changing market. His partners reassure this new and growing U.S. clientele there's no sleaze and no disease, just discretion and untainted meat. Mack knows he stands to make a fortune with this slight fine-tuning of his business. His Canadians, of course, want in on the first few buying trips. Why? Because they know exactly what 'look' appeals to sex-starved Puritan suburbanites."

"Sadly, there is such a pilgrimage" Wiesel said. "You notice a lot more Americans these days in our houses of ill-repute."

"Okay, it's a statistical reality," Hatch said. "But let's forget my partner's sick religious interpretation. There's no evidence for it, and even if there was it wouldn't help us with what we're doing. But Randall is right about Americans going abroad to buy sex, I'll give him that."

"Then gentlemen, Wiesel said, "it appears we have our starting point."

CHAPTER TWENTY-FOUR

In a professional audio room, Inspektor Wiesel introduced his guests to Dietrich Waldheim, known locally as Mack the Knife. "No latex gloves," Connor explained, declining to shake the crook's hand.

Mack was clean shaven and dressed for work. He'd selected his leather dress jacket, black silk shirt and tight trousers that afternoon from the catalogue of a local clothes shop. Wiesel managed to find someone at the station to polish his shoes to an ebony gleam, and to convince a visiting undersecretary from Interior to part with his flashy red tie. The overcoat and abundant gold jewelry that their man had been wearing at the time of his arrest, unlike his indoor garb, could be recycled without fear of arousing suspicion.

The most annoying aspect of Mack's preparation involved the gel for his spiked blond hair. He insisted on a certain brand, available at only one shop in Vienna. When Wiesel suggested an alternative, Mack pointed out that every girl in the place knew the smell of his spikes. A fuck-up like that could blow the entire act. Wiesel had been forced to send another detective on a minimal skill mission across town. Now, at least, his dirt bag seemed ready and relaxed.

"We're going to practice until it's perfect," Wiesel said. "With accompaniment." He switched on a high-quality recording of background noise, made the previous evening when the Casa Blanca was being prepared for business: chairs scraping loudly, staff cursing, rubber blades screeching over vast mirrored walls. A nasty mix of rap, disco and slow dance sifted through cracks in the work-sound symphony.

"Mack," Wiesel ordered, "into the glass booth. Pretend you're making the call."

"Yeah, okay. What if Majdak or Obie asks to talk to you guys?"

"Tell him you'll round us up, we're being treated to some of the house specialties. Have him call back in a few minutes."

"Alles klar," Mack said, "You got that background shit just right. If I rehearse, it's not gonna sound natural. Let's just do it."

"Your call," Wiesel said. "Your life. Randall, Hatch, put on those headphones if you want to listen. I'll translate. I'm good at this stuff. You'll think you're at the UN."

"Save the translation for afterwards, Lutz. My head won't survive."

"Understood. So, Mack, you ready?"

"What did I say?"

"Just don't lose your nerve."

"Shut the door."

Wiesel did just that, leaving Mack in a soundproof glass cage where you could hear him only through a headset. "Fucker deserves to be in a zoo," Wiesel said.

Hatch grinned. "I like your English. You sound like Randall on a good day."

"Shhh . . ."

Connor took a deep breath while the sleaze in the glass booth dialed a number in Slovenia. Tension, as suffocating as Memphis on a summer night, filled the room. Wiesel manipulated the dials on the console in front of him. Needles danced against a dim greenish backdrop. A gruff male voice answered.

Connor sat bolt upright when their snitch started singing Mack the Knife in German:

Und der Haifisch, der hat Zähne
Und die trägt er im Gesicht . . .

The man on the other end of the line bellowed something Connor couldn't understand. He had no idea if it was born of anger or amusement until he heard a raw laugh. He was about to lift his headphones and ask Wiesel what the hell was going on when Mack resumed his singing. The creep had a surprisingly good voice, as smooth as his hair gel:

Denn der Haifisch is kein Haifisch
Wenn man's nicht beweisen kann . . .

"Mackie Messer in the original," Wiesel whispered. "The imbecile thinks it's chic to use the English title for his sobriquet."

Connor stared at the glass booth. Their snitch was becoming more animated with every word. His interlocutor finally lost patience. A resounding verbal explosion brought the song to a quick end; the high-stakes conversation began.

Connor regretted for the first time in 40 years he had flunked high school German. Here he sat listening to the exchange that would determine whether he brought home the bacon, perhaps even whether he lived, and he couldn't understand one fucking word of it. He glanced over at Hatch, who wasn't trying to hide his frustration.

Ten minutes seemed like an hour. When Mack finally hung up Wiesel signaled him out of the booth.

"Perfekt."

"Ich weiß. Darf ich jetzt gehen?"

"Will someone please speak English?" Connor grumbled. "When's that guy calling back?"

"When he calls, okay?"

"Okay, Mack, you're done here," Wiesel said. "I'll have you dropped off near the club. One thing I want clear. If we don't get inside that Slovenian market for any reason, it's your fault. You know what that means. So make sure you follow the script and don't try any bullshit. We've got your lines tapped and undercover people around every corner. You take a piss, we'll know. Nothing changes until we're finished with Obruchev. Want me to repeat it in German or do you get the idea?"

"Hey, Wiesel, you weren't the only one who lived in the States. It's doesn't take a doctor degree to learn how to talk. They speak the same language in massage clubs as universities, only there's more after the talking ends."

***

"Gonna fill us in now?" Hatch asked when they were alone.

"It went better than we could have hoped," Wiesel said. "He told Majdak what the General already seemed to know: that increasing numbers of Americans were coming to Europe for sex, that it made sense to tap this "market of the future," that anyone stupid enough to invest the huge amount these Canadians had invested in the Casa Blanca would pay a fortune for girls. So Majdak's going to plant someone inside to keep bidding up the price."

Connor seemed skeptical. "Yeah, well that's all nice and cushy but it doesn't help with Ruski's refusal to deal with North Americans. Maybe this General Mud Dick is hot for the deal, but it seems obvious Obruchev'll nix it the second he hears Canadians are involved."

"He might if he caught wind of the details. He's apparently working the block himself as auctioneer. His regular is on vacation. Mack's smarter than I thought. He offered the General twenty percent of the total sale – a gift over and above, not a cut. I know, government funds, US and Austrian, but what the hell. This might be our only shot, and Majdak's greedy. He said he'd forget to tell the boss who you guys are. We'll dress you right and I'll do the bidding. You just sit there, point and don't say a word. We're in, meine Herren. That I can almost guarantee. Our challenge now is setting things up so we leave with more than girls."

"But we don't know when?"

"Mack didn't answer your question, and I didn't want him to. Majdak's calling tonight with your 'reservation.' It won't be long."

Connor stood, feeling like a new man. "The sooner the better. You know where to find us. Ready, Hatch? I want to see if your cake theory's any good."

"Maybe you should worry about my Slovenian theory."

Wiesel, for the first time that day, looked tired. Instead of trying to join his colleagues' banter, he phoned downstairs to arrange their transportation home.

CHAPTER TWENTY-FIVE

At three o'clock in the morning, on a dirt road near Trieste, Rasputin crossed an unmanned border into Slovenia. A short time later he arrived at the address Pimenko had given him. He could see that people were still awake in the two-story stucco mansion: the shutters were closed but light from the upstairs windows seeped through the cracks.

They were waiting for him. When he slowed, a spiked iron gate opened automatically. He drove around back and parked his muddy Skoda among the luxury sedans and expensive roadsters. His ugly duckling did not embarrass him. On the contrary, it reinforced his sense of superiority. He was not like other men, did not squander his wealth on the meaningless trinkets of Babylon. Rather he used it for things that would give him power over the testosterone-driven herd; things that would allow him to play a godlike role on earth.

The black night absorbed the glow from the windows. When he opened his trunk, he needed a flashlight to check on Teresa. She was restless, about to wake up. Using his body to hide his actions from anyone who might be watching, he gave her another injection. Then he walked to the nearest door, his small vinyl travel bag in hand. Before he had a chance to ring, a guard opened and invited him inside. "Welcome, Father. Director Pimenko is waiting. I will take you to him."

***

When the padded door closed Rasputin found himself alone in an opulent room. A long table stretched beneath the window. Silver ice buckets held bottles of vodka. Peaks of caviar adorned an elaborate topography of Western delicacies. Sybarites to the last man, these creatures with whom he worked . . . .

He was still on his feet, staring at the table and clutching his tawdry bag, when Pimenko burst in from the bedroom.

Cheerful and pink as always, he tugged the tie on his white terrycloth robe. Rasputin fought to ignore the carnal musk surrounding his presence.

"Nikolai Petrovich! I thought you would never get here. Where the hell have you been?"

"Sometimes one is called away on a special mission. Do you have my information?"

"Now, now, Father Nikolai, one must not rush such matters – especially on an evening like this. As you see, I am expecting important guests. So important my concern for their satisfaction required me to sample the entertainment in the bedroom. Young and inexperienced, but as delightful as the lilies of the field. Now I must evaluate the table. I would like you to join me and offer your opinion."

"You know I don't care about food or drink. Why are you wasting time? I asked you if you had the information. If you do, I have brought the second half of the payment. But I am in a hurry. Let us please dispense with games."

"Yes, yes, of course, my dear Nikolai. But do give me a moment to recover. Seventeen-year-old virgins, corpse-like though they are during the divine act, take a toll on an old stallion. We'll have a drink and conduct a brief tasting."

"Not I."

"Very well."

Pimenko strolled to the table, prepared a plate of assorted delicacies, poured a glass of vodka and let himself down in an overstuffed armchair. Rasputin watched in disgust as he ate lustily, washing down each mouthful with a large swallow of drink.

When he had finished, he smiled. "I have good people, Nikolai Petrovich. Not that it matters. Anyone works for the kind of money I pay. Fifty thousand dollars to an FBI secretary, that amount times four to a disgruntled agent. Cash, unmarked and untraceable. The money changers, my friend, have returned to the temple. And not only the temple. They are in every nook and cranny of God's earth. Tell your Father in Heaven when and if you get there. It's never too late to change sides."

"Did Sondheim and her accomplice show up?"

"Yes, but there was no child. They left a nearby tavern a few hours later in a FIAT with three other people – and a dog. Would you like me to have them followed?"

"I know where they are going, and the whereabouts of the child is no longer an issue. What do you have to report on the American police?"

"They're in Vienna. They think the fugitive is headed for Slovenia. A team will enter at Sentilj tomorrow night."

"Did you learn where they plan to begin their search?"

"Yes, Nikolai Petrovich. I suggest you watch yourself."

"The Heavenly Father performs that role."

"I wouldn't count on it. They're going to your place of business."

"For what purpose?"

"To pick up Obruchev's trail. They have this crazy idea he'll lead them to his fugitive, though they must know by now he never leaves the factory or his cousin's home unless he's on his way to the airport. Word is, they'll stay on him until they've exhausted all possibilities. The dumb bastards have no idea how long and useless a stay they're in for. Unless they stumble onto another plum – your business."

"It is not important."

"Not important?"

"They've tried before. The business is safe. You've given me the information I need." Rasputin made no attempt to explain. He dumped the contents of his travel bag on a sofa – four fat manila envelopes sealed and marked according to the type of currency they held. "You are a man of little faith, Pimenko," he said. "I should like to see you find peace in the love of our Savior."

"And I, Nikolai Petrovich, should like to see you ice skate in your frock. Perhaps next time I come north in winter you will indulge me."

"Good night, Pimenko. Go to the cathedral in Capodistria and confess."

CHAPTER TWENTY-SIX

Less than an hour had passed since they found the note. Fighting back despair, Kristýna made a superhuman effort to think clearly. Vesh's words didn't help.

"Go back to the Tavern," he repeated in Czech. "Stay. Have the ones who brought you get in their car and leave. Have them take along a man and woman dressed in your clothes. Where they go is not important. But they should go far and stay gone."

"But, Vesh, you're ignoring my concern. Without their help, William and I won't be able to get our own car tonight. We can't give the priest that kind of head start. Any hope of finding my daughter will be delayed for hours. That's not acceptable. Why won't you listen to me?"

He took her roughly by the arm. "You must do as I say. There can be no discussion."

"Then at least tell me why."

"You don't need to know. You don't need distractions."

"Vesh, she's my daughter. If anyone has a right to know, I do."

"Alright. This once. You are being watched. If you go with your friends, they'll be watched too. They can't help you anymore. Not with a place to stay, not with a car. You might feel like you're moving, but if you are being watched it's an illusion."

"I don't think I'm being watched. Where did you come up with this idea?"

"Listen, I know these woods like the back of a my hand. If I say you are being watched, then it is so."

"Watched by whom? The priest?"

"No. You feel when he is close. Besides he left with Teresa. This is a man I've never seen. He followed us from the place of the kidnapping to the river path. I'll instruct my men to make sure he doesn't come near the Tavern. The friends who brought you came with Fabrizio and his dog. Is this so?"

"Yes."

"Then they must leave the same way. Except you will not be in the car. Like I said, they will find a man and a woman who will wear your clothes. The spy will follow the car. He will think you and your man friend and Teresa's dog are in it. This will be your chance to get free."

Kristýna stared ahead at Djivan, who was trying to teach William how to walk Katja on her rope leash.

"Vesh, I'm sorry. We can't hide in the Tavern forever. If you're right, if we really are being watched, it won't take the person or persons long to figure out where we are. I'm sorry to disagree, but we're much better off trying to lose them in a car."

"Did I say you were going to hide in the Tavern? After your friends leave, I'll come for you. I'll bring you and your companion to my camp."

"In spite of the rule?"

"I said I would bring you to the camp. There we will decide how to get your girl back. But you must do exactly as I say. You must not follow the instructions in the note. They will lead you into a trap."

"But Vesh – "

"No more talking. I return home with my boy, you go to the Tavern. Tell your friends what you wish them to do. When I see Fabrizio's car leave, I'll come. Walk ahead now and tell all of these things to your companion. Stay on this path. It will take you where you must go. Djivan, come." Without looking back, Vesh took his son's hand and disappeared into the night.

Kristýna joined William and the dog. They kept to the trail that hugged the river bank. The rain had stopped. Banks of fog hovered over the water. The woods were deathly quiet.

"Will you please tell me what's going on?" William said. "Ever since you opened that pouch, you haven't said a word in English."

"Vesh says a man is watching us. So Vesh is meeting us at the Tavern and taking us to his camp. He's breaking the rule.

He wants to help. William, that man Vesh saw . . . there can only be one reason he was spying: to report on whether or not we had found the note."

"Speaking of which, I still don't know what the note was about."

"It's not intentional. It's all these languages. The papers in the pouch were tied together with scraps of Teresa's friendship bracelet. She was wearing it the night Obruchev kidnapped her and killed my husband. That tells me the priest is working for Obruchev."

"Kristýna, you're walking through the deepest puddles."

"I don't care. I know that priest is working for Obruchev. The bracelet proves it. The priest is taking Teresa to her grave."

"Calm down. The bracelet doesn't necessarily prove Obruchev's involvement. We have to keep an open mind until we're sure. Remember. Vesh thought you were a villain earlier tonight. By the way, you still haven't told me what's in the note. If we analyze it together I'm sure we'll find other possible interpretations."

Kristýna stopped in her tracks. "No, we won't, because there aren't any other possible interpretations. The priest wrote that he was trying to help me but that he was in danger too. He included a map of an abandoned farm in Slovenia. He says he leased the farm from the state. A priest with no money leases this huge piece of land just so he can have a place to deliver Teresa. Don't tell me you buy that. A church would serve just as well, if not better. I tell you, he works for Obruchev. He's trying to give the impression Obruchev is after him so I'll think we're in the same boat and walk into his trap. It's perfectly clear we're dealing with a setup."

"I admit it sounds like one."

"Another thing. The farm mentioned in the note is the same farm where Vesh found Teresa. Can't you see what's going on? The farmer was keeping Teresa while Obruchev was in the US. The farmer happened to die while Vesh was passing through. So Vesh took her. What else could he do? Obruchev found out when he returned to Slovenia. He hired the priest to find her and bring her back. He's using her to find me. If he kills us both, there are no witnesses to his other crime."

"You don't suspect Vesh is involved in any of this? I mean, the same farm, the – "

"Absolutely not. He couldn't just leave her alone after her guardian died. That part is pure coincidence. The other things aren't."

The lights of the Tavern glowed in the murky distance. Katja heard something. She stopped, lifted her front leg and pointed. Kristýna breathed a sigh of relief when she realized it was an animal scampering down the bank.

"So we have this farm," William said. "The farm where Vesh found Teresa but is now leased by the priest who just kidnapped her. He wants you to believe you'll find Teresa there. Did he give instructions?"

"Yes. Every morning just before dawn, starting tomorrow, I'm to wait on a hill nearby with a good view of the farmhouse. The hill is sketched on the map. When the lights come on, I'm to take that as my signal Teresa has been delivered."

"And if the lights don't come on?"

"Either the farm is being watched or he couldn't get there safely. I'm to stay away or I might be killed."

"And if lights do go on?"

"I sneak into the property. Teresa, if you believe the note, will be hidden for her own safety. Katja will pick up her scent and find her. That's why the priest says he left the dog. William, I'm starting to feel desperate again. What am I going to do?"

"First, you're going to understand that you're not alone. I'm going to stay with you until the end. That's what Gabriella would want, it's what I want and it's non-negotiable. We should start by talking to Vesh."

"William, no. I won't allow you to be pulled into this any further. I scarcely know you. People are going to die. If I'm among them, so be it. Any mother in my position would risk her life. But a stranger?"

"I will be accompanying you of my own choice, Kristýna. I made you listen to me in my study so that this issue wouldn't arise. We can work together and greatly improve our chances or we can be stupid. Believe me, these people would prefer us to be stupid. But that's not going to happen. So please. Quarreling wastes energy and time. We don't have that luxury."

They were close to the Tavern now, a glow in the misty night. She was about to protest his decision but burst into tears instead. He took her arm and held it firmly. "Not now. Weeks ago you were in a maximum security prison in New York. You've come a long way since then. Pull yourself together. We have a job to finish."

CHAPTER TWENTY-SEVEN

"The dog stays outside," Vesh ordered. "They're all asleep in back. Katja will go to Teresa's bed and try to find her. She'll disturb everyone."

"We'll tie her up," Kristýna said.

"No. Let her run free."

"If I do that, she'll look for Teresa in the woods."

"I know. Let her. I'll explain later."

After Katja ran off, they went into Vesh's RV and sat around the kitchen table. Plastic trinkets everywhere, Christmas lights taped to the walls, a dart board above the sink. Kristýna took comfort in the appalling décor, though she had no idea why.

"We change tongues now," Vesh announced in English. He put down bottles of grappa and slivovitz, glasses and ashtrays. "My friend here, he needing to understand all."

"I can translate," Kristýna said. "I don't mind."

"No. I speaking English. My family, my big family, all these Roma you see in camp, we go to England once and spend three year. I understand. I talk. Maybe not good like Czech, but good enough. William must hear from my mouth, not from yours. Okay?"

"Okay," Kristýna said. "But if you get stuck and need to say something in Czech, I'll be happy to translate. They'll still be your words. And if you don't understand something —"

"No more Czech. I say 'don't understand' if I don't understand. Now we think together as Rom and Gaye. Never happens. Maybe something come out, who knows. You, woman, you first to say ideas. Then I tell what is no good with them."

Kristýna nodded. "Okay, Vesh, my daughter is somewhere not far from here. With the grace of God, she is still alive. I must go in search of her. I have only the note and the map left by the evil spirit. I must go where he directs me. But not as he directs. I agree with you. It is a setup. But I'm telling you. It is not the evil spirit who is the mastermind – "

"Don't understand."

"It is not the evil spirit who thought up the evil plan. It is someone even more evil. It is the man I told you about before, the man who killed my husband. That man thought I would be in prison for the rest of my life. Otherwise he would already have killed Teresa. She saw what he and another man did. She saw them murder my husband. This evil man has bought the evil spirit. He must now kill Teresa. He must also kill me. If he doesn't there are witnesses to his crime. Believe me, I know how he thinks. He plans to kill Teresa and make me watch before he kills me. Maybe this is good. Maybe the priest has been ordered to keep Teresa alive so I can be forced to see her die."

"All possible," Vesh said, exhaling cigarette smoke into the airless room. He poured William a glass of slivovitz, as he had done on many nights at the Tavern. "Yes, very possible. Sounds to me like sick things Gaye doing every day to each other. I saw an evil spirit. I did not know about evil power of man with him. Make sense. Now we hear what you are going to do."

"I'm going to ask what I tried to stop William from doing. Vesh, I am going to ask that you to come with us. You love Teresa and have treated her as your own daughter. I want your help every step of the way – for both our sakes."

"I would like. But I cannot leave this my big family. Seventy people. If I go for three days, I have no more family when I come home. They do not understand what my father taught me, what his father and all his ancestors teach him. I make them obey. They do not know how to give the Gaye little scraps, like you giving dogs after meal. They do not understand we Roma must give scraps to keep freedom. They do not understand nothing. The Gaye want that we stop wandering so they can destroy us. I know how to keep us free. I do not know this from words. I know from watching my father and grandfather. I should go with you. I gave my word I would look after Teresa and I fail. But I cannot go. I cannot go even for honor. I cannot go find a girl you the mother will take and lose the rest of my family at same time. I am sorry. But you have a good man here. He tell you about his war picture taking, yes? That is helping. But now he must learn to think like Rom. He must learn fast. So tell me, William, do you have gun with you?"

"Unfortunately, no."

"Not good. I have no gun to loan you. We crossing too many borders. Gaye find guns, they use for excuse to take away our freedom. With no gun, you must understand how these evil spirits thinking. They probably not teaching you this at picture taking school even for Gaye war. You understand what I am going to teach, you be okay."

William drank another glass of slivovitz. "But Vesh, seriously, how can we defeat these men without weapons? You can be sure they're armed to the teeth. I know that for a fact. I've seen it up close."

"Yes, true, but no one saying you have no weapons. Just no guns. The farm where map sends you, I know that farm. We stay there every year. Zlatko the farmer has tools. Every kind of tools. Like think for mowing grass. What you call it?"

"Scythe?"

"Yes, that one. Some with long handle, some short. He have forks for hay and hammers and saws for cutting down trees. He have hunting knives and plenty other knives like Rom use. We have sharpened all of these things before he die. So you making plan when you get there and see. You choose right weapon. You make sure it is not weapon enemy seeing in his head. Then you come like poison spider. You hide. You think of trick that will make evil man have picture in his head. Wrong picture, understand. Wrong picture leads him into your trap. Best way, you turn trap he set for you into trap for him. He looking to catch you in his trap but he looking in the wrong place. Maybe you dig hole and cover it with hay. Maybe you put razors on inside of door. Maybe you have gasoline fall from bucket and throw burning rag. You find everything you need at this farm. Only way you lose, you follow dog like note say. This is why I tell you, let dog run. You do not use Katja. You come back for dog when you have Teresa. Even if you don't want, she make you come get

Katja. You do not need bring back car, not important. But with dog you have no choice. You have to come back."

"Car?"

"Yes, man. You are taking car. You taking car soon. Evil spirit must rest. He already have picture in head. Picture of woman on that hill waiting for light in house. He thinks now he have plenty of time. But he is wrong. You will be on farm tonight. You will not wait for dawn tomorrow or next day. You will not be on hill and you will not follow dog. Then picture in your enemy's head go fuzzy like bad TV. He is getting lost in mess in his head while you moving like poison spider."

"I'd still feel better with a gun," William said. "Is there any way to get one?"

"Why gun? You know about pictures. This is better. What do you know about guns?"

"Enough. War correspondents learn how to protect themselves. I would like you to help us get a gun."

"You have one," Vesh said. "You have one right now. What you do with it? I am the evil spirit. What you do with it, man? Maybe shoot me?"

"Why not?"

William reached under the table, as if he were going for a hidden pistol. Even before his fingers touched his lap he felt an ominous prick under his chin. When he looked up he saw that Vesh was holding a long narrow blade to his throat.

"Jesus, put that thing away."

Vesh smiled as he withdrew the knife. "This good lesson. I saw picture in your head. You did not see picture in mine. You did not even think to look for picture. Maybe you learn something. Too late to go looking for gun. You must use head to figure other way."

Vesh clanked his switchblade on William's glass. It made a sharp clear ring one might easily confuse with a signal for a wedding toast. Then he closed the knife, still smiling.

"Now you listen, yes? I have old car in camp. Ugly, rusted, diesel. But it go anywhere, this Mercedes. You driving like hell all night. You be near farm before morning. You hide car, then hide selves. Woman sleeps, man watches. Then other way around. When night come again you make plans for next morning.

"Now I show you car. I show you map for leaving Italy without border check. Then you go. Six hours till dawn. Maybe snow on pass. Like I say. You must be driving like hell."

"But Vesh," William objected, "I can't just take your car. At least let me pay you for it so you can buy another one."

"No. You are borrowing car. I gave my word to watch Teresa. You are helping me keep my word."

"Listen, I – "

"No more listening. No more talking. I show you car papers Gaye like. We put things for you keeping warm in trunk. You crossing mountains, maybe need. I show you and then you leave."

"Vesh, we really might not be able to bring back your car."

"Only a thing. Not important. Tonight we have the same picture in head. Picture of only thing that count. Picture of Teresa safe. You listen. We taking care of dog. Katja come back to us. When you have Teresa she is sure like hell asking for dog. You bring her to see us when you come for Katja. Everyone in camp love Teresa."

"Even if she's Gaye?"

"I tell you. She is lost Roma girl. Probably same with mother here. Better watch out."

CHAPTER TWENTY-EIGHT

"Cividale," William whispered. "Say good-bye to Italy. This is the last town before we come to the Slovenian border."

The cobbled square they drove across was empty. A clock on the medieval bell tower, lit in soft colors, displayed the hour at which it had stopped forever. Kristýna couldn't rid herself of the premonition that she was late, that for Teresa time had run out . . .

They left the last remnants of civilization on a two-lane highway, empty in the dead hours before dawn. The highway dwindled to a narrow country road, which soon bent into an endless series of switchbacks climbing toward the pass summit and Slovenian border.

William battled to see in the thickening fog, not easy with the single headlight of Vesh's car. He swerved toward the center line whenever he caught a glimpse of it, marveling at how far he had drifted to one side or the other without leaving the pavement.

He was wondering how he would stay on the road if he encountered snow when a vision from hell hit him between the eyes. Rounding the last turn before the border he was greeted by a battery of lights on high poles, piercing the haze like flares. In the swirling mist two rectangular buildings loomed. An Italian flag flew over the first, a Slovenian flag over the second. But the red and white bars used to block the road were raised. Vesh, thank God, had known of what he spoke: the crossing was unmanned.

***

The snow they had been lucky enough to avoid on the pass began falling in wind-driven sheets around dawn. "We should rethink our plans," Kristýna said. "Let's drop the complicated stuff and go straight to the farmhouse. The snow will cover our footprints, and anyone spying from a distance won't be able to see us."

William squinted into the blizzard, using the trees on either side of the road as his only guideposts. "You don't think the priest might already be there?"

"If he is, we'll have a good chance of surprising him in his sleep and rescuing Teresa. That's part of the reason I think we should take advantage of the weather. Worse case, we'll be on the farm before anyone expects us."

"But if the priest is there, Obruchev could be with him."

"Not a chance. He won't show up until shortly before the light in the farmhouse comes on. The note said that we should start watching for the light tomorrow morning. I promise you, Obruchev is not the type to spend twenty-four hours waiting."

"Unless he knows you as well as you know him . . . and is expecting us."

"He doesn't."

William smiled without taking his eyes from the road. "Good. What's next?"

Kristýna studied the map. "There's a road that comes in from the north somewhere up ahead."

"Somewhere? In this weather, the meaning escapes me."

"Sorry. I'll try to be more precise. After we've passed through the village of Idrija it's about three kilometers. I'll watch the kilometer counter. That way we'll know if we missed it and can double back."

"And when we're on it?"

"According to this map . . ."

"Which is how old?"

"New. Vesh must have bought it for his trip in the other direction. When we've gone about a hundred meters, all the land on the right side belongs to the farm. Hide the car the first good spot and we'll hike in."

By the time they found the turnoff it was snowing even harder. William parked behind an abandoned garage. Kristýna again examined the hand-drawn map that had been around the dog's neck. "Let's take the minimum with us," she said. "There's a barn close nearby. We can warm up in there, then make our way to the house."

***

They started their trek with nothing but a couple of ratty blankets from the trunk. The wind howled in the leafless trees, the snow stung their faces. Leaving the road they slid down the side of a deep ditch and clawed their way up the other side, only to snag themselves on a barbed wire fence invisible in the storm. They helped each other through, then leaned into the gale and struggled ahead. Minutes later, as the wind temporarily abated and the curtain of blowing snow became less opaque, they saw the silhouette of the barn not far ahead. They picked up their pace and covered the distance before the whiteout resumed. With frozen fingers, they felt their way along the rough wood of the barn's exterior until they reached the front. A heavy door was blowing open and shut. They glanced inside. A few observations, interrupted by the swinging door, convinced them the place was empty. William entered first, spun in all directions for a better look, then motioned Kristýna to follow.

Pale light spilled in after them. Tools and farming implements hung everywhere. The visibly clean cutting edges on the scythes and axes displayed their recent sharpening by Vesh's men. Labeled metal canisters lined a stretch of wall beneath shelves of random farm supplies, and horseshoes were stacked in neat piles on a work bench.

"My God, look at this," Kristýna whispered. "Come quickly."

William moved with her toward the object of her attention, stopping abruptly each time the door slammed shut and plunged the barn into darkness. He lost sight of her, only to find her still at last, standing on the steps of a large painted wagon with stout wooden wheels. A crooked smokestack jutted from the roof and kids' art covered the sides.

"She's been here," Kristýna said. "Teresa painted those pictures. I'd recognize them anywhere. In fact, she painted the whole wagon."

"What's inside?"

"The door is padlocked. But this is the spot, William. This is where the priest will hide her. This is where Obruchev will wait for me. This is where he plans to kill us. It's going to be difficult for me, but I know what I have to do. When the priest locks Teresa in there, I must stay in hiding. I must wait patiently like a tiger for Obruchev to come. If I try to rescue her too soon, we won't get far. He'll find us both. Are you certain you want to be here?"

"That issue we've already dealt with. But Kristýna, listen to me. Listen to reason. You can't just assume you know their plan. You might suspect . Fine. But there are scenarios you haven't thought of – probably hundreds of them. We'd be stupid not stay flexible, not to prepare for every contingency we can imagine, no matter how unlikely. I suggest we start by finding the farmhouse. You said yourself the priest and Teresa could be inside. We'll take a couple of these blades and check the place out."

"Yes, we'll check it out. And we'll of course prepare for all possibilities. But I'm telling you. This is where it will happen. Right here."

***

The only entrance door to the farmhouse was unlocked. When their search produced no evidence that anyone had been inside for weeks Kristýna became impatient to leave. "William, hurry up! There's nothing here to help us. We should get back to the barn while we can do so safely. If the snow stops, our footprints will be visible in the morning."

William was rummaging through the kitchen drawers, still hoping to find a gun. "Give me another minute."

"We don't have a minute. I'm in the main room looking outside. The sky's lighter. The snow's about to stop. We need to go NOW."

"Relax. I can hear the wind. It doesn't matter if the snow stops. The drifts will – "

"Please. Whatever you're looking for, we don't need it."

He had just closed the last drawer when something caught his eye. "Kristýna, I think you'd better look at this."

She appeared in the doorway, exasperated. He was pointing at an old-fashioned black telephone on the counter. "I missed it before."

"Missed what?" She approached reluctantly.

"These tiny wires." He traced their course with his finger, careful to avoid touching them. They were taped to the back of the counter and ran from the phone to a metal box the size of a book. Two fat wires came out the other side of the box, climbed the wall like ivy and snaked into a light switch whose cover had been removed.

"What is it?"

"A relay."

"I mean, what does it do?"

"Turns on the house lights when this phone is called. For Obruchev to signal you, he doesn't even have to be here. All he has to do is dial the farmer's number."

"I understand, yes. And it is good that you noticed this. But remember. The priest will bring Teresa to the farm before there is any call, before the lights go on. I think I understand."

"Kristýna, you don't. Don't be angry with the messenger, just think about it. They don't need to bring Teresa to the farm. They just have to make sure you believe she's here."

"Logically, yes, William. But it won't happen that way. Obruchev lives for revenge. He could have killed Teresa and me when he shot Arthur. It would have been a lot easier for him. Instead, he chose to kidnap my daughter and frame me for my husband's murder. It meant more to him to make me suffer in jail, believing Teresa's fate depended on my silence, than to dispose of us. It was an extraordinarily cruel thing to do. Now I've escaped his psychological torture by escaping from prison.

"Look William, I know he means to kill us this time. He can't take any more chances. But he won't do it until he has the pleasure of punishing me for my latest defiance. When that light goes on, he and Teresa will both be here. Maybe it doesn't make sense to you. But don't doubt me. The man's a psychopath. He's going to make me watch him put my daughter through an agonizing death I won't be able to prevent. That, William, is the reason for this setup – not because it makes sense. If he wanted, he could simply kill her and wait for the police to catch us. I'd be unable to prove I even know him, let alone that he's a killer."

"So why are the lights rigged? Why doesn't he just come with Teresa and turn them on?"

"Because he's not going to bring Teresa. The priest is. He's going to sneak into the barn when it's convenient for him and call from there when he's ready."

"Why? It seems more complicated than it needs to be. Why does this torture and killing that you find inevitable have to happen in the barn? Why not right here?"

"Because of Teresa's wagon. She painted it. She lived in it. If he makes me watch her die near it, he'll think he accomplished some kind of symbolic victory. He's a psychopath, as I have been telling you all along."

"So you're saying the only purpose of this wiring thing is to let him signal you from the barn?"

"Yes, William, that's exactly what I'm saying. He knows I might be nearby, watching with binoculars to make sure there isn't a setup. A trip from the house to the barn would be too risky for him. Hence the man he's paying, the priest. Now, please, let's go. We have things to do."

"Such as?"

"Hiding ourselves where we still have some kind of a view inside and out. The priest will bring Teresa. It could be an hour or a week. What's important is that he doesn't see us and alert Obruchev. You discovered the rigged light. I'm really pleased you did. That is the final proof I needed, the proof Obruchev plans to come to the barn rather than to the house. As I said, we'll have to leave Teresa where the priest hides her. It won't be easy for me, but it's crucial. It lets us turn the trap set for me into a trap for Obruchev. Vesh would approve. We can't predict when either visit will happen so we have to be prepared at all times."

CHAPTER TWENTY-NINE

Wiesel maneuvered the huge tour bus through the narrow cobbled streets of Ljubljana, avoiding parked cars and piles of dirty snow with consummate skill. "Pretty town," he said, glancing over his shoulder at Connor. "Most of Yugoslavia didn't get off this lightly."

"Watch where you're going, Wiesel. You're making me nervous. I can look at postcards of the place when I get home."

"Why did your Ministry give us this monster of a bus?" Hatch asked. "They could have come up with something smaller."

"We've got to consider our girls, gentlemen. If anyone deserves a few hours of comfort, they do. I haven't hit anything yet, have I?"

"Don't get cocky" Connor said. "One fuck-up and you'll turn this place into Sarajevo."

Wiesel laughed. European driving conditions always rattled Americans, even those who faced bullets for a living. It seemed to him absurd that men on a mission as dangerous as the one planned for tonight were worried about scraping street signs in a bus. But that's how they were, all of them, and no amount of reassurance seemed to help. Fortunately this all-American quirk was a poor predictor of behavior under fire: he'd never worked with a Bureau guy who'd folded in the face of real danger.

He said, "I'm sorry we had to come this way. General Mud Dick, as you call him, gave us specific directions an hour before we left. They apparently keep close tabs on their buyers."

"So where the hell are we going?" Hatch asked. "You never told us."

"An army base on the west side of town. It's been closed for a few years but Majdak and his units still pretend to use the repair garage. The soldiers you'll meet inside are most likely on Obruchev's payroll. They'll make us leave the bus at the facility during the auction. They'll no doubt search it. We've got nothing to hide. The paperwork is flawless and the counterfeit ID lab in the restroom is par for the course."

"Par for what course?"

"Normal equipment for big shots in the Trade. The ability to produce false paperwork on a moment's notice is a condition of survival."

"Yeah, okay, fine. But if the bus stays there how the hell do we get to the auction? More importantly, how do we leave with these girls we're supposed to buy?"

"According to Mack, they take us in their own vehicles – Tatras."

"Tatras?"

"Czech military transporters. I thought we went over this."

"Maybe we did," Connor mumbled. "We're just dumb Americans. You gave us too goddamn much to remember. Hey, slow down! You're gonna roll this thing."

"Let me worry about the driving, okay? We're almost there. If you've got questions, you should ask them now. We won't be talking for the next eight hours, at least not to each other. When they interrogate you, I'm sure they'll use their own interpreters."

Connor said, "And what if the snow prevents your undercover guys from getting the transponder on Obruchev's vehicle?"

"Then you're fucked," Wiesel joked. "Especially if you're worried about driving over here."

"Thanks, pal. Now go over this whole thing once more for your dummies. You took as much time as it takes Hatch to eat dinner describing how Obruchev doesn't go anywhere when he's here except to his cousin's place, the auction house and the airport. Why are you convinced it will be any different this time? About right here's where you got kinda vague, Wiesel."

"As I said, we received anonymous calls from around here somewhere that your story is correct, that Obruchev is breaking routine to go after the little girl and her mother. According to our friendly caller, they are both going to be in the same place at the same time in the foreseeable future – and Obruchev knows this."

Hatch said, "I don't like it. We don't know the caller. It could be a setup."

"That's right. It could be. In which case you'll be lured into a trap and assassinated. But my explanation seems a thousand times more probable, and Randall agreed earlier, whether he remembers or not. We believe it is a setup – not of you two but of the big boss. Someone wants Obruchev dead. There's no reason you can't oblige – after he leads you to your fugitive and her daughter."

"Listen, Wiesel," Connor said, "I'm with you on this, with you all the way. No more talk of my senility, got it? My main worry isn't that we're being set up. It's the homing device your people are supposed to put on the transfer vehicle. They're in a foreign country, their expertise is untested, at least by the Bureau, and the weather isn't exactly – "

"Randall, trust me. The transponder will be in place. If it makes you feel any better, it's the same device the FBI uses."

"Hatch, do you know what he's talking about?"

"Not a clue."

"Me neither. We haven't been trackers for years. How does it work?"

"You're serious? You don't know?"

"How does it work, Wiesel? What should we expect?"

"When he starts driving, you'll be able to watch his movement on a state-of-the-art GPS monitor. You still have to keep within a range of three kilometers because of the transponders range limitations. You'll see a warning light when the signal starts getting weak. Don't ignore it. If you lose him, you're unlikely to find him again."

"So we sleep when he does?" Hatch said.

"You sleep if he does. If he stops then starts to move, your receiver will shriek like a fire alarm. One of you should always be ready to take the wheel in seconds. Something else. You might be stuck here for a long time. The caller did not say when the girl and her mother would be in the same place.

Don't worry. Karl has stocked your jeep with everything you'll need if that turns out to be the case – food, blankets, petrol. You're set for at least a week."

"A week?" Connor sounded as if he were in pain. "Obruchev won't wait a week."

"Not if he has a choice but – "

"Watch out for that traffic island up ahead."

"I see it."

"Well, watch for the next one. Tell me something, Wiesel. I don't know why I didn't ask you before. How are we supposed to bid on these girls if we don't speak a word of Russian? That is the language they conduct their auctions in, right?"

"Right, but it's not a problem. A lot of buyers don't speak Russian. They've designed things to make talk unnecessary. You get a numbered paddle when you go in, like it's a normal auction. If you can't speak Russian, you hold up a piece of paper with your bid written on it. Everyone understands numbers. The auctioneer's assistant lists the bids on a chalk board. Confusion is impossible. Lift your paddles, but consult with me in English. I'll do the talking. That much I did tell you."

"Okay, maybe. But we don't want to stand there waving paddles like we're a couple of Memphis ladies in church. Who says, 'going once, going twice,' that kind of stuff?"

"Nobody. You'll be pleased to know it's precisely because of the language barrier. They use virgin candles."

"Virgin candles?" Connor grumbled. "What the hell are virgin candles?"

"Ones that haven't been used. The burn time's consistent, something that has to do with how they're made as well as with their size."

"So how big are the things?"

"Small. Three of them go into a miniature candelabra. They're lit one at a time. When the last candle goes out, the bid on the floor wins. No language needed, and the process stays orderly. They can do a lot of business each session, especially since the girls are sold in groups of five."

"All or none?" Hatch asked.

"All or none."

Connor fidgeted. "So let's say we have a bid on the floor that the chalk guy up front has written on the board . . . "

"Alright."

"We want to raise it. What's a reasonable amount?"

"That's where I come in. Give me a 'thumbs up' if you want to raise and I'll decide that. If I get no sign from you, I'll do nothing."

Hatch said, "I get the impression you've been to a lot of these meat markets."

"I feel like I have. That's because I've worked with so many buyers who get busted and tell all to get a plea. Their descriptions of Obruchev's methods are detailed and consistent."

"I never thought I'd be buying girls," Connor said. "You make it sound easy."

Wiesel slowed for the entrance to the army base. "Sadly, Randall, it is."

***

"So how many units is The Knife looking at?" Majdak asked Wiesel in Slovenian. "It sounded like a big buy."

"How many young ladies?" Wiesel asked in English.

"Depends on price and quality. Maybe thirty, maybe fifty. Me and my partner, we make the decisions now because we've put up the cash that's keeping Mackie afloat. We're planning to double the size of the club."

Wiesel's translation caused the general's bulldog mouth to bend into a smile. "You'll get a friendly reception. This morning's snow is keeping a couple buyers away, and the boss doesn't like warehousing bitches."

Connor and Hatch nodded. No one, not even wily old Majdak, seemed to smell a bust. The general treated his Western customers with kid gloves, limiting his search and interrogation to the minimum. Almost as an afterthought, he warned them not to speak English during the auction. The boss was old-fashioned. He didn't do business with North Americans. This was costly and stupid. Europe was reaching the saturation point when it came to Eastern pussy. Any fool could see where the next market was. So Majdak would work with them – as long as they kept their mouths shut and let their European partner do the bidding. Obruchev's right-hand man had decided to protect his Canadians in order to make a little on the side.

No doubt about it, Connor thought. The entire charade, beginning with Mack in Vienna, had worked like a charm. His Austrian colleague knew the ropes. Drexler had been right about that.

CHAPTER THIRTY

Around eleven o'clock, several uniformed men led Connor, Hatch and Wiesel to a waiting Tatra. The snowstorm had ended and the moon burned brightly in a cold cloudless sky. Wherever the snow had been cleared off cars and trucks, white frost glistened in its place. Everything sang of cold: the brittle ice underfoot, the doors that cracked when opened, the scrapers that grated on frozen windshields.

Soon they were underway. The defroster blew freezing air onto the passengers; the radio picked up East European disco music peppered with bursts of static. Connor shifted heavily in his seat and looked out the rear window at the truck bed.

The transport area of the military personnel carrier was dark but he could see its outlines in the moonlight. The canvas roof stretched over arched scaffolding. It sagged under the weight of snow. Wooden benches too close together for men left no doubt about how the girls would be ferried from the auction to their buyers. They would sit huddled in the cold like soldiers on their way to the front. Fear and death awaited them, as they would know the truth by now. But unlike soldiers they would not have the comfort of fighting for a cause. This whole business made him sick.

The first sign the heater might be working came as they turned onto a narrow, recently plowed road that ran a short distance through the forest to a guard house. A bar was lowered to block their passage while men in Slovenian Army uniforms searched the vehicle with halogen flashlights, explosive detectors and German shepherds.

The soldier in charge read aloud from a clipboard. Connor lifted his hand when he heard his Canadian name, already foreign to him, called out in a thick accent. Standing outside, he was patted down, searched by wand, then asked something in a language he didn't understand.

"Show him your cash," Wiesel said. "New customers must demonstrate their ability to pay."

Connor pulled out a roll of bills that elicited a stiff nod from the soldier. Moments later they were on their way, bouncing over plowed road, then pushing through deep snow in eight-wheel drive.

When lights appeared on the horizon Connor recognized the silhouette of a factory. Its smokestacks towered into the moonlit sky, belching dark clouds. He picked up a smell long forgotten, the smell of steam trains passing near his grandmother's house when he was a kid, the smell of coal. There was something unforgettable about that smell, something ominous.

Inside the factory weak light flickered behind filthy broken windows. You didn't need special powers to know that this was a place of nightmares.

He had read about the sex trade, had been lectured on it by his daughters, had listened to sanitized government descriptions of "trafficking in human beings." But words conveyed little of the horror. Wooden benches in the back of military trucks, dilapidated factories surrounded by guards, the smell of coal on a frigid winter night – these were the things that nudged him toward a painful awareness that civilization still ignored the atrocities it lacked the will to fight.

***

Stamping feet shook the makeshift grandstands. Whistles, hoots and cheers echoed through the vast littered hall. All of this in response to the first terrified teenage girls, hoisted hand in crouch on stage by a couple of punks.

Connor knew it would be bad, but this was unimaginable. He felt paralyzed by the images unfolding before his eyes. Drums of burning coal cast a reddish-orange glow over the naked bodies. Everything became a vivid blur: shadows of enticement, high-heeled shoes, gold ankle bracelets, hair in buns, hair falling in loose curls on adolescent shoulders. He stared in stunned sadness as the girls responded like circus animals to their trainers commands: hands over head, back stretch, legs parted, sex thrust forward, about face, toe touch.

Young flesh glistened with sweat – whether from heat, humiliation or terror, he didn't know.

A man stepped up to the block, a short man with broad shoulders, stout legs and a gut that looked to be more muscle than fat. He was bald, with a closely cropped band of gray hair around his large head. Connor recognized him from the photos the Chicago field office had assembled.

With him were two assistants, dressed in the same casual manner – open collar, khakis, heavy leather boots. One of the assistants set up an easel and, using clamps, attached a chalk board. The other readied a cashier's station, complete with cash register and a strongbox for the overflow. Obruchev, who appeared exhausted and impatient, launched into a gruff monologue.

English is the language of business, my ass, thought Connor. But he had a pretty good idea what this lowlife was saying. Wiesel had given him a sketch, gleaned from informants, of how the sessions began. This would be the reading of house rules, designed as much to titillate as to keep order. It explained, among other things, when the public rape of these helpless girls would be ordered and how the choice of rapist was made.

When Obruchev finished he fired his automatic pistol in the air, evidently to silence the crowd. It worked. Upon entering, the buyers had passed through metal detectors and been patted down. The boss was the only armed person in the factory.

The girls were ordered to resume their march around the stage, stopping on painted circles to provide explicit displays of their future market value, their sexuality.

Obruchev said something to the man at the chalkboard, who wrote down a figure: the floor. Then the boss used some kind of hissing ceramic animal to light the first of three small candles in the miniature candelabra beside him. Numbered paddles went up in all the bleachers. The figure on the chalkboard climbed toward 20,000 Euros as the first candle went out. Connor leaned forward and gave Wiesel the thumbs-up when the second candles was lit. The sum of 31,000 Euros appeared on the board in response to his colleague's shout.

One of the handlers slapped a girl in the face when she refused to simulate masturbation. A stomping of feet began in the bleachers and quickly rose to a crescendo. Men stood, waving their arms. Obruchev surveyed the horny masses, then glanced at the handler of the offending girl.

This would be it, Connor thought, a public rape as punishment. The girl, who seemed to have sensed as much, stopped refusing instructions and did as she was told. It took a while for the gladiatorial mood in the house to subside.

Obruchev lit the last candle. This time Hatch gave the thumbs-up sign. Wiesel hollered a sum in Russian as he lifted his numbered paddle. The chalk lackey wrote 35,000 Euros on the board. The candle flickered, a mad chatter rippled through the ranks of buyers, a guy with a bin Laden head and World Wrestling Federation body held up his paddle. Before he could shout his bid, the candle went out.

Connor handed Wiesel a roll of banknotes. Watching his colleague walk down to the cashier, he reminded himself that these girls were among the lucky ones. They had jobs waiting for them in Austria, legitimate jobs similar to the ones they had been promised by the swindlers. Whether they had already been through too much horror to lead a normal life, Connor didn't know. He usually thought Bureau psychologists exaggerated the impact of emotional trauma on long-term mental health, but when it came to these girls, exaggeration seemed impossible . . .

***

Four hours and two public rapes later, they were preparing to close for the night. The auction participants had dwindled by half, some having left with five girls – the minimum permitted – others with as many as fifteen. Connor and crew had already caused a minor sensation with their shopping extravaganza. Several buyers were angry, believing they had driven up the prices. Others were curious about their identity. It was definitely time to go.

But there was a problem. Departure required a buyer's personal appearance on stage to ask the boss to arrange transportation back to the base for himself and his purchases. From what the Vienna group had observed, it was wise to pick the moment carefully. If you approached Obruchev when he was busy, you could count on drawing anger and attention to yourself – not a good idea. Right now he was definitely busy.

A driver who had just returned from the army base stepped without permission onto the stage. Incredulous, Obruchev reproached him harshly. But he relented when the soldier waved an envelope. The soldier strode to the block and handed it to him. Obruchev read the epistle a few times before cramming it in his pocket. After a tense fidgety silence, he roared something in Russian.

The chalkster reloaded the candelabra. Obruchev lit candle number one. An oriental buyer who had yet to make a purchase raised his paddle. "Forty-two thousand Euro," he said in butchered English. "But not dark-haired one. Dark-haired one no client want in Japan. Blonde only. Name of my club, Blonde Only. Cannot cheat customer."

"Fuck you," Obruchev shouted, too overwrought to pretend he didn't speak English. "It's five or none. You've been here. You know the rules."

No one else had come forward by the time the third candle went out. "You've scared off the other buyers," Obruchev bellowed. "What do you want now? To wiggle your way out of your bid? No way, pal. You've bought 'em."

"Forty-two thousand, no problem. Just don't want dark-hair one. I make you gift of her. Can't use her in Japan. We got whole country of dark-hair whorings."

"Get up here and pay for what you bought."

"Hey, don't go weirdo. I pay for five. Never say I don't. I pay, only you take dark-hair one as gift. Then your peoples take me to place."

Obruchev drew his automatic pistol and matter-of-factly shot the dark-haired girl through the head. He pulled the black lever that started the conveyor. The door to the incinerator went up automatically. The remaining buyers fell silent.

"Okay, happy now? I make slant happy, yes? Get your ass down here and put her on the conveyor. I got brunettes up the ass."

The little oriental man scampered onto the stage like a disoriented rabbit. He rolled the naked girl with half her head blown off onto the metal conveyor, then stared at the blood on his hands and trousers. "Hey, Mister, you got something like towel? You fucking crazy man. You don't have to shoot. I make you gift. I . . . "

Obruchev relieved him of 42,000 Euros, took a few steps back to avoid the splatter and dissected him from crotch to throat with a stream of soft-tipped bullets. He kicked what was left of the corpse onto the conveyor and watched it accompany the dead girl down Bogdan's path to the incinerator. "Anyone want to bid on the remaining four," he said in English, looking more relaxed than he had all evening. "This man isn't able to take possession of his wares." The house was silent until he realized no one understood what he had said. He repeated himself in Russian.

Shouts erupted, the shouts of men who thought they could get a deal. Wiesel, knowing they had enough evidence to convict Obruchev of murder as well as "trafficking in humans," quickly outbid the lot. When he had paid for the last group he requested immediate transport to the army base.

The boss called General Majdak to organize the larger-than-usual delivery. They hadn't gone far when the general asked politely for the 20 percent commission Mack had promised him.

***

At five o'clock on a frigid winter morning in Slovenia, a tour bus with 39 teenage girls aboard pulled into a secluded rest stop. Connor and Hatch got out. Karl, Wiesel's undercover man, held open the door of his waiting jeep, gave precise instructions in English, then casually boarded the bus. While Wiesel cruised toward the Austrian border with his girls and undercover agent, Connor drove to a hidden spot near the factory exit and parked. He turned on the receiver. The homing device was working, the vehicle to which it was attached was stationary. The man they hoped would lead them to Sondheim was finally in their sights.

CHAPTER THIRTY-ONE

Teresa woke from a kaleidoscope of drug-induced dreams. The ceiling spun so fast she got dizzy, and it didn't stop spinning until she sat up and held her breath. She was on a bed with ruffled sheets, fat pillows and a bright quilt of pretty squares made with needlework. Everyplace she looked there were cuckoo clocks, dolls, music boxes and painted figurines. The carved wood around the windows and ceiling made her think of the gingerbread houses she'd seen a long time ago in children's books.

She tried to figure out how she had gotten here but her mind was blank. The very last thing she remembered was playing newspaper games with her brothers at the train station. Then all at once she knew: she was dead! God had put her in this funny-smelling house. But it wasn't really a house; it was Heaven. That's why it looked so strange.

Maybe she could find her dad. She remembered him pretty well, better than she used to. That probably meant he was close. She was about to start looking for him but she got dizzy again and felt like she was going to be sick. She tried hard not to throw up on the pretty quilt and after a while she was okay.

She slid off the edge of the high bed. Some slippers that looked like rabbits were on the floor near where he feet touched. She noticed she was wearing a dress. It was a bright red dress that reminded her of the children's clothes her mother had shown her a few times – clothes her mother wore to special things like birthdays when she was a little girl.

The dress had shoulder straps and flowers everywhere made from sewing, just like the squares on the quilt. It was nice here but she started to wonder whether it really was Heaven. Things came back to her now that had happened after the newspaper games at the station. Like Vesh warning her about the evil spirit and Katja running off at night when they went to do dishes in the river.

She'd forgotten her dog! This was the first night she had spent without Katja since she went to live with Uncle Bogdan. If Katja wasn't here, she didn't like Heaven.

It was bright. She rubbed her eyes. If it really was Heaven, she thought, the brightness would be on account of angels with haloes or Jesus with a big sun around him. But that wasn't the reason. Here there were just plain lights. They had cords and one of the shades was even crooked.

She saw a bathroom with the door open. She needed to use it so she went inside. When she came out, a man she didn't recognize was waiting for her. The man looked sort of like he worked in Heaven. She had seen him and his friends painted on the walls of her mother's church. He had a flat round face as white as if Aunt Michaela had dusted it with pastry flour. His blue eyes seemed to make holes in her. He had a long pointed beard and wore a white priest collar and black satiny shirt.

Staring at him, she realized he looked even more familiar than the men on the church walls. The sudden memory of where she had seen him terrified her. It had been at the train station with the ugly boats out front. He was always watching her, standing up against a big stone pillar staring at her the whole time she asked Americans for money.

He was the evil spirit! He was the ghost who had tied up her dog and stuffed her in the trunk of a car! She tried to run but her feet wouldn't move. She tried to scream but not a sound came out of her mouth. He stepped toward her, smiling.

Finally her feet came unglued. She ran into the bathroom and slammed the door. It bounced open. She tried again, then saw a big black shoe that kept the door from closing. The evil spirit was coming after her!

He pushed open the door. He spoke Czech, like her mother sometimes did. But she was too frightened to understand what he was saying. She tried to scream. This time her voice worked. She screamed and screamed and screamed. The evil spirit didn't come any closer. Instead he pulled a folded-up piece of paper out of his pocket and opened it up. At first she wouldn't look at it. But he held it so close to her face she finally opened her eyes. The evil spirit was holding up a picture of her mother! It was the same picture from the newspaper she kept under her cot in Vesh's trailer, but it wasn't all wet and muddy from her dog.

"Teresa," the evil spirit said, "I am sorry if I frightened you. I'm going to take you to your mother now. She is coming to pick you up at a place you already know. But you must behave if you want to see her. You can't scream or act afraid. Some bad people are looking for us, so we must be very quiet and very careful.?"

"I know who you are. You're – "

Rasputin touched his collar. "I am a priest. Did Vesh tell you I was something else?"

Teresa shook her head yes.

"I am sorry. I tried to talk to him but he wouldn't listen. He is a stubborn man. He did a bad thing but he didn't know it was bad. He was trying to help you. Instead he took you from the farm just when your mother was coming. Farmer Zlatko told you your mother was coming, didn't he?"

Again, Teresa shook her head yes.

"This might be hard for you to understand, but you should know God's will. I was entrusted with caring for you until she arrived. When I got to the farm you were gone. I went looking for you because I had promised your mother you would be safe. It took a long time to find you in Italy. But when I finally managed, the people you were living with didn't believe me. They wouldn't let me take you to your mother. They said you belonged to them. They are not bad people, they just didn't understand. They invented stories to make you afraid of me. I had to take you the way I did to save you. But this story has a happy ending. Now you're safe, and if you are very quiet while we travel you will soon see your mother. Do you think you can you stay quiet even if you're still a little afraid of me?"

"Where is my dog? What did you do with my dog?"

"Katja is fine. She's with your mother. That's how your mother will find you. I will hide you from the bad people so they can't find you, but Katja will make sure your mother knows where you are. Now, do you think you can be good and travel with me in the front seat?"

Teresa said she could but she was secretly afraid. This man was only pretending to be nice. He hated her. With Vesh it had been different, even when he was mad. She always knew Vesh loved her. She didn't trust the evil spirit. She didn't believe he would really take her to her mother but she didn't know how to get away from him.

He said, "Come now. You must meet my mother and eat something. You haven't eaten in a long time. You have been asleep all of last night, and all of today and part of tonight."

"I don't want to meet your mother."

"You must thank her. My mother loves little girls. My sister died when she was your age. My mother collected all of these nice things for her own little girl's room before God called Beta to Heaven. Whenever we move to a different house, my mother makes a room just like Beta's old room in Russia. No one was ever allowed to sleep in Beta's room until last night. No one before you was ever allowed to wear her clothes. That's why you must thank my mother."

Teresa refused to take the evil spirit's hand but she went with him to the kitchen. She didn't know what else to do. When she passed a row of windows without curtains, she saw that it was night outside.

A clear moon lit up the fields and mountains. As far as she could see the ground was white with snow. Where the evil spirit had grabbed her, it was muddy. There hadn't been any fields either, just woods. He must have taken her a long way from the camp. She started to feel sick again.

While it was still dark and the moon was high, the evil spirit's mother dressed her in red boots, a stocking cap and a big fur coat. The old witch kissed her before the evil spirit led her away. Teresa was inside a nightmare she couldn't escape.

They drove in the evil spirit's white car for a long time without saying a word. The roads had lots of snow and ice on them. Sometimes the car went sliding halfway across the road but they didn't have a wreck. That's because there weren't any other cars out, not even one. She was about to fall asleep when the evil spirit turned onto a small road. She saw Grandfather Zlatko's farmhouse in the distance, lit by the moon. Its windows were dark. She was wondering if her painted Gypsy wagon was still in the barn when she felt a tiny prick in her thigh. The evil spirit had given her another one of those shots . . .

***

William gently nudged Kristýna. "Wake up. Car lights."
"What time is it?"
"I can't see my watch. I'd say three-thirty or four."
They had chosen a stall that was positioned to give them a view of the farmhouse, then punched tiny nail holes in the barn wood so they could see out. A white car was approaching along a drive that had been plowed by a neighboring farmer just before dark. The car stopped in front of the farmhouse. They watched a shadowy figure climb out and shovel snow off the stairs to the house entrance. Kristýna held her breath when he walked around to the passenger side of the car and opened the door.

"Obruchev?" William whispered.
"Too tall. It's the priest."
The man picked up a little girl, who was limp as a rag doll, and started toward the barn.
"Is that her?"
"Yes. She's either hurt or drugged. Look at the way her arms are hanging."
They crawled over deep hay to the front of the stall. That afternoon, while making their final preparations, they had covered the gap at the bottom of the stall door with Vesh's rolled up blankets. Through tiny gaps between the blankets they could see most of the barn's interior. But with the barn door closed it was much too dark to see anything.

That changed when the man from the car kicked open the door. Moonlight flooded in, giving Kristýna a look at her daughter's angelic face. Thank God. She was alive. Her color was good, her fingers moved involuntarily.

The priest turned on a flashlight and climbed the steps to the wagon. With Teresa slung over his shoulder like a sack of grain, he fished a set of keys from somewhere inside his religious garb and opened the heavy padlock. Seconds later he came out of the wagon alone, locked it up and left the barn.

Kristýna expected him to return to his car and drive away. Instead he walked down the plowed path to the farm entrance and waited. A few minutes later a car similar in appearance to the one he had abandoned picked him up.

His white Skoda parked out front would, she thought, give the impression to anyone who came that the priest was either in the farmhouse or the barn. Why this was important she had no idea.

Her mind and heart began the tug-of-war she had anticipated. Teresa was only several steps away. She was alive; they were alone. She and William could easily fashion tools from the farm implements they had assembled as weapons, break into the Gypsy wagon and free her child. The desire to do just that was almost irresistible. But she knew, as she had known when they devised the plan, that taking Teresa before Obruchev was dead would make them easy prey. There would a tearful reunion and several hours of closeness. But it wouldn't take the man long to hunt them down. The end, once he found them, was predictable. This tug-of-war she must let her mind win.

They had practiced the murder a hundred times. Their plan was foolproof. All she had to do was wait right where she was until he arrived . . .

"William," she whispered, "promise me you won't let me do anything stupid. If Teresa wakes up, if I hear her . . . well, it's just that I know myself. I could lose my head and try to go to her. You mustn't let me do this, even if you have to restrain me. Can you promise me that?"

"Of course, even though I'm sure it won't be necessary. You might feel the impulse, but it won't go any further. But, Kristýna, this raises another issue that's been bothering me. If I'm strong enough to restrain you, which I am, I should be the one who strikes Obruchev first."

"No. When I see him up close I'll be stronger than both of you together. Let's leave the plan as it is. Three steps and he's a dead man. If he's still breathing, you finish the job."

***

After dropping off his accomplice, Rasputin drove the white Skoda that had picked him up at the farm to the army base. He stopped at the guardhouse and waited for a Tatra returning to the auction. Greeting the driver of the first vehicle to appear, he handed him a sealed note. The driver initially refused to accept it. But Rasputin explained that it was imperative Obruchev receive the note at once, regardless of what he was doing, and that whoever brought it to him would most certainly earn a promotion. A second lost could mean disaster for the boss and his business; a second gained could mean yet another decade of prosperity. When the driver asked for further explanation, Rasputin fixed an otherworldly stare on him and said, simply, "Go."

CHAPTER THIRTY-TWO

The son-of-a-bitch was fucking with him. The time and place of the exchange made this totally clear – so clear, in fact, that he was certain the bastard wanted him to arrive with a head full of questions.

Obruchev was blind with rage, crazed with frustration. Ever since he had left the plant he'd been trying to devise a theory that would reveal the hidden meaning of Rasputin's bizarre note, a theory that would allow him to plan a devastating countermove.

But the road had become a ribbon of ice. Just staying on it required total concentration. Instead of moving toward a checkmate, his thoughts fell into a vortex of circular reasoning.

He cursed viciously when he missed a turn and ended up in a roadside ditch. Snarling and lurching the eight-wheel-drive Tatra eventually pulled him out, but not before his fury had risen another notch. He'd better calm down, he thought, or he'd blow a gasket before he handled unfinished business. That would be a goddamn shame.

The isolated country roads were dark, deserted, treacherous. Driving more slowly now, he lit a black Russian, inhaled deeply and managed to relax. If he kept his speed down and his temper in check, he could get back to mental chess. No way the holy freak had something up his frock that Stepan Obruchev couldn't foresee . . .

His Tatra slid, he realized he'd let his speed creep up. Bad idea. There was absolutely no rush. He didn't plan to arrive until he had some idea of what he would find.

So where had his thinking brought him? Not far enough. This was clearly a setup, or at least Rasputin wanted him to believe it was a setup. Weird? Maybe if you considered Rasputin normal.

From the seat beside him he grabbed the rumpled sheet of paper, careful not to lose control of his 30-ton Tatra when he reached for the interior lights. Where was his confidence? No one could trick him if his mind was clear. No one. Frustration created a cloudy mind and, with it, vulnerability. That was something he could not afford to forget.

Obruchev waited patiently for a straight stretch of road, then reread the note.

"My car will be parked in front of the farmhouse. I won't be there when you arrive. I am to be picked up by a local worshiper to conduct pre-dawn services. I will return shortly."

Maybe, maybe not. Obruchev glanced at the road, then continued reading.

"In the meantime settle your affairs. The child is inside the Gypsy wagon in the barn. I chose this place for two reasons. I knew you wouldn't want me to bring her to your work and I learned she had spent a lot of time in that wagon while living with Zlatko. You can be sure that her prints are everywhere. Do not shoot the lock off. If you do, you will leave evidence of foul play.

"Go to the farmhouse. The stairs are shoveled, the door is open. The kitchen is to your left as you enter. Beside the cellar door you will find a cabinet for dishes. In the smallest of the three top drawers are several dozen keys. The one you want, the key to the wagon's padlock, is marked with a blue florescent cross.

"I beg you, Stepan Mikhailovich, take this key into the barn and use it. If I still haven't returned by the time you complete your affairs, wait for me in the farmhouse. We will conclude our business there. If you do not feel comfortable with this arrangement, please depart with my blessing. We will meet again before the day has passed."

The road bent into an endless series of curves. Pine trees laden with snow hugged the sides. Pre-dawn fog swirled in the beam of his headlights. Driving, even slowly, took all his concentration. No problem. He'd seen enough of the note to remember its contents, enough of the map to find Zlatko's farm without looking at it again.

The narrow road crested the hill, descended in tight switchbacks, then ran arrow-straight across open fields.

Back to the drawing board. He was being lured to the farm. He was supposed to suspect a setup. What, exactly, did this mean?

Christ! He was making himself crazy again, just as Rasputin had no doubt intended. He couldn't know what awaited him until he got there. He would be better off trusting his instincts, remaining aware that anything or nothing might happen. If the holy pervert was playing more than a mind game, Stepan Mikhailovich Obruchev would find out soon enough . . .

***

"He's stopped."

"He's stopped before."

"Only for a few seconds. This might it be it, Randall."

"Don't get excited. He's probably taking a leak. We're back too far anyway. Let's close the gap to one point five kilometers. If he's still not moving, we'll have to reconsider."

"Didn't you look up ahead?"

"What? We're in a foggy forest with two foot visibility. There is no up ahead. You're seeing things."

"You're not seeing things. When we came over the last hill, we came briefly out of the soup. I had a bird's eye view of what's below. We're approaching a valley floor with no trees and no fog. In the moonlight the whole area is visible to the naked eye. So do us both a favor, okay? Stop before we get there."

"Okay, Hatch, don't get worked up. It's not like you."

When the road widened Connor eased the jeep to the right, careful to keep all four wheels on the plowed surface. He stopped, took a deep breath and stared at the monitor. The blinking red dot that marked the Tatra's location had stopped moving. Hatch was right. This could be it.

***

Twenty minutes earlier Rasputin, shivering in a hunter's blind near the factory, felt the earth shake when Obruchev's military transporter rumbled by. He waited to be sure Pimenko's information was sound, that the FBI was on his tail. When a jeep not belonging to the business sped by a short time later, he took out his cell phone, dialed Zlatko's number and hung up. He redialed several times to send an unmistakable signal to the girl's mother, whose nearness to the farmhouse he did not doubt. Satisfied that all had gone according to plan, he pushed his way into the branches that hid yet another car and started the engine.

***

"Well?" Hatch said.

"Let's go. You were right."

"Thank you, Randall. It happens from time to time."

Connor was about to say something when they came out of the fog, rounded the last curve and began a straight gradual descent. Farmland stretched in all directions, as white as polished ivory under the moonlit snow. Hedges or rows of trees broke the vast expanse into the familiar patterns of cultivation, separating pasture from pasture, farm from farm. A few remote dwellings announced the existence of life, sleeping life.

"What the hell time is it?" Connor asked.

"Five thirty. Still a couple hours till dawn. I think I know where he stopped."

Connor tried to look at the monitor and drive at the same time. "Where?"

"Watch the road. We're coming to a dead end. Well, not exactly a dead end. A T-type intersection with another road running at right angles to this one. The electronic map doesn't show driveways, but he's apparently turned into one nearby. Or plowed his own. He's several hundred meters from the nearest road."

Connor turned off his headlights. "How far to the T?"

"About a kilometer."

They had reached the valley floor, losing their panoramic view. "What can you tell from your map? Did he turn right or left on this so-called driveway?"

"Right."

Connor felt his heart beginning its pre-battle drumbeat. "Then we'll pull off up ahead and take the final stretch on foot" He patted the breast holster and 9 mm Glock automatic pistol beneath his coat. It had been waiting on the seat, along with one for Hatch, when they got into the jeep. Good weapon, good holster, good fit. He was ready. Christ, was he ready.

Hatch turned around to rummage through the various equipment Wiesel's man had left in back. Connor was about to say something when he caught a glimpse of the intersection. He cut the motor, coasted to a plowed tractor path, turned in and stopped.

"Let's go."

"Hold on. A couple minutes could save your life. They left us vests and night goggles. If I could – "

"Let's go, Hatch. Fuck the vests. It's too cold out here to put them on. Bring goggles for yourself if you want. I'll take a flashlight."

"Someday, Randall . . . "

"Someday, what?"

"Your impatience is going to catch up with you."

***

Still no sound from Teresa.

For the better part of an hour, since they had seen the kitchen lights flash on and off, William and Kristýna had been glued to their peepholes in the side of the barn. Time passed with agonizing slowness. They were about to return to their system of sleeping in shifts when the ground began to tremble. She grabbed his wrist as they watched a huge military transporter rumble through the main gate of the farm. The stall shook as it approached, rattling the tools and pans hanging from the walls.

A loud crash caused them both to jump. The personnel carrier rammed into the back of the priest's Skoda and knocked it several car-lengths forward. Kristýna reached for the pitchfork, but without taking her eyes from the peephole.

"What the hell's going on?" William said. "The driver's climbing the steps to the farmhouse. He's not coming to the barn. Are you sure it's him?"

"It's him," she said. "I don't know what he's doing but he'll be here soon."

***

Just like that fucking asshole, Obruchev thought, hitting the gas and blasting Rasputin's wreck away from the front door. *The freak shovels the steps, then blocks them with his car so I'll have to walk through even deeper snow.*

To hell with trying to be quiet. If anyone was in the place, the sound of crunching metal and exploding glass would have alerted them. He depressed the thumb plate and pushed. The door was unlocked but it didn't budge.

He pushed again, harder. This time it flew open, accompanied by the screech of hinges and brittle crack of ice. No one had entered or left the place for a couple of hours, that much he could be sure of. It was cold, but the door would need longer to freeze shut as tightly as it had.

Before entering, he drew his automatic pistol. The fact that no one had come in or out didn't mean no one was waiting for him.

Should he use the flashlight he carried in his pocket? No. That would turn him into a beacon. He'd be better off darting in unpredictable directions, working his way thoroughly but cautiously through the house until he was satisfied it was empty . . .

He lunged inside, hurled himself to the floor and rolled behind a sofa. No one fired a shot; his wounds were limited to a few splinters from the rough-hewn planks. Better yet, he could see. Moonlight brightened by snow poured through the unshuttered windows, illuminating the parlor. He got to his feet and locked the door. Someone outside could be watching him. He didn't want a surprise visit. Quickly, efficiently, he searched the house.

All clear.

A short corridor led to the farmer's kitchen. A kerosene lantern stood on the wooden dinner table. Counters that doubled as cutting boards lined the walls. The primitive iron sink, black hooded stove and standing cabinets reminded him of his childhood kitchen in Kursk .

He flung himself to the side when he first saw the door to the cellar. How the hell had he missed it the first time through? Someone could be hiding down there with an assault rifle, just waiting to burst into the kitchen and blow him to bits. That goddamn chess game the priest had initiated must still be going on in his head . . .

He looked at the door again and felt a wave of relief. He'd completely forgotten it had been mentioned in Rasputin's note. That's why he hadn't bothered with it. His instincts were in charge, his reactions were on auto-pilot. This round was his.

Adding to his confidence, he now saw that the door was blocked from opening into the kitchen by a massive steel bar resting in iron cradles lag-bolted to the hardwood jamb. The door was reinforced by broad metal bands. He'd heard about how the army had routinely transformed farm cellars into torture chambers during the breakup of Yugoslavia. They'd done a hell of a job with this one.

A cabinet for dishes stood beside the door, just as Rasputin had indicated. The key to the Gypsy wagon was supposed to be inside.

He pulled open the smallest of the top drawers and immediately spotted a blue florescent cross. Smiling, he put the key in his pocket. So far, so good . . .

He was about to leave when he had an annoying vision of St. Seraphim kneeling over his grave. Jesus! What was this supposed to mean? There was no one in the farmhouse. He could turn on the lights if he really felt spooked.

In fact that's exactly what he would do. The switch was above the counter, scarcely visible in a tear-shaped pool of shadow. He spun quickly, pushing his butt against the butcher block counter, and surveyed the room in the dim light. Empty, of course. So why the hell did he feel something was about to happen? Why were the superstitions from his youth gathering like a lynch party in some obscure part of his brain? That fucking freak had cursed him from afar.

The moonlight, so helpful to this point, had become an otherworldly glow, summoning the demons of his subconscious. As his left hand moved toward the light switch, his right hand tightened its grip on his gun. Light, pure artificial light, would restore his sanity.

His fingers touched the switch. He flicked it, holding his breath in anticipation of instant deliverance. But the artificial sun did not rise.

Feeling almost frantic, he turned toward the counter and squinted at the switch. In the hellish glow he could see that the cover had been removed. He gave an audible sigh of relief. There was no black magic here, no ghost of Bogdan, no icon waiting peacefully for his demise. The goddamn switch was broken.

To prove to himself that he wasn't insane, he placed his pistol on the counter and pulled out his flashlight. When the beam hit the switch, he saw wires leading from the open box to the telephone.

Light off, gun in hand, he again turned to face the open kitchen. No one. But there were new questions, ugly questions. The light had been tampered with. The wires connected the light switch to the telephone. Could he, by flicking the switch, have sent a burst of current down the phone line, a high-tech telegram announcing his presence? Was this the setup? If so, it was the work of man, not demons. The work of man he could handle.

He ripped the wires off the phone. In the same instant he knew he had been right. That flick of the switch had given some kind of signal. He saw two men approaching from the main road some 200 meters away, hiding behind carts and hedges before crossing open areas. They must be feeling the rush of the kill right now, he thought. They had him trapped; they could not fail.

Obruchev was again in his element. He had a plan. He strained to lift the heavy bar from its mounts. The thing was a length of railroad track strong enough to keep Sampson in the cellar. Breathing heavily, he stood it on end and shimmied it into the narrow gap between the stove and cabinets. When he lit the lantern, it was still lost in darkness.

Why not have some fun, he thought, after the hell he had just been through? Why not make certain his assassins saw exactly where he was going? It wasn't necessary. They would follow his fresh boot prints to the end of the trail in any case. But it would be amusing. In fact, the amusement had already begun. He could imagine them now as they spotted the pale fire of the lantern. They would watch him putter around in the kitchen, believing him oblivious to their approach.

He would never stay in one spot long enough to provide a target. Frustrating for them, but they'd get over it when they saw him open the cellar door and disappear into the basement. All the while, he kept moving unpredictably, kept denying them a shot.

They would be close by now, perhaps 100 meters. They would rush the house, trapping him in the cavern below. Or so they thought.

What would they feel, he wondered, when their self-gratification changed to white-hot terror? How would they react when they realized they were going to die a slow, horrible death?

These things interested him. Too bad he wouldn't be able to conduct an interview, post-mortem . . .

CHAPTER THIRTY-THREE

"I think I can hit him from here," Hatch whispered.

"Too risky," Connor said. "If you miss him we announce ourselves. If you kill him we lose our only lead to the fugitive."

They were crouched behind a snow-covered pile of firewood no more than the length of a football field from the kitchen window. "How close do you want us to get?" Hatch asked.

"His army truck."

"It's light as day out here, Randall. He'll see us when we move."

"If he turns around. He hasn't so far."

"That doesn't mean he won't. Give me a chance."

"Listen, Hatch, you haven't even fired that gun yet. You're not going to practice here . . . Jesus! He's going into the basement. Move!"

They sprinted to the Tatra and worked their way toward its rear. Connor signaled Hatch to stop, then dropped to his knees and glanced around the back of the truck.

"Shit," Connor hissed in frustration. "Can you believe that? He closed the door behind him. Why would he close the goddamn door?"

"Some people close doors," Hatch said. "What difference does it make? We wait here until he comes back upstairs. The rest will be easy."

"Who's says he'll come back up? He might sleep down there. He might keep his girls down there. His auction buddies might show up for a party while we're standing around like ice statues. We don't know shit. We're going to proceed accordingly."

"Okay, Randall. I'm waiting for orders."

"Stay here. Wound him if he shows. I'll circle the house and check if there's another way out of the basement."

"If there isn't?"

"We're going in after him."

***

Obruchev closed the cellar door and took off down the stone steps, intentionally leaving the cavern dark. At the bottom he directed the beam of his flashlight on the path he had taken. Perfect. His boots were still wet; they left distinct prints. He walked a random course through the cavernous cellar, grabbing a can of machine oil as he passed a storage shelf. His exit, when he made it, would have to be silent.

Near the foundation wall loomed an ancient furnace, its tangle of crooked pipes rising to the ceiling like branches of a dead oak. He walked toward it, examining the floor for dust. None was visible.

Behind the furnace, he took off his boots, tied the laces together and draped them around his neck. He felt his wool socks. Dry, cold but dry. He took a few steps, then stopped to check if he'd left a trail. No dust, no moisture, no footprints. He smiled to himself: things were finally going his way.

After locating the fuse box, he yanked down the main lever to cut off power to the house. Darkness, when those two idiots got down here, would force them to move slowly.

At the top of the stairs, he oiled the cellar door hinges and sat down. He knew he might be here a few minutes or an hour, but he didn't care. His usual impatience had given way to an icy calm. When the assassins Rasputin had dispatched to kill him showed up, he would be ready.

***

Connor returned from his reconnaissance tour. "Let's go. He's got no way out of the cellar except the one you're looking at. Even if he comes up while we're at the front door, he's still caught in the house. We don't have time to waste. His pals could show up any second."

"Randall, I think we should give it five minutes. He's an easy shot from here. Once we get inside, we're facing an unknown situation."

"If he was coming up, he'd already have come. Let's go."

"Five minutes, for Christ's sake. At least let me wait here. When he hears you breaking in, he's not going to stay down there."

Connor, still out of breath from his hike through the deep snow, puffed steam into the night. "What's wrong with you, Hatch? We don't know who else is in the house. We break in together. Come on."

Connor trudged off, using the tracks he had already made. Hatch, cursing under his breath, holstered his pistol and followed.

***

Obruchev reacted instantly when he heard gunshots. Using the move he had rehearsed a hundred times in his mind, he burst from the cellar, quietly closed the door and ducked into the pantry. They would not walk past this enclave if they followed his boot prints into the basement. But he was done taking chances; he used the auditory veil of their loud entry to fashion a hiding place behind sacks of flour.

It wasn't long until he heard them enter the kitchen. From the echo of their footsteps he knew they were moving in the right direction. He smiled. He couldn't resist.

***

Connor and Hatch approached the cellar door, pistols sweeping every corner and cabinet. Hatch gestured with his gun at the one-way boot prints. Connor gave a thumbs-up. Their years of working together made words unnecessary.

They paused at the door jamb. With clock-like ticks of his pistol Connor synchronized their actions. On three Hatch opened. Connor glanced down the long staircase, jerking his head back by reflex. No one. With his flashlight he surveyed the murky cavern beyond the bottom of the stairs.

Nowhere a gunman might hide. So far, so good.

Hatch put on his night-vision goggles and handed his partner the extra pair he'd brought along without Connor's knowledge. Connor grunted his thanks as he adjusted the fit. This way they could approach in darkness; no need waste time finding the light switch.

They started down the stairs, hugging the walls to either side, pistols steadied with two hands. They stopped before the last step to regroup.

Connor was certain they would be fired on when they made their move into the cellar, fired on while they were still silhouetted by lantern light from the kitchen. But if they reached the basement floor unhurt, the tables would abruptly turn: two men with night vision versus one without.

They spun into the cavern at the same moment, ready to cripple anything that moved.

Nothing. The staircase was solid, no place beneath it to hide. The cellar itself had a few metal shelves, but there were neither partitions nor pillars. The furnace offered the only cover in the entire place. They would find their man behind it. He was hopelessly trapped.

They approached slowly from opposite sides, backs to the dungeon-like walls. Obruchev could either bolt into the open or give himself up. There simply were no other options.

For some reason he did neither.

Connor and Hatch met behind the dormant beast. In the same instant the cellar door to the kitchen slammed shut. Their night goggles needed a modicum of light to function. The total blackness rendered them useless. Two loud clunks followed. They could hear movement on the tile floor upstairs.

***

When he heard the men reach the bottom of the stairs, Obruchev ventured out of the pantry. Still without boots, he shuffled to the spot where he had stashed the length of railroad track. Lifting it carefully he stood and listened to them move further into the basement. When they stopped walking, he charged the cellar door, kicked it shut and lowered the massive beam into its brackets.

So much for his assassins.

He put on his boots and ran to the Tatra. When he returned with a 50-liter can of diesel fuel, bullets were already pinging against the iron bar and penetrating the thick door above and below it.

Obruchev poured the fuel onto the kitchen floor. The puddle grew quickly and spread toward the crack at the bottom of the cellar door.

He took the lantern from the kitchen table, backed up a safe distance and hurled it against a wall. The liquid beneath burst into flames. Good that it was diesel and not gasoline. It would burn more slowly. Why rush things when he was having fun?

He would now visit the barn. The girl might be there; she might not. Rasputin was dead in either case. Already he could see the shock on the holy freak's face when the man he believed to have killed showed up for a friendly chat . . .

***

Connor ran his finger horizontally along the line of bullet holes he had shot in the door. "So what's your conclusion looking at these?"

"Same as yours," Hatch said. "There's a Charlie bar. When we aim above or below, the slugs penetrate. When we hit the bar they don't. We're lucky we haven't caught a ricochet yet."

"So our way out is obvious?"

"Unless the bar can't be lifted. You've seen those U brackets that close at the top."

"No, I haven't. We know the bar's location from that line of bullet holes. We'll shoot out a rectangle of door beneath it and lever it up. If we're dealing with the kind of brackets you describe, we'll enlarge the rectangle and use our hands to shift it sideways. I hope you brought extra ammo from the jeep."

"I did, Randall, in spite of your protestations."

"Good. Don't ever listen to me."

"He's back."

Connor was about to comment on his bad hearing when something crashed against the kitchen wall. "Shit."

"What's that smell?"

"Diesel. Jesus, Hatch, it's coming in under the door."

Connor tore off his coat and tried to stuff it into the crack. The material was too thick. The fuel encircled their boots as it continued its flow toward the next step. "Let's go. We can stop it at the bottom."

They piled coats, sweaters and hats on the lowest step. When they looked up, the bullet holes in the door flickered with light. Moments later fire was in the cellar. It roared down the stairs on a river of fuel.

Connor looked at the ceiling. Wooden joists. Goddamn wood. The blaze on the stone steps would burn itself out, but if it ignited those beams, they wouldn't have much time before the inferno above crashed down and consumed them.

As they fled toward a cooler part of the basement, the joists above the staircase began to smolder. Connor saw a Saint Vitus' dance in orange on dungeon walls. He remembered how he had felt as a bible-belt kid. Hellfire, boy. That's your future unless you bow down before Him.

Well, fuck it. He hadn't bought the prophecy then, and eleventh-hour conversions weren't in his nature.

CHAPTER THIRTY-FOUR

From the near total darkness of the barn, peering through the holes they had punched in the wood, Kristýna and William caught sporadic glimpses of Obruchev's indoor prowling. What he was doing remained a mystery – before and after he lit the lantern on the kitchen table.

They were each lost in thought when two armed men hit the ground with a thud near the log pile between the house and barn. The smaller man aimed a pistol at Obruchev, whose unpredictable movements made him a difficult target. From the behavior of the big man, it was clear he didn't want any shots fired from that distance. A heated discussion ensued; tatters of whispered American English drifted to them on the silent dawn.

William tensed. The larger man looked familiar. Where had he seen him before? For the life of him he couldn't remember.

Obruchev left the lantern burning, retreated into the cellar and closed the door after him. The Americans sprinted through the snow to the military transporter. William cupped his hands around Kristýna's ear. "That big bastard . . . I just recognized him. Genoa. American FBI. We, Gabriella and I, were watching you from a distance while you were there with Lucio. So tell me please: what the hell is going on?"

"I'd be guessing. But one thing seems clear. They've finally figured out who Obruchev is and Obruchev knows they're after him. He's luring them into a trap. This isn't going to turn out the way we hoped."

William returned his attention to the peephole. He watched the big agent trudge around the house while the small man waited behind the military truck, ready to put a cap in Obruchev if he came up from the basement. But when the big guy returned Obruchev still hadn't resurfaced. After another animated exchange, the agents stormed the front entrance.

Suddenly William saw things through Kristýna's eyes. A shiver went down his spine. It was a trap. It was also a disaster in the making.

The FBI broke into the house, none too subtly. While they shot up the lock and bashed in the door, Obruchev slipped out of the cellar and hid in a pantry.

When the agents entered the kitchen they moved toward the basement stairs. The small man was examining the floor with a flashlight, leading the way as if he had discovered some sort of a trail. Clueless, they descended into the cavern.

Obruchev walked out of the pantry as if nothing had happened. He lifted a fat iron bar from the space between the refrigerator and a free-standing cabinet, closed the cellar door and dropped the bar into brackets on the door jambs.

William had never been a big fan of law enforcement, having encountered for too many years what seemed to be their indifference to his cause. Now, watching the prison door slam shut on real human beings, he felt empathy. These were just a couple of regular guys trying to do their jobs. They didn't know the truth, didn't know they were on his and Kristýna's side. But they were, which made them allies.

Obruchev ran to the truck. Instead of driving away, he returned with a large canister of fuel, dumped it on the floor and hurled the burning lantern against the wall. William closed his eyes: this was something he didn't need to watch.

As flames engulfed the kitchen, Obruchev returned to his truck and tossed his pistol onto the front seat. Before William could rejoice, the shithead pulled an Uzi from a compartment in the door and jammed in a fresh ammunition clip . . .

William struggled to keep his voice low. "Kristýna, he's coming! He's trapped the two agents in the cellar and set the house on fire. He's got a machine gun."

She had been a whirlwind of activity during his vigil. Now she took his hand and placed it on a pitchfork she'd propped against the wall. She handed him a coil of rope, guiding his wrist to the spot she wanted it tied. Kicking off her boots, she took off across the straw floor, peeling off loops of rope.

The barn was dark. He didn't know exactly where she had gone until he felt a gentle tug on the line. She was on the other side of the barn door. He understood. Dropping to his knees, he tied his end of the rope to the base of the stall.

He heard rustling, like the approach of a snake. Kristýna reeled in slack; the rope writhed in the hay. When she pulled it taut and secured it, they had their first line of defense: a trip wire. He grabbed the pitchfork, ran his fingers across the barbed prongs, tried different grips.

Incredible, he thought, taking up position at the front of the stall. She had prepared them for battle in the blink of an eye. She'd given them a fighting chance.

***

In the darkness Kristýna acquainted herself with the stall in which she had taken cover, reading its contours with her hands like a blind person probing a stranger's face. As she began her search a weapon, she came across a sledge hammer that weighed a ton, an unwieldy pair of sheers and a rake that was too awkward to use. Then, as time grew short, she nicked her palm on a razor-sharp scythe hanging from the wall beside her.

It was small and light, the handle short, the curved blade about the length of her forearm. Perfect, she thought.

Sucking the trickle of blood from her palm, she moved to the front of the stall and took a deep breath. She hiked up the long Gypsy skirt she'd worn from Vesh's camp, tightly retied her belt and waited. Should she pray? She didn't know.

***

The door swung open. Obruchev stepped inside as if he would crash ahead, then abruptly stopped. Quickly, unexpectedly, he backed off.

Had he noticed the rope? She didn't believe so. It was straw-colored, low to the floor, scarcely visible even in the light that came in through the open door. Besides, his gaze when he had focused on the loft, the stalls, the places where an assassin might wait. He was not looking down.

She couldn't see him; he was behind her. But she knew he was studying the Gypsy wagon, the tractor parked to its left, the horse-drawn plow between the two . . .

Without warning, he stormed ahead and fired several shots into the stalls nearest the wagon. But again he stopped just short of the rope.

She could see him clearly now through a crack in the stall. She watched his massive bald head dancing in the flames from the farmhouse. She shuddered. He carried a short compact machine gun made for small spaces. Equally horrifying was the hand-sized flashlight he took from his pocket. As soon as he turned it on, the beam began probing the corners and crevices where she planned to hide if William failed.

They had thought of so much . . . and yet so little. It was obvious he would come with a light. How had they overlooked the first thing they should have planned for?

No time for questions. Her mind, which had screamed in silence for him to take the next step, now begged for him to wait. William would succeed. But if he didn't . . . if he didn't, then her backup plan was worthless.

Improvising, she stayed hidden when Obruchev barged ahead. His shins hit the rope, he went down hard. His automatic rifle and flashlight landed beyond his reach. Struggling to keep her breath silent, she saw William rushing toward him, pitchfork raised.

Obruchev must have smelled the attack. He swung a leg at William's feet and upended him before he could strike. The fork fell harmlessly onto the hay; both men leaped for the gun. Obruchev caught William by the arm, spun him around and knocked him unconscious with a crushing blow to the jaw. He grabbed the gun and stood, hoisting William to his feet.

Obruchev wrapped a thick arm around the limp man's chest. With his gun pointed toward the open area of the barn, he dragged him backwards into a stall. To Kristýna's surprise he started bellowing.

"You're gonna wait right here," he shouted. "I'm tying you up with my belt so you don't go on any walks. Face down, pussy. Hands behind your back. When you wake up we're going to have a little chat."

Kristýna, scythe in hand, made a frantic dash for the flashlight. Keep talking, she prayed as she dropped it into her pocket and circled back toward the barn door. Go on, Obruchev. Talk yourself all the way to your grave . . .

Several barefoot steps in the snow allowed her to grasp the rough wooden handle of the barn door. Hinges screeched, darkness returned. Obruchev's curses exploded in a stall not two meters away.

Kristýna knew her destination. Moving like a cat across the open area of the barn, she found the tractor and crouched behind it.

Obruchev to burst from the stall, bellowing in white-hot anger. "Thank you, Kristýna. Thank you for leading me to her. Don't mind me. I'm coming out now to see if the kid's where you seem to think she is. Then we'll have our chat, just you and me. I want to know where I can find Rasputin. Your partner, right? You'd better be able to tell me."

Obruchev began to search the stalls, kicking open doors and spraying bullets inside. The gun's snout hissed fire, cleaving the darkness like lightning on a black night.

When he wasn't shooting he resumed taunting. "Kristýna, you didn't leave, did you? You didn't just walk away from a custody battle. Kristýna . . . Oh, Kristýna, your little whore baby's here, isn't she? If you haven't run off, we've got just about everything we need for a hell of a show."

He unloaded a few more rounds into a stall, then fell silent. Her heart stopped. She could hear him treading heavily toward the Gypsy wagon. She tightened her grip on the scythe as the first wooden step creaked under his weight. Desperately she began casting about for something to throw. She found an empty oil can. Not perfect, too light, but it would have to do.

She crouched, switched the scythe to her left hand and launched the can as far as she could. It landed with barely a sound in the hay beyond the wagon. Obruchev spun instantly and opened fire, alert to the tiniest noise. In the flashes from the gun she could see how close he was to the wagon door.

She felt a wave of panic. What now?

As if in answer, a second more substantial object landed near the spot where the can had hit. Obruchev laughed rather than shoot. "You'll have to do better than that, bitch."

William had gotten free! He was signaling to her! He was . . .

A volley of machine-gun fire split the wagon lock and sent splinters of wood in all directions. Debris hit the stalls, the loft, the plow. Some of it fell on Kristýna, tiny daggers.

Teresa finally woke from whatever drug the priest had given her. She cried out at the top of her lungs.

Obruchev laughed again. "Looks like I was right. What's new?" He kicked in the door with his boot. "Teresa, little Teresa, come see your Uncle Bogdan. I have a present for you."

Kristýna screamed.

Obruchev turned and blasted the tractor, his grin hideously distorted by the dragon tongue of fire leaping from the gun's muzzle.

But Kristýna saw something else, something that restored her hope. William, pitchfork in hand, had crawled to a cart less than five meters away.

Obruchev closed the wagon door, shut the hasp and backed down the steps. "Kristýna, you disappoint. We had all the elements of a good play. Now it's turning into one of those pieces of shit my wife drags me to in Chicago. Let's make a few improvements. Stay behind that tractor. I'll start a fire under the wagon. The whore's child can't get out. I shot off the lock, not the latch. Once the blaze starts, we'll have real suspense. Will you come out and try to save her? Will you run for your life when the inferno spreads? Surprise me. That's what good plays do."

He took a cigarette lighter from his pocket, flicked it on and held it beside his face. "So how do I look? We had some good times together. Maybe we should have some more. I mean right here in the hay, nice fire behind us and all. It's a cold winter night. Like my proposal?"

Darkness returned. She could hear him kicking hay into a pile under the wagon, could hear Teresa crying for help.

Had panic crippled her mind or was the problem real? It seemed that wherever she went, however she approached, she would be visible the instant he used his lighter. Knowing him as well as she did, she had no doubt he would be watching for her.

She found a piece of wood blown her way by his shooting. It was small, insubstantial. She tossed it a short distance from the tractor. Though it landed softly as dust, he heard it. The kicking stopped, the tiny flame of his lighter filled the barn with a dim glow. She was thinking clearly, thinking right through the panic.

Yes, he would be equally prepared for a soundless approach. She could almost feel his mind at work. He would stop kicking hay and light the place up at unpredictable moments. If she left the cover of the tractor, he would kill her.

At that moment an eerie glow again filled the barn. Obruchev carefully examined the area between the wagon and the tractor, then went back to building his pile, whistling with soft arrogance as he worked. There was simply no possible way for her to reach him undetected.

But there was. He had missed something. The next time Obruchev's lighter gave her a glimpse of him, she saw that William had moved closer, apparently during his blustery outbursts. If Obruchev opened his mouth again, William could crawl within striking distance.

Talk, you son-of-a-bitch! Say something. Anything!

He did, but it wasn't what she wanted to hear. "That should do it, Mother Whore. Let's not waste time. I'm ready for you now. I'm horny as hell. I'll start the fire. Then you'll come here, lie down and spread your legs."

When he again flicked on his lighter, Obruchev was squatting near the pile of hay. He had gotten careless.

William lunged forward and drove the pitchfork into his back.

For a moment Obruchev looked too stunned to move. Then he whipped the machine gun over his shoulder and fired blindly behind him. William dove for cover.

Obruchev clicked his lighter back on and held it to the little pile of hay he was trying to set afire.

Now!

While he tried to ignite the damp straw, she crept in a wide semicircle behind him and brought the scythe down on his wrist. He let out another howl and dropped the lighter. It went out, the fledgling fire went out, an awful stillness returned to the barn.

As Obruchev staggered to his feet, he opened fire at the side of the wagon. William grabbed the handle of the fork sticking out of his back and twisted him to the side. The bullets flew wildly, hitting the loft, the ceiling, the stalls. As the gun flashed, Kristýna saw the barbed prongs, slick with blood, protruding from his chest, saw a partially severed hand dangling from his wrist.

How could he still be standing? Standing and dangerous.

He slung the Uzi over his shoulder again, forcing William to let go of the fork. Hoping for a lucky hit, he opened fire at the wagon.

Kristýna threw caution to the wind and pounced, swinging the scythe in a low, savage arc. It hit one of his calves above the boot. She felt a slight rubbery resistance as the blade sliced through muscle and tendon, then felt the jarring collision of metal and bone. He tumbled backwards onto the pitchfork handle, yelling and gurgling. The machine gun bounced down the wagon stairs.

She switched on the flashlight she had pocketed after Obruchev hit the trip wire. William saw the gun immediately, picked it up and handed it to her.

Obruchev flopped onto his side. She pressed the barrel to his forehead and pulled the trigger. He had saved her one bullet, the last in the magazine. It was his final gesture, and his most generous.

***

Kristýna dropped the Uzi and ran to the wagon. When she flung open the door Teresa stood directly in front of her, paralyzed by fear. Her mother picked her up and hugged her as tightly as she dared. The void in her heart that had existed since that hideous day in Cold Spring Harbor filled with the warmth so ruthlessly stolen from her. "Darling . . . my . . .

precious little girl . . ." She could say no more. Tears streamed down her cheeks.

Teresa – dazed and still half drugged – immediately became hysterical. She stuttered, cried out, kicked. Kristýna held her away so she could look into her eyes. "Sweetheart, it's me. Everything's alright now."

"The bad guys," Teresa choked. "The bad guys, Mommy. They'll find us."

"No, Sweetheart. Hug me. Try to calm down. I'm going to show you what I did to the man who killed your father. He's the bad guy who tells the other ones what to do – like when he told that man to shoot Daddy. He's dead now. He's on the floor beside the wagon. We're going to go look at him so you know for sure. There's nothing else to be afraid of. Do you want to go see him?"

"I'm scared, Mommy."

"Kristýna! I forgot those FBI guys. They're in that burning house. I have to try – "

"No, please! You'll die if you – "

She guessed he didn't hear her or wasn't listening. He was running and had already reached the barn door.

CHAPTER THIRTY-FIVE

William fought his way through the deep snow. When he reached the Tatra, the farmhouse was engulfed in flames. He leaped inside the truck, turned the key, waited for the glow light to go off and started the giant diesel.

He had seen them go down the stairs; he knew exactly where they were trapped. Could they still be alive? He didn't think so, but his mind forced him to pretend.

He jammed the long gearshift lever into a position he guessed to be reverse. When he popped the clutch, the huge personal carrier lurched forward, demolishing what was left of the Skoda. He tried another gear. This was it, this was reverse. He inched backwards and stopped. You have to have a plan! Think!

There was deep snow on the canvas roof that arched over the truck bed, snow on the cab, snow almost everywhere but on the hood. With any luck he would have a little extra time before the side tanks exploded. His fear of an explosion morphed into a vision of sending giant chunks of concrete down the stairwell when he rammed an interior wall, killing the men he was trying to save.

What the hell was wrong with him? They were dead already. If not, he was their only hope.

He popped the clutch, turned the wheel and crashed into the blazing farmhouse with the massive rear bumper of the truck. The exterior kitchen wall crumbled. A piece of roof fell. The Tatra stalled, mired in a heap of flaming debris.

Too cautious, too damned cautious!

He restarted the engine, saw and engaged the eight-wheel drive lever, jammed the gear shift into reverse and lurched over the fiery heap. The truck stopped. The inside of the cab was already hot. He struggled for breath as he popped the clutch and hit the gas again. This time the back of the truck crashed into the cellar, wedging itself in the stairwell.

With smoke seeping into the cab he couldn't see, could scarcely breathe. Groping around for something that would break glass, he remembered he had seen a pistol on the seat.

Not there now.

He found it on the floor and used it like a hammer to knock out the back window. When he climbed through, the jagged shards stuck in the window frame ripped his clothing and clawed at the flesh beneath.

He landed on the floor of the truck bed, cracking his head on a bench as he went down. Pain? This wasn't pain. He slithered toward the open end of the truck, vaguely aware that the smoke was less dense, the heat less searing. The canvas arch had created a partial seal between the main floor and basement.

He rushed down the stairs, shouting and choking at the same time. Part of the house fell with the force of a landslide into the cellar, casting fiery light in all directions. At that moment he saw them then, heaped in a corner, dead or unconscious. He grabbed the big agent by the arm and shook him. The man opened his eyes for a second. They were the eyes of a dead man, but he had opened them. He was alive. William kicked the smaller man, whose body reacted with a jerk. Both alive, both dying fast. He'd heard of super-human strength in situations like this. He hoped it wasn't a myth.

It was. He dragged the big man to the stairs but could go no further.

Another piece of house crashed into the basement, creating an inferno near the smaller guy. Burning timbers landed on his legs. William rushed to him, kicked the wood aside and hoisted him over a shoulder. This one he could manage. He carried him up the stairs, heaved him into the truck. The man groaned. Still alive . . .

Cracking sounds came from above. William glanced up. Jesus Christ! The part of the house over the staircase was about to come down.

What should he do? Cut his losses and fly. He would leave the big man. But even as he made his decision, his legs defied his mind's command. He found himself at the bottom of the stairs without knowing how he had gotten there, found himself slapping the big guy so hard the blows echoed above the roar of the fire.

There must have been a pocket of air at that point because the agent stirred. William got him to his feet, wrapped an arm around his neck and started hauling him up the steps. The man went down hard again and again but always fought desperately to get back up. Somehow they reached the top, weaving like drunks.

William pushed the agent's shoulders over the edge of the truck bed, lifted his feet, shoved him forward and jumped in after him.

The truck was jammed into the stairwell and tilted slightly backwards. There was a problem. When and if he broke loose, his load would slide off the back.

The ceiling started to come down with an earsplitting crack of joists. In the blinding light he noticed a recessed tailgate that must come up to secure cargo. He wasn't mechanical, he had no idea how to raise it. But a button to the side seemed promising. Choking uncontrollably now, he pressed it. The gate began its slow trek to the top. He didn't wait, couldn't wait. He pressed himself into the cab, where visibility was nil. He'd left the motor running. Jesus Christ! He had been pouring carbon monoxide into the cavern.

What difference did it make? A big difference. It cut a second off the time he needed to get out of here.

He engaged the clutch and pushed the accelerator. The big diesel strained to dislodge the truck bed from the stairwell. No luck. He pushed down the clutch and accelerator together, let the engine rev to the max, the popped the clutch.

The Tatra broke free and crashed into the open; he kept his foot pressed to the floor until they were halfway to the barn. When he finally stopped and squeezed through the shattered rear window into the truck bed, he found the agents gasping like fish on a dry river bank. The canvas roof was on fire now. God only knew what the temperature in the fuel tanks was.

The gate, the goddamn rear gate. One of the agents kicked a red button to his side and it started to go down in slow motion. He waited, waited when he could have run, until the gate clunked to a stop. Wiping the sweat from his eyes with a charred shirt sleeve half blinded him, but he was able to roll and push both men out the back. They hit the snow like sides of beef. He jumped down after them and dragged them behind the wood pile where their folly had begun.

The truck was in flames now, and soon exploded in a mushroom cloud of fire and smoke. He waited until the debris finished raining down, then went to work on the FBI. They were still gasping. He packed snow on their foreheads without a clue if it would help. He pushed on their chests, wishing he'd listened to Gabriella and learned CPR. "Come on, motherfuckers! I've got the woman you're chasing. Don't die before you catch her!"

The big agent opened his eyes. He reached around, grabbed his colleague's limp arm and shook it. "Hatch, wake the fuck up!"

***

Connor, still wobbly, pushed open the barn door, letting in the cold gray light. William followed, supporting Hatch at the elbow.

Kristýna sat on the steps of the Gypsy wagon with her daughter, playing some kind of a game with lengths of straw.

Connor took a deep breath and prepared to give the speech he dreaded. Before he uttered a word, he saw a body on the ground with a pitchfork protruding from its back a few meters from where he stood. He looked around for a cane, accepted William's arm, and took a few uncertain steps to get a better look. William pushed the pitchfork with his foot, levering the body around until so the face was visible. It was Obruchev, no way to mistake the guy for someone else.Grasping William's arm more tightly, he kneeled as if by instinct to examine the dead man's wounds. A pitchfork in the back, a leg and hand nearly severed, a bullet hole ringed with powder burns on the side of the forehead.

Connor thought of own daughters, of the auction he had attended, of the countless crimes on this monster's hands. Justice had been done, vigilante justice. In his years with the Bureau, Connor had never found himself in such an awkward position. And yet he still had a job to do: bring his fugitive home. He felt nauseated, from the fire he told himself. Now wasn't the time to start doubting his judgment. As distasteful as it was he knew he didn't have the luxury of choice. Pulling away from William, he staggered over to Hatch.

William went to Kristýna, who kept her eyes down, not bothering to interrupt her little straw game with Teresa. There wasn't room for him on the steps of the wagon, so he stood with an arm on the rail and waited for the inevitable pronouncement.

"You're under arrest," Connor said. "I'm sorry, but you'll have to stand trial in the U.S. for your crimes."

"Crimes?" Kristýna said angrily. "I've done your work for you. Is that the crime? I've put this horrible man out of business. Perhaps that's it. Or was it saving my child, this little girl you had written off?"

Teresa hid her eyes. "Mommy, I told you more bad guys would come."

"I don't believe these are bad guys, Sweetie. They just don't understand. I'm going to make sure they do. Then they'll leave us alone."

"Goddammit," Connor said. "This is hard on everyone. Do you have to make it harder? There's not a jury anywhere in the US that's going to convict you. The DA knows this. He'll cut you a deal. If he refuses, simply demand a trial and I guaranteed you'll walk. But for now, you're under arrest."

Kristýna stood, along with the Uzi she had covered with her skirt. She pointed the rifle at Connor's chest. "We're under arrest? You'd better tell your heart to wake up."

Connor winced. Those were the exact words Betty had used when she left him. "Okay, tell me what you want."

"For you to disappear. Now."

"We can't," Hatch said in a bureaucratic monotone. "And it wouldn't help you if we did. Police all over the world are going to keep searching until they find you. And I assure you they will, sooner or later. Why would you choose to run when we can clear you in a couple months?"

"Because I don't trust you. Do you blame me?"

"Mother, let's go. I told you already. I want my dog."

"Teresa, please."

"I want my dog."

"She wants her dog," Kristýna said.

Connor softened. "A hound?"

"She's a hunting dog, Mister Bad Guy."

"I see. I had a hunting dog when I was a boy. Ms. Sondheim, will you put down that gun?"

"No. Listen, both of you. I can direct you to the dog if you will have her flown to New York. There's also an old Mercedes car that needs to be returned to the man who loaned it to us. He's the man who's keeping the dog, so it won't be a detour."

"We can't just – "

"Shut up, Hatch," Connor growled. "You can't. I'm in charge, remember? I, Ms. Sondheim, will do the things you ask, and I'll do them gladly. Just put down the gun. I want you to be clear about this. We're trying to help. We're trying to give you a second chance at life. Okay, I admit you got a raw deal from the system. We can't change the past. The future's a different story. Now please, for you own sake, I suggest you cooperate."

She hesitated, then handed the Uzi with the empty chamber to William. "Give this to the agent, please. He can't make a proper arrest without a weapon."

CHAPTER THIRTY-SIX

Inspector Lutz Wiesel got drunk on Christmas Eve and stayed drunk for the next two weeks. The Slovenian bust, instead of making him an international hero in the fight against the Trade, had damaged his reputation and set back his career.

Connor and his fugitive had been gone only a few hours when the Stapo, together with crack elements of the Slovenian criminal police, launched a pre-dawn raid on factory. Wiesel, anxious to show the world one of the worst East European markets in young flesh, had invited journalists and police observers from all over the globe.

But the abandoned factory he had described to police and journalists such vivid detail turned out to be just that – an abandoned factory. Gone were the checkpoints, guard towers and razor wire fences that had surrounded it a few days earlier; gone the stage, bleachers and holding rooms; gone was the Ljubljana office with its plush carpets and tasteful artwork.

All they found was General Majdak, whose lifeless body swung by a rope noose beneath the Cobbler's Bridge. When the sun rose that morning, it cast his elongated shadow onto the ice-choked River of Seven Names.

They cut him down from below. His frozen corpse landed with a brittle crack on the deck of the police barge, setting free a note pinned to his trousers. The morning breeze picked up the note and sent it gliding like a swallow among the spires of the medieval city.

When Wiesel and his cops, accompanied by an increasingly skeptical throng of reporters, finally succeeded in catching it, they read the account of a suicide as convincing as it was false: Majdak explained how he had disgraced himself by participating in an ugly scam. The Western defense contractor who was allegedly renovating the factory had deceived the entire Slovenian government. Majdak, who had made the illusion possible through his role as intermediary, knew when the Westerners left that he had only one option.

The suicide note, along with vague references to military honor, contained an apology to the citizens and officials he had duped. Nowhere was anything mentioned about the brisk traffic in young girls. The press, with its usual perspicacity, concluded that Wiesel had invented a tall tale to thrust himself into the limelight. The Ministry of Justice, now in possession of a busload of girls hauled out of Slovenia without the knowledge or consent of the government in Ljubljana, decided to drop the investigation.

When Wiesel begged his boss at Interior to call back the Americans to corroborate his story, he was placed on unpaid leave. The girls, whom the nightly news portrayed as prostitutes trying to sneak into Austria, were deported to their countries of origin.

***

Two months later Rasputin opened his new facility in a small village in Moldova. The company's upscale office in Chisinau attracted so many teenage girls only the most attractive received a second interview. While the impoverished and unsuspecting sex slaves of the future awaited their chance in lines that snaked day and night through the town's historic center, buyers in record numbers queued up for the first midnight auction.

Pimenko, who had quadrupled his fee, served as Rasputin's new adviser. Once again, the irreverent Russian proved worth his weight in gold. He delivered a high official of the Ministry of Economics to perform the services that had once been Majdak's domain. He also brought to the business a new breed of buyers, Ukrainian men from across the Dniester who preferred not to send their girls West but to keep them locked up in Odessa and Kiev. Adeptly using the Internet they had cracked the North American market. Sex tours in the East were now the rage, offering image-conscious suburbanites, television evangelists and "family value" politicians a safe haven in which to enjoy erotic treats unimaginable at home.

As profits soared, the threat of police intervention plummeted. From Rasputin's vantage point deep inside the former East Bloc, growth projections for the global sex market presented all in the Trade with reason to rejoice. As he looked out over a full house of buyers and prepared to put the first group of girls on the block, Rasputin felt an overwhelming sense of virtue. He could not help but smile as the girls, instruments of Evil on earth, mounted the stairs. They were naked except for the jewelry and the high heels they had been instructed to wear. He recited the house rules, took out his ceramic gargoyle and lit the first of three virgin candles. The floor was 30,000 Euros or its equivalent. The first offer came in at twice that amount . . .

For a moment, Rasputin's mind wandered. He saw his adolescence in Novgorod. His voice had been a gift from God; his solos in the Sofia Cathedral had brought worshipers from as far as Moscow. Then everything changed. He quit the Church the very next week as planned, opting to serve the Almighty on his own. But for reasons incomprehensible and deeply troubling to him, he also lost his urge to sing.

It wasn't until this night, almost three decades later, that he again felt the burning desire to exercise his gift. Instead he waited for the next bid.

EPILOGUE

She was in the same courtroom from which she had escaped last October, sitting through a noon hearing. Today's legal formalities didn't frighten Kristýna. An official agreement by all parties had been reached in the matter of People v. Sondheim. What did frighten her was the realization that she would be released from one prison into another. The paparazzi and tabloid press would be on her trail the moment she stepped outside, and they would be even more relentless than the FBI or Obruchev.

She'd read everything she could get her hands on about Princess Di and how that poor woman had been stalked and hounded to the point of insanity. It was going to be the same with her, given her crazy new celebrity. Wherever she and Teresa tried to start a new life, it would be in the company of hordes of these disgusting news vermin.

She looked around, hoping memories of her escape would dilute her anxiety. But there were no memories. In fact, she scarcely recognized the place. During the post-trial hearing from which she had fled, the courtroom had been packed. Now it looked almost empty. The crotchety old judge was on the bench. She counted among the others a court reporter, a bailiff, a dour man from the D.A's office, a US attorney and a few journalists in the gallery who had learned of the court's last-minute scheduling change.

Sure, everything looked a little different, but she still recognized the setting. Why wasn't she able to summon forth a little bit of the terror she had felt during her escape? Why wasn't she able to feel anything other than the dread of what awaited her on the outside?

A large man in street clothes stepped inside through a door at the front of the courtroom, flipped his badge at the judge and sat down beside the US Attorney. Finally some sort of mental distraction, though not the type she had been looking for. The man was Agent Connor.

"Turn on the husher," Judge Bremer roared. "Let's get this over with before the pals of these reporters find out what's going on. I don't want the entire city press corps in here. All of you attorneys, to the bench. The Defendant too. Now!"

The machine designed to keep juries from hearing sidebar conferences began to whoosh as the prosecutors, lawyers and Kristýna hurried forward. Judge Bremer's dyspeptic stare settled on the Assistant D. A. "Your response to Defendant Sondheim's motion to set aside the original murder conviction."

"Your Honor, in light of the – "

"I said, your response. We all know she didn't do it."

"Your Honor, the People do not oppose the motion."

"Do you plan to retry the Defendant?"

"No."

"Good. So ordered. State's position on Defendant's motion to set aside escape charges."

"Your Honor, Defendant has agreed to enter a guilty plea of attempted escape in exchange for time served since her return to New York."

"Do you wish to enter a guilty plea, Ms. Sondheim?"

"I'm not guilty of anything."

"The hell you're not," the judge erupted, hushing the husher. "You up and ran out of my courtroom. That's a crime. Counselor, I thought you'd settled this with your client."

"I have, your Honor. She doesn't understand. Give me a moment."

A few seconds into the frantic whispering and gesturing that followed, the judge whacked his gavel. "Hurry the hell up."

"Okay, guilty," Kristýna said under her breath.

"What?"

"Guilty! Satisfied?"

There was a moment of silence, as if a contempt citation might come roaring down from the bench. But Judge Bremer had evidently decided that he wanted this particular matter out of his life forever.

"Guilty of attempted escape," he growled. "Is there a good reason I can't sentence you now and accept the plea?"

No one objected.

"Very well, then. So ordered."

"Okay. What about federal charges? When and where do you guys in D.C. plan to settle this matter?"

"No federal charges were ever filed, your Honor."

"Then, Ms. Sondheim, you are free to go. Now please do just that, and don't let me ever see you in my courtroom again."

The judge retired to chambers, moving not like the lion he had always been but like an exhausted old man.

Kristýna felt paralyzed. She sat motionless, unable to stand, while everyone else headed toward the tenth floor window to watch the throng of TV and newspaper people massing below. Almost everyone. Agent Connor was still gathering up some papers at the prosecution table.

Kristýna looked at her hands, then back toward Connor. He was making his way toward her between a row of benches. He slid an empty chair beside hers and sat down. "I sure as hell am relieved we're not in a Slovenian barn. I thought you were going to shoot me."

She didn't smile, just shook her head as if she hadn't heard him. "All of those years with Arthur," she whispered, "all of those years when I had the first real name I had ever had since I'd been in America. No one cared who the person was behind that name. Then my life went totally to pieces and what happens? Everyone cares. Why is that, Agent Connor? Why do they all of a sudden care?"

"You're asking me to figure out people? Sorry, Kristýna, but I've officially given up on that. So let's talk about the easy stuff. You know, stuff like the vultures waiting for you outside and how you're going to deal with them."

"That's your idea of easy?"

"Well, let's put it another way. You can understand them all you want and they'll still be there. Or . . . "

"Or what?"

"You can let me help you, no strings attached."

"Why, Agent Connor, would you want to help me? I made your life pretty miserable for a long time. At least that's what the prison psychologist said."

"You listened to that jerk? Look, you didn't shoot me in the barn, that's why."

"There weren't any bullets in the gun or I would have."

"Well, then, I guess you'll have to go it alone."

She grasped his wrist. "No, wait. I can't. I'm changing my testimony . . . isn't that what defendants say? I wouldn't have shot you, regardless. That's the truth."

"I know," Connor said. "Now let's talk business. You got a raw deal from the system, and I'm part of the system. I want to do something to make . . . well, I know I can't make it up, but to make your future a little better. I can get you out of here unnoticed, and after that I can give you another chance at life. I can do those things if you'll let me. For you and for Teresa."

"By putting me in some kind of witness protection plan?"

"Nope. You don't qualify. You're not testifying against anyone. You're not in danger of being killed. You're a free woman."

"Free? Like Princess Diana was free?"

"Yes, like Princess Diana. Exactly like Princess Diana. Do you want to hear the offer I came to make or not?"

"I don't understand. You want something in return. People don't do things like you are promising, not without a better reason than the one you gave me. I know more than you think about you."

"Sorry, but you don't know the first thing about me. If I were the type who always wants something in return, I sure as hell wouldn't have gone into law enforcement. Let's forget about needing to understand. I'm going to go over the specifics of exactly what I'm able to do. Then you decide whether you want in. Okay?"

"Yes, okay. Sure."

"Forsythe, the Head of the Bureau, owes me a favor or two – not small ones, either. His career depended on someone bringing you home, and he wanted me. Only I was on leave. So he made a few vague promises to induce me to sign on for one last fugitive job. The promises got more specific as your release date approached. I guess you could say I blackmailed him. Or you could say I lied. Whatever, I got what I wanted. This was the Bureau's help in doing something off the record and unconventional, something for you and your kid."

"I'm supposed to believe that?"

"You believe what you want, Kristýna. I'm out of time. There's an FBI helicopter on the roof pad waiting to take you to a small airport. There's an FBI Gulfstream waiting to fly you to Oklahoma. There's a special unit ready to create a new identity for you and Teresa. You'll have to give up your names, sorry about that, but at least you'll be in a place where the vultures will never find you."

"There isn't such a place."

"You're wrong. A fishing cabin in the Ozarks."

"A fishing cabin? With you, I suppose."

"With me. Sort of. When I'm not working. The cabin's big. Actually it's a home on a lake. There's room for a separate unit for you and your daughter. There's money for that, and for a decent private school nearby for Teresa, and for all the furniture and décor you want. You and me, we won't even have to speak. If I'm there at all, I'll be reading or fishing. You make your own life. We have disguise experts for when you want to travel or go to a university or just go shopping. We have . . . well enough about the things we have. Either you risk it and come with me or you don't. It's your call. I have to go. Michaela and Teresa are expecting me. So is the pilot, and so is Agent Hatcher."

"What? My sister and daughter are in the helicopter? Why did you do that?"

"Because the press will be wherever they are the moment you're let out. I had to round them up when I did. If you come, Michaela wants to fly with us to Oklahoma to check things out. She's as wary as you are. Remember, you and Teresa are free to return to New York if you aren't happy with what you find. Like I said, Kristýna, it's your call."

Connor's chair made a screeching noise on the floor as he shoved it away from the table and stood. He didn't look back, he wasn't the type. He was almost at the door through which he had entered when he felt her hand on his arm

They didn't say a word all the way up the private elevator to the roof. But their eyes met, and neither one of them seemed in a hurry to look away.

The End

Made in the USA
San Bernardino, CA
13 June 2016